The Harpoon Gun

Books by
VASSILIS VASSILIKOS

VASSILIS VASSILIKOS

THE
HARPOON
GUN

Translated by Barbara Bray

HARCOURT BRACE JOVANOVICH, INC.

New York

Originally published in Greek by Editions 8½

ISBN 0–15–138800–8

Library of Congress Catalog Card Number: 72–79925

Printed in the United States of America

B C D E

To Mimi

Contents

3

Self-slaughter

1

THE HARPOON GUN

Thanassis

The Greeks abroad were gradually growing more and more apolitical. The work that should have been everyone's was now done only by the resistance organizations, castes closed at the top. But who wanted to be a mere member carrying out orders when anyone might hoist himself up to the heights of authority? It was logical enough: since the leaders had failed, why not become a leader yourself and see if you couldn't do better? And that was why, chiefly abroad, there were a lot of small independent groups all savaging one another in xeroxed publications and so adding to the general confusion, which in turn contributed to the process of depolitization.

As a student had summed it up the previous evening, talking about the colonels, "Why resist them? Why even oppose them? It's playing their own game, recognizing them as our legitimate counterpart. And making ourselves theirs—so they can tell their bosses, 'Look who'll replace us if we go.' "

"What do you suggest, then?" asked Thanassis, nervously clutching at his iced beer.

"Ignore them completely," said the student in the old flannel suit. He couldn't send it to the cleaner's because he had no other. "And when no one opposes them any more they'll have lost their reason for existing. 'No existence without resistance . . .' "

A theory Thanassis found original, though peculiar, to say

3

the least. But since he didn't know the student, he didn't judge him too severely. Charilaos told him later that the student hadn't been at all like that at first, at the beginning of the dictatorship. He'd been among the most active and revolutionary until the members of the organization back home had been arrested and had to pay for it while he'd only been sentenced in his absence. It had demoralized him to be free while the others were in prison, and he'd taken up with women, like the pretty English girl over there playing it cool.

"Now I understand depolitization," said Thanassis. "It's a subconscious guilt reaction." Then he added, "Look at the girl—she's just the sort we need."

Thanassis had seen everything fall apart around him, the left concentrating on settling accounts with its own past, the center fragmenting over the controversial personality of Andreas. Disintegration spread like an ink blot, while his brother, whose monstrous sentence of twenty years for distributing leaflets had been regarded as purely symbolic and deterrent, would soon have served a quarter of his term. Hence the need for spectacular action.

"The Paraguayan commandos did us a good turn when they bumped off the German ambassador," he'd said to Charilaos. "Now if we take any of theirs they'll give us whichever of ours we want." And then his brother would be free, and the rest of the world would know there was a Greek resistance.

All he needed was a girl to use as bait. The "zealots" who were to do the deed were all ready in Athens. Every time he saw a pretty girl he would whisper to Charilaos, "Hey, don't you know one like that?" until finally Charilaos started to wonder if it wasn't just a pretext for staring and commenting like a yokel on every skirt that walked by.

Charilaos looked at him. Thanassis was a good-looking

youth, with eyes intense as two olives and a melancholy most apparent when he was silent. He smoked cigarette after cigarette, and had a characteristic way of letting the tip lie there on the red lips before puffing out the first ring of smoke. Like a prewar train before it has worked up its regular rhythm. It was in those short silences, while the tip of the cigarette rested still dry and unassimilated on the fresh lips, as alien as a sea shell caught between someone's toes, that Charilaos sensed his sadness over all the misfortunes that had struck his family since they had arrested his brother. And Thanassis was having a hard time abroad. He'd been brought up in middle-class comfort, and now there were times when he was reduced to eating vegetables he dug up himself from allotments and boiled over a gas ring. That was why Charilaos had invited him to dinner this evening.

"How do you see it, then?" he asked, helping himself to a piece of goat's cheese from the abundance left on their table by the waiter.

It was the time for confidences. When the stomach was well lined it was imagination's turn—as when society ladies ask artists to dinner, plying them with food so they will later entertain the guests with examples of their talent.

Thanassis, after initiating him into the principle that a secret known to more than two people is a secret no longer, told him everything. What worried Charilaos most was whether the girl would run any risk. Absolutely none, Thanassis insisted—she would leave by the next plane, before the news of the kidnapping had even broken. And there was not even the need to hook a big fish—a bream or a mullet would do, as long as it was an American bream, or a mullet belonging to the Sixth Fleet.

"Just one thing—" began Charilaos.

"I know," interrupted Thanassis. "No need to talk about it. The colonels are good lackeys. They'll hand over the men

5

we ask for as fast as they can. The American ambassador will give the order. Don't worry."

"What I mean is," said Charilaos as he paid the bill, "in the unlikely case that the colonels refuse to obey their masters, can your zealots—I have to know about this—are they prepared to pull the trigger?"

"They are prepared to pull the trigger," said Thanassis. His face glowed.

"You'll hear from me in Rome," said Charilaos as they parted.

Ethel

Ethel von Cintra was French, but of unusual parentage—her mother was Polish and her father a German who'd been persecuted by the Nazis. She was born in America, where her parents still lived, but she preferred Europe, away from her family and closer to her roots. In Paris she worked for a film company whose main office was in New York. She was bilingual from the cradle, multilingual by education, and looked as French as if she'd stepped straight out of the last issue of *Elle*. When Charilaos called her up and went over to her office, she was overjoyed to see him.

Their friendship was as old as the dictatorship. Ethel had been living, then, with a Greek actor trying to make a career for himself in Europe—a dark, handsome boy, not very bright, but with a temperament that elicited her maternal instincts. She'd met him at a cocktail party where, learning that she worked in films, he'd made a date with her for the following day, thinking that if he could sleep with her she'd get him a part in a movie. He came from a poor family in Piraeus and had left Greece with the object of making good abroad so as to find work more easily at home. Charilaos had known him in Piraeus, and it was through him he'd met Ethel one evening.

The actor used to disappear without trace from time to time, and then Ethel would phone Charis, as she called him, to see if he had any news of him. She was attached to the actor because, unlike Frenchmen, who were blasé, he was passionate and tortured her a little; and there were unexpectedly good things about him, too. But, as she told Charilaos, it was very hard for her to find him a job with so many actors out of work and the French movie industry going through a crisis. She'd introduced him to a few producers and directors, but they'd said his French wasn't good enough. Once he'd been given a test, but on the very day he was to sign the contract he'd found himself replaced by someone who'd probably slept the previous night with the director. Subconsciously he blamed Ethel for his failure to worm his way into the establishment. He even suggested that if she'd only gone to bed with some heterosexual director—there were still a few left —she could have gotten him a job. In short, their relationship was beginning to sour, and it was at this critical period in Ethel's life that Charis came to be a real friend to her. As a Greek, he took the place of the boy and made the final separation less painful. It came in a stupid way, like all separations. The actor owed Ethel some money, which she asked for because she was strapped, and he denied ever having borrowed it. Thereupon, in her flat, amid cries of "dirty thief" and "lousy whore," the idyll had come to an end. In the next few days Ethel noticed that various little things were missing. As for the actor, he had vanished completely, until Charilaos phoned her one day to say he'd seen his picture in a Greek paper. He was playing the lead in some run-of-the-mill Greek movie, and the caption said he'd been a success in several films abroad. He heard her laugh bitterly over the phone.

After that Ethel and Charilaos met often. And each time Ethel was eager for news about how things were going in Greece. She was civic-minded by family tradition, a Jewess opposed to Dayan, and the colonels annoyed her as much as the armor-plated mosquitoes from a nearby dump that kept her awake when she stayed with her girl friend in the country. Once they invited Charilaos there, and it was then she told him she was prepared to work for the resistance. She'd been to all the Greek demonstrations in Paris and contributed what she could to all their appeals; and, just as you get to like a certain kind of cooking, she'd come to prefer the Greek problem to all the others.

Then Ethel changed her job, and Charilaos went to Germany. When they met again a year later the views they exchanged about the future were somewhat glum. The actor cropped up in the conversation from time to time, but like the shadow of an object whose relation to the light neither of them could remember. He was now a celebrity in Greece.

That was why she was so glad to see him that day after he'd phoned. Charilaos found her looking quite different. Her hair was done in chestnut and a new style: straight back over the temples and behind the ears, then falling in loose crescents about her neck and over her shoulders. She was alone in her office except for a sort of dragon on the desk, aglow with flashing green, red and amber lights, with apertures between to show which lines were free, and plugs like those on a dentist's chair—a kind of Minotaur, with Ethel playing Pasiphae to the boss, who must be lurking behind the leather-padded door.

"You couldn't have chosen a better day," she said. "Only outside appointments this morning. So let's go."

He offered her a cigarette; between her fingers, it turned

into something elegant. She shut a couple of drawers, pressed a switch on the dragon as if to mesmerize it into immobility while she was away, pulled down the blind, put on her dark glasses, and emerged, displaying ravishing legs in wide-meshed stockings, which a daring mini highlighted like an arc lamp.

They went to the nearest pizzeria. At this hour it was full of business people from nearby offices, but they managed to find a corner where they could talk: a table for two next to where the cutlery was kept, so noisy no one else had taken it. They ordered a Neapolitan and a Margherita, with one beer and one Coca-Cola, and he described the plan, including all the details she needed to know. It was up to her to find the victim who was to serve as cat's-paw. He described the haunts in Glyphada Beach and Bucarestiou Street where sex-starved Americans got drunk and cheated on their wives. She would never meet the zealots themselves. She would only deal with a contact. He gave her the telephone number and a password: *"Tou îpa paré méros."*

"It doesn't mean anything in French," he explained, "but in Greek it means 'get going.' And it sounds like 'Tupama-ros.' "

They smiled. Ethel was supposed to be taking her vacation the following month, but she could take it earlier. Naturally, the organization would pay all her expenses. It would be like a month's paid leave.

"I've always been looking for an excuse to go to the sea and the sun," she told him, her hand gripping his wrist like the strap of a watch that ticked in her pulse and had its works in her head. The two pizzas landed in front of them like a couple of flying saucers or two land mines neither of them was eager to set off.

Ethel was the first to say "I'm starving" and dive in.

Charis followed, hesitantly.

"Who else knows besides you?" she asked after she'd appeased her hunger.

"Thanassis, in Rome," he said.

"No one else?"

"No."

"Is the contact married?"

"No."

"Okay then," she said and paid the bill.

The Cash

Charilaos put a call through to Rome to tell Thanassis the good news: the "person" had agreed. At the same time, he gave him the vital statistics: bust and waist measurements, weight, color of hair and eyes—she might have been a candidate for Miss World. All they had to do now to keep up appearances was get the money as quickly as possible. Thanassis promised to see to it.

He made the rounds of the people he knew, Greeks long settled abroad and foreigners who'd been made aware of Greece by the dictatorship. He asked them for money for a very serious "matter" that had to be seen to "back home." But the people he knew told him they were fed up with giving money for plans that never materialized. It wasn't that they didn't trust him, they said, but they'd learned from experience that money meant for the resistance always ended up financing the travels of the resisters. So they suggested first of all cutting down the toing and froing. Just let them have the date and time and place of some definite "action," and then they'd really know there was a solid setup and hand over the money. He went to see three people in a row and they all gave him the same answer, as if they'd arranged it between them.

"First a guarantee you're not a crook like the others, and then the cash," they said. But how, how? It was the first time he'd asked for money. And he wasn't like the others. And how could he move about without money? They told him, "Get started first, and then we'll invest." He told them, "I can't get started if you don't give me anything." They told him, "We've given a whole lot already, and nothing is happening." He told them again, "I'm not like the others."

The resistance organizations collected money for the families of political prisoners, for the setting up of underground presses, for posters and leaflets. That, thought Thanassis, was how a takeover started: they let themselves in for playing opposition on the enemy's own ground. What was needed was to reverse the terms, upset the board and force the enemy to play on another. That was what he believed. What gave him courage were the names of twenty-one political prisoners who would be liberated, among them his brother, if . . .

He told Charilaos to wait a bit longer. He'd have a last try in West Germany.

There's No Worse Feeling . . .

Ethel's new passport was ready. It had been faked by someone who'd been in the Algerian resistance and was now one of "theirs." Her bags were packed. The contact had already photocopied the list of twenty-one names to be given to the foreign press and the statement that was to accompany it. Everything was ready, or nearly; all that was missing was the accursed money—that sixth sense which, as someone once said, sets the other five in motion. The date of Ethel's vacation was approaching, and Charilaos still hadn't dared call her to tell her the real reason for the delay. Ethel had to know that she wasn't being sent barefoot among thorns, that behind the *Tou îpa paré méros* there were solid people whose apparent absence was made into real presence by their money.

There's no worse feeling than giving yourself up entirely to an idea when the man who personifies it keeps out of the way, doesn't call you, doesn't answer the phone when you call him. So it was that, two days before her vacation actually began, Ethel irrupted into Charis' attic. She found him lying there, unshaven, under a poster of Guevara with a cigar between his teeth. Some soup was heating on a spirit stove. The bare room with its uneven floor, the dim light, the bust of Lenin on a set of dusty shelves—all proclaimed the absence of any woman.

She sat on the edge of the divan. Her mini left uncovered the classic legs, centripetal in form and marble in texture, in the flowered stockings with a run in them, that necessary flaw in the artificial through which a breath of humanity can enter. For in this, Ethel was like all the French girls of her age who were Maoists: they revered uniformity as much as Mao did, and dressed according to the one-year plan of the Lin Piaos of fashion, the Chou En-lais of the revolution—Cardin, St. Laurent and Dior. Yet the run in the stocking, the flaw, gave the leg back the humanity it had lost under the openly provocative mini. And Charilaos could recognize it as hers and nobody else's, just as, while watching beauty contests where you could hardly tell one competitor from another, he'd often been moved by an appendicitis scar in the right lower corner of the belly. . . . She sat on the edge of the divan and asked him straight out whether it was for financial reasons he hadn't called her. Charilaos started by saying no, he had other problems, but when she pressed him, he had to admit it. At that moment the soup boiled over and Ethel ran to the stove. But she didn't know how to turn it off. Charilaos got up and snuffed the flame with the lid.

Then he fetched two plates. The bare room, the austerity, Greece on posters—these all moved her deeply, and she tried to offer to pay for the whole operation herself. But Charilaos wouldn't hear of it.

"Out of the question," he said. "Absolutely out of the question. That's our responsibility. You're offering us your services free. But we're the organization, and—"

"*Tou îpa paré méros,*" she murmured in her halting Greek.

She came over. Now she desired him. She hadn't yet told him how much he attracted her, under his charmless "intellectual" exterior. The actor might have been her Adonis, but in the end his beauty had left her cold. She wanted something more flawed, more human. The vases she liked best in museums were those stuck together bit by bit with glue. Since the dictatorship she had relived the tragedy she had gone through herself when she was a little girl—the tragedy of the refugees, the emigrants. In spite of her apparently unmarked surface, she had a great deal of feeling, a great deal of compassion, for every diaspora and for every fugitive. She came over to him and was just about to tell him not to worry when the phone started to ring and got him out of the dilemma. She heard him speaking conspiratorially in Greek. He told her an official representative of the junta was coming to Paris and they were getting up a demonstration against him.

"But how are we to set about it? The French police are always looking for an excuse to expel foreigners. It's a junta that functions here too, according to the laws of capitalism. . . ."

She looked at the poster of Che. The joy of the future shone already from his eyes.

Finally Charilaos admitted they were having difficulty raising the money for her traveling expenses and the flat they had to rent for her. He overcame his shyness and produced the list of the twenty-one who would be liberated if Ethel lured a member of the American army into the hands of the zealots. He read them out. For Ethel, of course, it was only multisyllabic sounds, like electronic music, but she was intoxicated by the ring of his voice. Might not these incomprehensible noises be the names of the Brazilian political prisoners now enjoying the sun of Algiers? There was a fourth part of the Jewish diaspora in her own veins, and she felt irresistibly attracted to the Greek, who for so long had regarded her as merely a potential unit in the resistance. There's no feeling more exciting to a woman conscious of her own magnetism than to be seen by a man not as a sexual object but as a maker of history.

There was a knock at the door. It sounded like a signal, but it was not. Charis had just been saying how he went about Paris as if in enemy territory and how he still kept to the rules of the underground. So now he signaled her to hold her breath. There was another knock at the door, then a voice.

"Let me in, Charis. It's me—Thanassis."

Charis leaped up and ran to the door, first unbolting and then unlocking it. Thanassis entered, fresh from Rome, radiant as the sun. He had the cash. Some workers in West Germany had contributed it anonymously. They'd put in an extra day's work and got together the required amount so as not to be outdone, as they had said, by the Fedayin.

They really let themselves go in the attic. Charilaos wound up the old gramophone and put on a *rebetiko*. Then he rushed round the corner and bought a bottle of Algerian wine described on the label as "a velvet lining for the stomach." And cheap—the cheapest—one franc sixty. Meanwhile the soup had got cold. He started to weave across the uneven floor, dancing the hassapiko, and the tenants below banged on the ceiling with broom handles. Then they went out and through a side street to Boulevard Saint Michel, where Charilaos bought *Ta Simérina* at a kiosk; all the other Greek papers were sold out. Then they went down by the river, and there, by the moored barges and the passenger steamers, they gave final instructions and exchanged final vows. And there too, for the first time, Thanassis and Ethel kissed. For several days he could feel the touch of her lips on his cheek, and he tried in vain to imagine the captain or colonel who was going to enjoy it now.

Hélène MacGibbon

Orly really is elegant, thought Charilaos. France may be going further and further right, but it's redeemed by its elegance. The Paris of the future will be a huge hotel for connoisseurs of the arts, fashion, and food. The Paris of the Bastille, the Commune, the Liberation, and of May '68 will no longer exist. The workers will have been pushed out to the suburbs, and what's left will be an empty shell, an echo chamber of revolution, an academic mausoleum for tourists. He was leaning on the barrier separating the crowd of passengers from the crowd of those they were leaving behind and watching Ethel as she waited in the queue at passport control, dressed like a model out of the latest fashion magazine. She had to go through two checkpoints, one for currency and one for immigration, and she mustn't arouse suspicion at either. Since the devaluation of the franc, passengers were allowed to take only a certain amount of money out of the country. Ethel had ten times that amount knotted up in a little handkerchief which she kept like a talisman in her bosom. It was money earned by the sweat of the Greek workers in Germany, and the tickle of it against her skin gave her courage; it was destined for the cause. She also had the false passport, made out in the name of Hélène MacGibbon, French nationality, sculptress. So Charilaos was relieved when he saw the inspector reach out and stamp it. And Ethel—he could imagine her smile—put the passport back into her sumptuous python bag, and with her ticket and boarding card in one hand, picked up her purple traveling case with the other and set out for the endless corridors leading to the gates for take-off. Only at the last moment, when the loudspeaker announced her flight, did she turn, before disappearing into the labyrinth, and give him one of those looks of understanding that can go with you for a lifetime.

Charis sauntered away from the barrier and glanced up as if casually at the big clock, between an Indian turban and the felt hat of some technocrat. The Air France Athens-Nicosia-Beirut flight was about half an hour late because of a token strike in traffic control. Then he strolled over to a newsstand and was staggered to read in *Figaro* about the assassination of Gheorgatzis in Cyprus.

Ethel was sitting in tourist class between an elderly lady who looked like a Greek from abroad and a man who told her he was traveling in the Middle East in aluminum. The lady, who spoke French with a heavy accent, used the delay in their flight as an opportunity to observe how she simply couldn't understand strikes, hijacking, boycotts, and all the other things of which there was no danger in Greece thanks to the revolution of April 21. "You'll see for yourself," she said. Ethel made no comment either way. She was bored. And as the old lady, the wife of some shipowner, chattered on, she turned politely towards the man, who had a cigarette in his mouth, ready to light it as soon as the red light went out. Immediately afterwards he got out a thermometer, suspended it in the air for a moment, read it, and complained to the stewardess about the dreadful heat.

It was quite a pleasant flight. The businessman's conversation was a revelation about how capitalism was eating up this part of the Mediterranean. When the Greek coast ap-

16

peared below, Ethel couldn't resist getting up and looking down at Ithaca through the porthole. The last time she had been in Greece was in 1965. She felt as impatient now as she had then to reach the sea, the sun, the untamable light.

She was greatly impressed by the new Hellenikon airport; the view from its windows encompassed the whole plain of Attica. She went through customs like a dream, by dint of exercising her charm on the inspector and another man in plain clothes, and took a taxi straight to the Hilton. On the way she noticed all the new apartment buildings that had invested the shore and how the filth from the sewers had pushed back the sea itself. Even more noticeable were the battleships of the Sixth Fleet, refracting the sun like the Carthaginians' burning glasses at the siege of Tripolis.

Colonel George Foster

Colonel George Foster had replaced his colleague John Willis, known all over Greece for the famous affair of what the papers called "the modern Medea": he had cheated on his wife, and in a fit of hysterical jealousy she had strangled her three children with a nylon stocking. She was first put in a mental home, then sent back to Texas; no one ever heard any more about poor John Willis. So the colonel who succeeded him, George Foster, was very sensitive on the subject of women and took the same precautions against discovery he would have if he were fighting in Vietnam.

He had been in Greece more than five years, not counting an intervening year spent at NATO headquarters in Izmir; there was a rule forbidding anyone to spend more than three consecutive years in one post, in order to avoid local complications. Because he was in charge of the mess at the American base at Hellenikon—known all over Greece as the PX—

the risks in his case were obvious. The post was the last in a career of more than twenty years in the army. When he retired he was going into the Chariot Food Corporation. This was a Greek-American company named after the Charioteer at Delphi and run from Boston, which did the catering for all Onassis' ships and planes. He was to be taken on as an expert in management, with special knowledge of the insatiability of the Greeks.

He had two children, and his wife belonged to the Association of American Wives, which in addition to giving tea parties once a week also made efforts at philanthropy. After the king's unsuccessful countercoup, the ladies of the AAW were in a quandary and were forced to devote themselves, fortunately only for the time being, to providing dowries for underprivileged girls. Mrs. George Foster distinguished herself so much in sorting out the chaos left behind by the queen mother that the clerks at the Ministry of Social Welfare called her Frederika the Second.

They lived at Glyphada, behind the church, in a villa found for them by the army, with a private garden and a garage to protect their tires from the homemade bombs which, according to HQ, the anarchists or some such had been in the habit of planting as a protest against the American invasion of Cambodia. But how were they, in Greece, responsible for what their compatriots were doing elsewhere?

Mrs. Foster never bought anything in Glyphada—not even sugar, not even eggs. She drank only boiled water from the mess. This was not because her husband was in charge of it, but because in the special school in Washington for army wives she had been told to avoid local products. Goods produced by indigenous elements might always be dangerous— not properly canned, or infected. Heaven knows they didn't do it on purpose, but their technological backwardness made them dangerous. After all, that was what the Americans were there for—to civilize them. It used to be the missionaries; now it was the military. Of course, they'd been told they weren't going to some underdeveloped African country, but to Greece, to the cradle of civilization, as Durant called it, which through various historical vicissitudes had unfortunately come to be backward, underdeveloped, left behind by history. So they mustn't show any "distaste," but simply be very careful about indigenous vegetables, lemons, eggs, bread and water. Nothing, absolutely nothing, they were told in Washington before they left, was to be relied on.

Mrs. Foster hadn't needed to attend any special school to discover the lamentable quality of "local goods." She only had to go to some party or reception, and as soon as they found out her husband was in charge of the mess all the other ladies, especially the Greeks, fell upon her like carrion crows. For the natives, the PX was like Allah's paradise, a bower of bliss with mountains of Uncle Ben's rice—"foliage of dream, and dream of foliage." Not only were the things there a mere third of the usual price, but they included products not to be found in even the best Greek-American grocery stores in Athens. Ketchup and Tabasco and assorted steak sauces, big tins of Maxwell House coffee, cases of Kentucky bourbon—because of these, respectable judges', doctors', lawyers', bankers', industrialists' and jewelers' wives ran after her as if she were manna from heaven. When they succeeded in getting Howard Johnson ice cream, with its countless flavors, from the mess, they would organize a poker game in its honor. They were ready to sell their souls for the right to enter the base—ladies in very comfortable circumstances, not at all like beggars to look at, who gave Mrs. Foster their telephone numbers and invited her to drinks after dinner, so much so that she was obliged to limit her relations with the local inhabitants in order not to be always refusing.

George Foster's office was in the American Mission building next to the Military Aid Fund, and during the five years in all that he'd spent in Greece, driving home every evening along the coast road, he'd killed only two locals: an old man crossing at the traffic lights and a boy fooling around on a bicycle. He was in the habit of going about 75 miles an hour, and there was one part of the boulevard where he couldn't resist the temptation to accelerate. So the two accidents had happened there, between Trocadero and Flisbo, with the speed going up and up and the colonel still stepping on the gas. Of course, he wasn't prosecuted, because as a foreign soldier he wasn't subject to local law, even though the two victims died before the ambulance arrived. All that remained was his remorse, which as a Catholic he made a great deal of, cultivating it in the hothouses of the Church, remorse being such a valuable reminder of man's unworthiness compared to divine perfection. Also as a matter of course, he had discreetly paid compensation to the two families, but alone with God he called down retribution on himself for these sins. For these and these alone.

He didn't regard is as a sin to lay the women who worked in the mess. The Church forbade divorce, he was conscientious about his job, and he liked to supervise everything personally, so there was no reason why he shouldn't check on the cleaning women, these fiery natives, queens who could play the flute better than the king. There was an unlimited supply. In conquered capitals like Saigon, Djakarta, Athens and Ankara there were far more applicants than jobs; in addition to material advantages, collaboration with the occupying power meant protection against the arbitrary power of the local police. And so Colonel George Foster, without having really intended it, had even laid girls from the best Athenian families, who'd taken off their panties for the simple reason that their mothers had told them not to bother to come home if they hadn't hooked a job in the mess. Even girls in love with someone else found themselves in the unfortunate position of having to exhibit their underwear to Colonel Foster, who couldn't help being reminded that his predecessor, Colonel Willis, had known the same martyrdom and that it had ended up by making his wife a Medea. But George knew what was what and never went with girls who had any connection with his own circles. More important still, he didn't rent an apartment. When necessary, he just used to borrow a friend's key. He wasn't really either a mother's boy or a swinger. The creature he liked best after his children was his dog, Dick, which he took out to breathe the air of the chase on Hymettus whenever he could and on inspection tours of subsidiary messes at other Greek bases. Wherever he went—Idzedin, Crete, Oropos, Corfu, Kavala, or Nea Makri, near Marathon—Dick was his inseparable companion.

Colonel Foster would sometimes put in a brief appearance in the mess at Glyphada, but he took no active part there; it was near home, and he didn't like to be too near home. His children went to the American school at Kifissia, where the number of pupils had doubled since the "revolution"; many prudent parents had taken their offspring away from Greek schools and sent them to American ones, where instead of learning poems by Solomos, Palamas and Makriyannis, they heard about Lincoln, Longfellow and Whitman. Every afternoon the school bus took them home to their own doors, limiting as far as possible the danger of kidnapping.

Such, in short, was the life of the George Foster family up to the inauspicious day when the Colonel met Hélène MacGibbon in the Nineteen Bar.

The Solitude of Charilaos

Driving back from Orly in the Air France bus, Charilaos couldn't decide whether he was upset by Ethel's departure or by the assassination of Gheorgatzis. They got rid of him because he knew too much, he thought. Now that things no longer depended on him he felt like a deserter. His role was now only that of a spectator. Others would be pulling the chestnuts out of the fire; others would be taking the risks. He really ought to be there, underground, in disguise, following what went on, instead of . . .

He didn't know any more about the "others" involved than what Thanassis had told him, that they were ready for anything and that the contact was a citizen above all suspicion. As for Ethel, he knew her well enough to know she wasn't a secret agent. She hadn't entered the business through the door that agents are in the habit of using.

Back in his attic he warmed up some coffee, then lay on the bed and waited for the time to go by. He imagined Ethel being questioned by the immigration police, being tortured to make her give away the people who'd sent her. His brain, sick with inaction, imagined all the tortures he'd heard or read about being practiced on Ethel's fragile body. Whenever his imagination threatened to go too far, he remembered with relief her foreign passport.

Had he fallen in love with her without realizing it? Was he jealous because at this moment—it was beginning to get dark outside—she was in Athens, in his own city, in his own country that he had thirsted for so long? What was it that was oppressing him like this?

The gong on the radio announced the same news bulletin as an hour ago, with minor modifications. Israeli aircraft had bombed Egyptian bases on the Suez Canal. Cairo had announced two Phantoms shot down. Tel Aviv had denied it: all their aircraft had returned unharmed. The same news that had been churning out ever since the accursed day in June 1967 when the Greek question had been totally eclipsed. He realized he'd go mad if he just stayed in his room worrying

"Would you toss over the middle pages with the apartment ads?" said the one with the mustache. "We'll be going back soon so we might as well start thinking about where to live."

"You're an optimist," said the hippie.

"Hell," said the little roly-poly, getting angry. "In a month you'll be sunning your ass at Baxé-Tsifliki."

"'Sweetie from Salonika . . . ,'" sang the ladies' man to annoy him. "Tell us what you've had to eat today."

"What I've had to eat today is of no interest," said the little roly-poly.

Everyone stopped talking. He was going to do his bit.

"Just sausages and chips. But what I *could* have eaten is what you mean—a nice filet mignon? And do you know a good way to do it? You tenderize it for a couple of hours. Then you cover it with chopped onion and start cooking the whole works in a skillet. On another burner you make a sauce out of diced mushrooms, carrots, celery, onions, parsley, olive oil and tomato paste. And on a third flame you fry some potatoes in pure olive oil. As soon as the steak's about ready, you pour the sauce over it, take it off the gas, and flame the whole thing with Courvoisier, so the flavor of the meat and the sauce combine. Then you dish it up with the potatoes arranged around and a bottle of Mouton-Rothschild."

"Stop, stop," said the one with the mustache. "I haven't eaten since the day before yesterday."

This was the fat man's favorite act. No one knew if he was really a good cook or only good at describing a meal. He always said you ought to go to the market first thing in the morning to get the best, which at least implies going to bed early at night. Yet he was an inveterate night owl.

Charilaos felt stifled. He'd come here only for the pleasure of *not* telling them anything, just to feel inside him the secret that would soon be a secret no longer. And now he

like this. It would be better to go out and mix with people in the streets and shops, blow the cobwebs away. The best thing of all would be to go to a movie.

But first he wanted to share his anxiety with someone. And since the only person he could speak to was Thanassis, he dialed 10 twice and asked for Rome. After giving Thanassis' number and his own, he asked at the last minute how long the call was likely to take. "Two hours," said the girl on the switchboard. "No, thanks, then"—hastily. "I'll cancel the call." "Cancel the call," echoed the operator and cut off even before he'd hung up. Two hours was too long to wait.

He went out. One change on the Métro and he was among the cafés frequented by Greeks—not his friends, of course, but people he knew, and others he called "amphibians" because they spent the summer on the Greek coast and the winter in Paris, the "intellectual center" of Europe, playing pinball. In Greece they were regarded as up to date because they'd seen the latest work by Beckett or Glauber Rocha, not available there on account of the "situation." (The amphibians never spoke of "coup d'état" or "revolution," only of the "situation"; this got them out of taking sides.) The Greeks in Paris who had really suffered for their country tried to find some room more than four yards square, where they listened wistfully to music, watched television and scoured newspapers from home. Some of the more sober ones decided to start a family and from then on had their children to worry about.

He went in. Among them he hoped to withdraw more completely into his secret. And there once more he found the amphibians, together with the "monophysites"—those who'd burned their bridges and could not go back—playing pinball in pairs, unloading onto the insatiable machines all the rebuffs of exile.

"What's new?" someone asked him idly, his eye on the ball bouncing spasmodically here and there off the rubber cushions. And without waiting for an answer he bent right over the machine, which was now emitting pings and flashes, as if trying to stop the ball from going through the goal and disappearing down the abyss. He let go of the table with an oath and picked up his beer from the bar while the next player took his place.

"Nothing," said Charilaos. And he imagined them all in a few days' time, feverishly examining the business from all angles and wondering "who was behind it." And he would listen and take part in their conversation and their theories. . . .

"Have you seen *Le Monde?* They've let out another four hundred."

"No, I haven't seen it."

"They've killed Gheorgatzis," said another, with *Apoyevmatini* opened in front of him to the arts page. Then he went on, "It seems Lambéti's putting on a new play."

"Who's this Tzékos they're talking about?" asked someone reading over his shoulder and smoking like a chimney.

"The Kokotas of the cinema. Another star that's come out since we left."

"He's a young actor," explained an amphibian, "who claims to have been in lots of films in Paris. People'll swallow anything there."

This man had nothing but contempt for the Greek people, who were ignorant of all the important movements abroad. He went back just for the swimming and was disgusted by the "deplorable level" of art, preferring the simple fisherman of the islands to the "pseudo of Kolonaki." The monophysites had given up contradicting him long ago. The law of co-existence in the aquarium of the café forbade head-on collisions. Three years had taught everyone resignation.

The bell rang to announce a free turn. Everyone gathered around the player who'd struck it rich, trying to inspire him

to fresh successes. Before the dictatorship, he'd had a shop in Aegion and business had been good, but one day he'd spoken out of turn and had to leave. He'd worked as a house painter for a while, gone hungry, and now he turned his frustration against the pin tables. Beside him an amphibian dressed like a hippie fiddled with the cross around his neck.

Charilaos finished his glass of Beaujolais and ordered another. Drinking soothed him. He reflected that Tzékos w[as] none other than his friend the actor, Ethel's ex-lover. But [he] hadn't said anything because the subject was connecte[d] however remotely, with his great secret.

"You're very absent-minded today. What's up?" said [the] first player. It would soon be his turn again, and he [had] brought his beer over near the pinball machine.

"Nothing. This sultry weather makes me feel a bit d[ull]" said Charilaos. But why did the resident café informer [want] to single him out today of all days? He looked rather l[ike a] Moroccan, with his little suit and tie. He'd been coming [here] for a long time to drink his coffee and read his paper. A[t first] they'd taken him for a spy from the embassy—he was a [real] type of informer from before the coup—but late[r they] learned he belonged to the narcotics section of Interpo[l. That] didn't worry anyone; nobody was really hooked on dru[gs. All] the same, it worried Charilaos that the man should bot[her him] today, as if he could read his thoughts.

"Anybody else dead today?" This was said as he [entered] the café by the little roly-poly who'd become their [regular.]

"No one we know, anyhow," answered the one [with the] paper.

The little roly-poly had a morbid mentality. He u[sed to say] that we and everyone we knew would be dead bef[ore we got] back. And as necrophilia goes with gluttony, h[e loved] bemoaning the dead only to gloat over prospective [ones. But] others knew him and got along with him all right[.]

wanted to leave, to go a long way away, to vanish into the womb of a cinema showing some endless film without an intermission.

The Meeting

On that fateful afternoon, Colonel George Foster left his office as usual at one o'clock. He went past the Zonara, its sidewalk tables seething with tourists now, unlike last year and the year before when they'd stayed away on the pretext of the crisis in the Middle East. He waved to two or three of his colleagues sitting there waiting for the shuttle, the service car that delivered them home, for though Americans don't usually take a siesta, the special schools they pass through before being sent out to their colonies urge them to adopt local customs in order to appear less alien. So they, too, had a little snooze before going back to their offices in the afternoon. Some were in uniform, but most were in civilian dress to avoid "provocation." There were also a few Greeks, including five girls who worked in the American offices of the Aid Fund. Two of them looked like caryatids, with hair in Grecian knots behind and noses like antique statues before the vandals chipped them. He greeted them and walked on, as was his habit, toward the Nineteen, a hundred yards down the street.

The bar, owned by a Greek-American, was built below street level. Its habitués were members of the Military Mission, local pimps and a certain type of woman; and it had come to be a sort of "private" club. Only members were allowed in, and these included several agents of the Defense Intelligence Agency, also mostly Greek-Americans. After the April 21 "revolution," the bar had acquired the reputation of being a hornets' nest of secret agents of all nationalities, but it was convenient, close to his office, and—now in summer—cool in the middle of the day.

Here he saw her. Her legs were crossed, uncovering the thigh so that a hint of white could be seen gleaming between the two inviting petals. She was using a gold cigarette holder, and her hair fell loose about her bare shoulders. Two or three strangers ogled her from their stools at the bar without quite daring to go over. She couldn't have been there long; the waiter was just bringing her a gin fizz. The colonel raised an eyebrow at the barman to see if he knew who the new arrival was, and the barman, a gay type, shrugged his shoulders. The girl was leafing through a French fashion magazine.

Enveloped in the cellarlike coolness, his eyes soothed by the soft shadow after the dazzle of the concrete outside, he suddenly felt the blood rush to his head, and snorted like a bull. He wasn't the sort to wait for things to happen. His motto was strike while the iron's hot; hit and run. As the beautiful stranger fitted another cigarette into the long holder, he seized the chance for the classic approach and offered her a light. She accepted it, and he sat down beside her.

"Waiting for someone?"

"No."

"French?"

"Yes. And you?"

"American."

"A tourist?"

"No, I work here. And you?"

"I'm a sculptor. I'm here . . ."

"To see the Parthenon."

"That's right."

"What's your name?"

"Hélène. What's yours?"

"George. Can I buy you a drink?"

"No, thanks."

This dialogue took place at a quarter past one. At half past two, Colonel Foster phoned, from the exclusive ground-floor studio Hélène had rented, to tell his wife he wouldn't be home for lunch. Something unforeseen had cropped up: Admiral Rivero, chief of NATO's southeastern fleet, was arriving the next day on a tour of inspection, and he had to get ready for it.

"But the Sixth Fleet left today," objected his wife. "How can the admiral be arriving tomorrow?"

As he explained later to Hélène, his wife's reasoning was so naïve he couldn't help laughing.

"I can see her point," said Hélène, lowering her eyes. "But you must be an important person to be able to use that sort of excuse."

The blond wig and artificially halting English made her seem just like the French girls who play sexy roles in Hollywood films.

"I'm a brigadier general," he said, promoting himself a step in the hierarchy to seem more important in her eyes, the color of which varied depending on the pair of contact lenses she happened to be wearing. Anyway, it wasn't altogether a lie; that would be his rank on retirement.

"Which branch?"

"Commissariat."

She looked disappointed.

"But I fought in the Korean war," he said, and lost no time showing her his wound. As he undressed, she told him her father had been killed in the Second World War fighting under General Patton. She had a great admiration for soldiers; perhaps it was subconsciously connected with her father?

Before he left, he discreetly put ten dollars under the ash tray. He made her promise to meet him the next day at the same place, though it would have been better to find another hangout to prevent any gossip from reaching his wife's ears. And, guffawing loudly, he told her the story of his predecessor, Colonel John Willis, and of Medea.

The Studio

The studio was at the foot of Mount Lycabettus in a building finished only a few years ago. If you went in from Ippikou Syndesmou Street it was on the third floor, and if you entered from the ring road that circles the hill it was at ground level.

Ethel used both entrances. The first was the main one, and there were two janitors on duty, a man and wife, nice people. From there, she had to take the elevator to the third floor. But if you went in by the back through the kitchen door, you didn't see a soul, except perhaps some couple resting in the bushes on the hill. To get into the studio this way you had to go down a few steps and along a metal catwalk over a gully. The building, just beside the Doxiadis Institute, was a kind of dagger in the breast of the mountain, and they'd had to dig a moat to protect its rear against subsidence. After the catwalk, you had to go up a few more steps to reach the level of the door. She'd had no difficulty finding the studio; the agency understood at once she needed a separate entrance for professional reasons. Seeing how good-looking she was, they had no trouble guessing what the profession was. The place was fully furnished, and it had a refrigerator, a radio, and a telephone. Of course, the rent was a bit steep, but this was one of the most fashionable parts of Athens, and there was almost no noise except the hum of cars along the ring road. There was no further construction going on in the neighborhood, and the pure air from the hill was balm to lungs polluted in Paris. She'd paid in advance for the whole of the current month and for two more months besides. So, in fact, she'd paid for the whole of the summer.

Two days after she moved in, and before she'd even met the American, a plain-clothes policeman came from the Immigration Bureau. He spoke a little French and asked various questions about the purpose and length of her visit to Greece. As she made coffee in the big electric percolator, she answered politely that she'd always dreamed of coming to Greece, and friends who'd been here before had told her it was cheaper to rent a small apartment for the whole season than to pay by the day in a third-class hotel. She also told him she didn't believe any of the things people said about his country abroad. This pleased him especially, to judge by his smile. He asked what her job was, and she said she was a sculptor but made her living as a model. He asked her if she knew any Greeks, and she said yes, she knew several who lived in Paris. And some French people who lived on the island of Hydra had invited her for a weekend. As he left, the man apologized for his intrusion.

"Don't think we like bothering you," he said. "But our enemies plot against us from abroad, and we have to take precautions."

He left a card with his office number in case she should have any problems.

The apartment next door seemed to be unoccupied, and the sound of footsteps in the one above stopped around ten at night. The only thing that worried her was that if she switched off the lights and looked from behind the shutters she could see a man in plain clothes quartering the hillside. But it was probably someone from the vice squad, she thought, looking for Peeping Toms among the bushes.

The Contact

It was the contact who had suggested the Nineteen Bar the first time she saw him. She'd phoned him at his store and arranged to meet him at the Hilton. She was to wait for him outside on the opposite sidewalk. He would pick her up in a Ford Taunus and drive her to the beach. She was to be carrying a copy of *Elle.*

The contact had a leather-goods store in Pandrossou Street. He was thirty-five, with a slight paunch and frizzy hair; he seemed like a typical petty bourgeois, with his regular tavern, his quiet life, his policy of minding his own business. Once a right-winger, he'd later seen Andreas Papandreou as the symbol of his generation. But he'd never joined the Center Union party; he had always mistrusted them. So he really was, as Thanassis had said, a citizen completely above suspicion. He'd accepted the dictatorship like everyone else—passively. His first reaction had been, "Thank God I never committed myself." So they'd never bothered him, and he, for his part, had kept his mouth shut. Naturally his business nose-dived the first year, but he was ready to swallow even that. Until the moment came that marked him and determined his life forever—the evening they had suddenly arrested Thanassis' brother, Aristides.

Aristides had been with him at school and business school. They were more than friends, almost brothers. He himself had only sisters; it was to get them safely married off that he'd had, every now and then, to repress his feelings. In Aristo, he'd found a soul mate. Aristides had always been restless, searching, gnawed by inner dissatisfaction. Despite his success with women, for he was handsome, he was never at peace. Immediately after the coup, he had embarked on illegal activities—printing and distributing leaflets—though, of course, he never alluded to all this specifically, so as not to implicate his friend. The contact used to say, "You'll just kill yourself for nothing with this paper war." So each went on in his own way, not interfering with the other.

Then suddenly, last summer, one evening when they were going to see a "quality" movie at an open-air cinema in Patissia, he'd left Aristo for a moment at the corner opposite the theater to go and buy some cigarettes. When he came back—it couldn't have been but three minutes later—he found him in the clutches of the secret police, being shoved along on his knees towards a waiting van. He didn't go over. A glance was enough for them to understand each other. He walked on, affecting indifference, but observing the scene out of the corner of his eye: Aristides, his friend, being dragged into the car, bent double under jujitsu and karate blows. They must have hit him in the genitals, for Aristo, a very brave man, was yelling with pain.

He went straight to someone he knew in the Asphalia, the secret police, who was from the same village in Thrace as he was, and tried to find out where they'd put Aristides. The man had trouble tracing him because it was the military, not the secret police, who'd taken him. But he found him in the end and told the contact the official charge against him was distributing leaflets. According to the file, Aristides' defense was that he'd just picked up three leaflets in the street; otherwise he'd have had more of them on him.

The contact was shattered. And when he finally got to see Aristides three months later in Military Hospital 401, he found him unrecognizable, a skeleton with two broken ribs and feet cracked and swollen like old leather. And the quiet citizen vowed to himself that one day he would avenge his friend.

His work made it possible for him to travel abroad, for be-

sides selling manufactured goods in Pandrossou Street, he imported hides from Turkey and retailed them in Western Europe. He was a long-standing member of the Rotary Club
and had given a lecture on "the evolution of the treatment of
hides and skins from Homer to the present day." The talk
had attracted favorable attention in the press, and he always
took some clippings with him when he had to go to the
Ministry of the Interior to get permission for a trip abroad;
he'd foolishly omitted to get a five-year passport before it
was too late. The Rotary badge in his lapel and a couple of
one-hundred-drachma notes slipped to the official concerned
dissolved all difficulties.

His secret metamorphosis from bourgeois to revolutionary
surprised even himself. But his decision was made once and
for all. Nothing would ever stop him now. Repression is
merely abstract until it happens to you. Then, for the novices,
those who've never been touched before, it takes on a primal
horror that makes them its implacable enemies. This is what
happened to him that mild summer evening on the way to the
cinema with Aristides to see a "quality" film.

His main concern the next time he was abroad was to meet
Thanassis. He had had several addresses for him, and finally
tracked him down in Rome, frequenting, without joining,
various resistance movements. Thanassis had put him up at
his place, the apartment of a girl friend he had in Rome at
that time, the gentle and voluptuous Graziella. And there they
had agreed to organize something sensational, original, something after the heroic model of Panagoulis. For both of
them, Panagoulis had taken on mythical dimensions; his
desperate bid to kill Papadopoulos had seemed to them the
only thing to do—the only thing that, if it had succeeded,
would have produced some results. The Paraguayans who
had liquidated the German ambassador had prepared the
ground, Thanassis had said. The thought of a kidnapping had

begun to form on the horizon, like clouds generated by drought. Thanassis had already lined up the two zealots—his friends Sakis and Lakis. What had still been missing was a girl with guts.

And now he was driving her to the seashore in his Ford Taunus. They passed the airport and stopped near Alimo on a public beach where a mass of parked cars formed a kind of metal dike. They undressed and went into the water. Once away from the beach, he began to talk to her. It was there he told her about the Nineteen, where important people used to meet. If she went there she might . . . He spoke in halting English. Every so often the wash of a Chris-Craft going by between the flags or waves whipped up by the cool noon breeze would make him swallow a mouthful of salt water. He'd splutter, and then go on with renewed excitement. He watched her enjoying the feel of the sea, in her rubber cap covered with rose petals. She was scared by the touch of a medusa as they concluded their secret contract over the mute, conspiratorial water. As they walked back over the beach, she gave him duplicates of the studio keys and said she wouldn't see him again now until after the fish had taken the bait. The only thing she asked him was whether everything was ready and if they had more than one hideout. He said everything was arranged. Then she asked about the very last thing she wanted to happen: if, in case of necessity, the boys would pull the trigger. The contact nodded. He dropped her at the Hilton, at the spot where he'd picked her up.

The Cry

After the visit from the man in the Immigration Bureau, Ethel was afraid they might bug her telephone, and she de-

cided to go to the shop and tell the contact in person that "the
fish had taken the bait." It was a stifling hot July afternoon,
and she waited until the sun was behind the tall buildings and
the balconies threw deep pouches of shade. The flag on
Lycabettus, with the Phoenix of the "revolution," betrayed a
rising breeze. She went out in a sleeveless dress and exercise
sandals—she'd strained a tendon swimming.

On her way, she noticed the bellies, the sweaty shirts, the
sunburned faces. The only people left in the capital now were
those who hadn't been able to go away on vacation. She saw
no signs of hardship or impatience with the regime. Most
seemed to demonstrate the proverb "He who has nothing
has nothing to lose." With some bitterness tinged with a
gentle irony, she thought of Charilaos in Paris, reading the
latest news about Greece in *Le Monde*, about arrests and
economic crisis and all the rest of it. According to the secret
poll she was taking from their faces, people wouldn't approve
of the "plan"; prisoners were made for prison as surely as
cards were made for women's tea parties. Here—and again
she was judging from externals, because she didn't speak
the language—here everything seemed to obey some other
rule, some almost climatological pattern, which her friends
exiled in the West seemed to have forgotten about.

It was at this point, when she'd crossed Constitution Square
and was beginning to go down Mitropoleos Street, just at the
corner where Evanghelidis' photography store used to be,
that she heard a cry coming from the other side, near Papa-
spyrou's pastry shop, and turned around to look. The cry
had passed like an electric shock through the otherwise in-
different passers-by and a few tourists finishing their ices. She
would have taken it for a screech of brakes if she hadn't
turned in time to see someone being hustled away. Normally,
it would have had no effect except on the people nearby,
who'd seen what happened. But Ethel was glad to note that the

whole square had been galvanized; even ticket collectors poked their heads out of the trolley cars instead of giving the signal to start. So she concluded that under the misleading surface of acquiescence something was surging, something lying deeper, that had been uncovered by the cry, sinister as a shark's fin cutting through the quiet bay of Argosaronikos. Police in plain clothes swarmed around the El Al office, so, not wishing to show how interested she was, she walked down Mitropoleos towards Pandrossou Street.

When she walked into the shop on the pretext of making an inquiry, the contact showed his astonishment by a dilation of the pupils, which at once narrowed into a look of resentment. He came over and said they didn't have what she was inquiring about. Two young men who were sitting on the counter stood up and examined her. She realized her blunder from the contact's nervousness; he was drumming his fingers agitatedly on his little paunch.

Only a few days later she learned, much to her relief, that the two young men were also in on the secret—when she saw them, still in the same bright sports shirts, aiming the trident of a harpoon gun with untrembling fingers at the heart of George Foster.

The Zealots

Sakis and Lakis, the two assistants in the shop, were two boys who asked questions. They were old friends of Thanassis in Rome and had been in secret correspondence with him since the very first day of the coup. As a matter of fact, it was Thanassis who had suggested them to the contact when, during his third trip abroad, they had decided to go into action.

Lakis had been on the point of joining the Lambrakis Youth at the time of the coup. Sakis had been apolitical before, but he was one of those who were rudely awakened by the dictatorship. Seeing no other hope, they'd decided to study for themselves—books and ideas that they hoped would help them out of the blind alley of inaction. They were young enough not to have got on the files in the "prerevolutionary" years, yet old enough not to be satisfied with mere mockery, the usual resource of the weak. Naturally, at the local cinema they might make fun of the newsreels showing the deputy prime minister laying the foundation stone of a new church, or they might laugh to hear the prime minister talking away in his own incomprehensible jargon. But that wasn't enough. And when the contact suggested their coming to work with him, whom they remembered vaguely as a close friend of their own friend's brother, Aristides, they agreed with alacrity. Not only was it a temporary solution to the money problem, but also, when they'd put the shutters up in the evening, they could listen in safety to the Deutsche Welle from Cologne.

As for the contact, he'd arrived at praxis not through ideology—for him, Mao meant only a lotion to prevent falling hair—but because he had what he considered the good fortune to be able to go abroad often and see the so-called resistance movements as they really were. He'd met them through Thanassis and had come to the melancholy conclusion that nothing was to be hoped for from the Greeks in exile. Taken one by one, they all had charm and real, anguished sincerity; but as a group they were finished, incapable of agreeing among themselves on a common platform. To someone like him, eager for a lead, they gave the impression of being engaged in some pre-election squabble, giving no thought to the real power in the land—in this case, some admiral of the Sixth Fleet or top general in NATO.

Sakis and Lakis eagerly awaited his return from every trip abroad to find out if there was anything new. But, so as not to depress them, he concealed the sad reality. "You saw So-and-So. Aren't you going to tell us what he said?" they'd ask. But what was he to tell them? That the night he saw him he was looking for a place to sleep? Or that the party had told them to agree among themselves before even coming to discuss things? What was he to tell them? That the Greeks abroad had adopted foreign values and talked about home as if it were an already distant country—not in words or thoughts, still less in feelings, but in practice? It was inevitable. The law of emigration was operating as it always does. And while Sakis and Lakis were expecting the others to produce the tongs for pulling the chestnuts out of the fire, the contact, who knew there wasn't even the shadow of an idea of a tong, avoided talking to them frankly, because he knew it would only make them isolate themselves even more and ask questions more hermetical and unanswerable than ever. So he drank down his wine at a gulp to avoid speaking of what he didn't want to tell them, and they sat and pondered, saying "Yes, we heard it on the radio" or "Yes, we read that in the underground press."

Abroad, life went on, touched by the Greek question only when it became an object of domestic consumption for the purposes of local politicians. All vied to express in words their distaste for the "bestiality of the colonels." They could then go on, by way of redressing the balance, to attack the invasion of Prague. In their minds, the two went together; both could win them votes. The contact had learned abroad the truth of Flaubert's remark that human nature has inexhaustible reserves of indifference.

Everything was now poised for the kidnapping: the two houses, the car, and the weapon—the latest model of harpoon gun with an extra-powerful spring. Should their victim happen to be armed, they would take his gun, so that if the kidnap attempt failed they would at least be spared the charge of possessing illicit weapons. All they were waiting for was the news that the fish was hooked; then they were ready to harpoon him.

They didn't know that the woman who had come to the shop was the bearer of the great news. Later, when they saw her dashing to the telephone and pretending to believe they were burglars as they aimed the trident at their victim's heart, they laughed at the thought of that sticky late afternoon when they'd taken her for a tourist.

Mrs. George Foster

Mrs. George Foster knew she'd never be a modern Medea. Not only did she dislike the play, but also she didn't love her husband as her predecessor, Mrs. John Willis—who had strangled her children with a nylon stocking for revenge— had loved hers. But she sensed that another woman had seriously entered her husband's life; he'd recently begun titivating and scrutinizing himself in the mirror, taking great care shaving, and being lavish with aftershave lotion.

At home in Asheville, North Carolina, she'd have consoled herself by going to see a psychoanalyst. But that was a luxury beyond the reach of army wives in Athens. True, since the "Willis affair" a psychiatrist specializing in the psychology of officers' wives had been engaged, but he had so many patients you had to call for an appointment at least two weeks in advance. Besides, she'd met him at the home of a major they knew, and he'd made an unfavorable impression. So she threw herself into her efforts at the Association of American Wives, and even considered taking weaving lessons from a lady in Kifissia to soothe her nerves. She was also expecting her parents to come over next month to see their grandchildren for the first time, and the thought of having to show them the Acropolis and Sounion and Delphi made up for her present inactivity. She needed to get out, so she wouldn't have to think.

Her best friend, whose husband, a captain, was an expert in antiguerrilla warfare, wrote poetry. She was intelligent, sensitive, cultivated. She was younger than Mrs. Foster and had no children, and she often entertained the local intellectuals. She'd even taken a fancy to one of them, a quiet Athenian who wore glasses and was always asking her for tins of coffee, cigarettes, peanut butter, and bottles of gin. Mrs. Foster knew this because her friend got the stuff at the mess, on presentation of a chit from her. It was to this exquisite creature that Mrs. Foster went and opened her heart.

Her friend also suffered from *angoisse* and pointed out that the best way for her to avoid metaphysical anguish was to suffer in the body. Since Mrs. Foster had two bad teeth that needed extracting, she might as well have them attended to now. But when she arrived at the dentist's, she learned that all her teeth were bad, no doubt because of the local water, and that she would have to have false teeth.

"But I've never drunk *their* water," she exclaimed.

"That's not the point," said the dentist. "Even when you drink it boiled in coffee or tea, it still contains harmful ingredients which attack the pulp of the teeth."

And so, one fine day, Mrs. Foster made the great decision and found herself completely toothless, delighting in her own ugliness, and giving her husband further reason to be unfaithful to her. But what sort of a state were her parents going to find her in when they arrived? Arrived to visit the historic country which, as they said in their letters, "now had a government that was really one of ours." She would look older than her own mother. And there was George, doing setting-up exercises every morning in front of the open window. He said he wanted to lose twenty pounds. Who *was* this woman who'd turned his head?

41

Though she'd never particularly cared for the local people, whom she regarded as white Negroes, and though she had a special hatred of all the women, she couldn't resist the temptation to phone one of the girls who worked in the Mission on the same floor as her husband. She was a pretty brunette, just like a caryatid, who wore her hair in a knot; Mrs. Foster had met her at a reception held in honor of the new ambassador.

They arranged to meet for tea at the smaller Flokas'. The Greek girl came heavily made-up and dressed to kill. To have tête-à-tête with her boss's wife flattered her vanity no end.

"I want to talk to you woman to woman," said the boss's wife, offering her one of the long triple-filter cigarettes that were the exclusive privilege of those "belonging to the mess." "Someone has turned my husband's head—some woman I don't know, and . . ."

She burst into tears. Some of the other customers, for the most part elderly gossiping Greek ladies with blue-rinsed hair and lorgnettes, turned around and stared curiously at the weeping foreigner. The Greek girl, accustomed to serving in the American occupation forces and used to colonial dramas, took her tenderly by the hand.

"I've never sunk so low," said Mrs. Foster when she'd got over her first distress. "I can't blame him. Since I had all my teeth out I'm so ugly he has every excuse to . . . But I've never asked another woman to act as a spy for me. Never. Never."

This, of course, was a little white lie to spare her pride. Her husband was not being unfaithful to her because she'd had her teeth out; on the contrary, she'd had her teeth out because he was being unfaithful to her.

"My real dentist's in Asheville, North Carolina. For the last twenty years I've gone to him whenever I happened to be there. But just for once, I made myself go to an army dentist, and this is the result."

She kept herself from smiling so as not to reveal her red gums.

"I understand him absolutely, of course. Men are all the same. Though maybe yours are different—maybe they know how to love a woman better."

The girl shook her chignon.

"But ours are still little boys. They come straight from their mothers to us, and at first they take us for another mother. Until they are awakened sexually and get to know other women. But it isn't their mothers or the other women who pay. It's us, the American wives."

"How can I help you?" asked the Greek girl, who still didn't understand the real point of this tête-à-tête.

"I want you to follow him. If you can. I want you to find out who it is he goes out with, who it is he . . . ."

"But I hardly ever see the colonel. He just opens my door and says good morning when he comes in. I don't know where he goes or who he sees. And besides, in my position . . . I mean, one of my superiors . . . ."

"He's going to open a grocery store in Boston when he leaves the army. He's in with the Chariot Food Corporation," said Mrs. Foster desperately. "We'll have our own place then, and you can come work for me—double pay if . . . ." Then, with a gleam of madness in her eye, she added, "I presume you yourself are not the person in question."

She saw the chignon swooping towards her.

After her unsuccessful approach through the local "help," Mrs. Foster began to weave frantically at Kifissia.

The Solitude of Thanassis

Because of the postal strike in Italy, there was no hope of his getting the letter by which the contact was to inform him of the date and details of the kidnapping. According to their code, "wedding" was to signify the kidnapping, "son-in-law" the victim, "fiancée" Ethel, "best man" the contact himself, "witnesses" the zealots, "honeymoon" Ethel's escape, and "guests" the twenty-one political prisoners. Thanassis looked in his box every morning; there was never a sign. Nor had Ethel written to Charilaos in Paris. Whenever he could bear it no longer, Thanassis would go to see a couple he was fond of who'd just come back from East Europe.

The wife had been in the maquis, and after the civil war, like others from her village in Epirus, she'd gone to a socialist country, where she'd studied, taken her degree, married and had children, without ever losing the look of those who live in the mountains or her warm, country expression. With her brats, as she called them, always at her apron strings, she reminded Thanassis of the earth mother, the mother of mothers, the matrix of all life.

The husband was a Greek from Egypt, who'd also found himself in East Europe after the civil war. Unlike the Greeks from Greece itself, he was a cosmopolitan and had knocked about the world. This had given him a rare buoyancy, which he still kept even after fifteen years of dreary, colorless living among the "red aliens," as he called the Greek political refugees. The couple's dream had always been to get to the West. Of returning to Greece, even before the coup, no question. They just wanted to get away—not as defectors biting the hand that had fed them for fifteen years, but just simply, openly to get away. And about two years before, they had managed it. Now they lived in Rome, five of them in a two-room apartment. The husband worked his fingers to the bone in whatever job he could find; the wife worked hers to the bone in the home.

Thanassis was drawn to them and often went to see them. As a family, they radiated the warmth he missed so much. So when he couldn't stand being alone any more, and especially this evening, with the strike, he'd drop by to see them.

The wife was in the kitchen frying potatoes in oil, the way she knew he liked them. Though small, the kitchen was perfectly equipped with an automatic washing machine, three-shelf refrigerator, and an electric oven. She came and gave him her little finger to shake, then withdrew to her lair to get the children's supper.

The husband was shifting a heavy bookcase he had made himself out of planks and bricks. Jack-of-all-trades, he called himself. With three children, he had to watch expenses. But that was better than having everything provided by the state on condition you kept your mouth shut. His long years in East Europe had made him loathe bureaucracy, both the new class of leaders and the new class of slaves that had grown up on the Soviet model in the satellite countries. No one went hungry, but man does not live by bread alone. . . . "Right, Thanassis?"

And Thanassis gave him a hand with the bookcase.

"I've brought this back," he said, laying on the table Kostas Botsis' book on the Greek partisans in Tashkent.

"Oh? What did you think of it? You noticed how he shines the Bear's boots?"

"I learned a lot of things I'd never have dreamed of," said Thanassis.

"Such as?"

"The Greek partisans' difficulty in adjusting to the Soviet way of life."

"What he writes is nothing compared to the reality," said the other. "I'll tell you about it some other time."

"I was very interested, too," went on Thanassis, shoving the last shelf into place, "in the account of the relationship between the shepherd from Epirus and the Soviet woman. He had an awful inferiority complex."

"I already told you: aliens, red or otherwise, don't fit in anywhere."

His wife came out of the kitchen.

"Well?" she said to Thanassis, offering him the first of the fried potatoes straight from the pan. "It's more than a month since you've been here. . . . But you're not in very good form today. What's the matter?"

Her intuition was infallible.

"Not bad news about your brother?"

"No. No news. My mother was the last to see him. She wrote that the Red Cross isn't allowed to visit them any more."

Then they and the children sat down to eat, watching a variety show on TV at the same time. He told them about the "chaotics," the latest splinter of the outlawed Communist movement in Greece. There was another splinter group that was even further out, he told them. It was called "the balcony," because it considered itself above even the chaos. The differences between the two groups were minimal, he added. The only consolation, if you could call it that, was that these splinters were beyond the official split and belonged neither to the pro-Soviet nor to the anti-Soviet party. At about midnight, Thanassis left to catch the last bus.

Suddenly, he felt his shoulders flag under the burden he'd taken on. Where was he going, where was he heading for, walking barefoot like this among thorns? No problem if all went well. But if it failed, what would he, emerging unscathed, feel about Sakis and Lakis and the contact? He remembered the student he'd met in Paris who'd turned away from politics out of guilt because he was abroad and free while the others were in prison. No, he himself would never give up, never, so long as his brother was in prison, so long as Greece was a prison. And he raged again against the official left, which was once more on the defensive, begging for amnesties, the same rigmarole that was interrupted in 1964 only to be resumed again in 1967 in the same words, almost for the very same prisoners. No, it was too much. That was why he clung to the couple from the East—they knew the real situation from the inside. And for them it was too late to draw back. A life given to the party can't be canceled just like that. But they were in sympathy with him and with all the young people who at this moment found themselves outside all the old bankrupt groupings.

Lying with the radio on, his eyes open, he dared not think of the impact the kidnapping would have if it succeeded. Other countries would think the Greeks had an organization like El Fatah or the Tupamaros. No one would ever know they were still alone, barefoot among the thorns. Like Charilaos, he felt as if he were a deserter in the hour of battle.

"The Fullness of Time . . ."

While Thanassis tossed and turned on his bed in Rome, Sakis and Lakis waited, disguised, in the darkness in Ethel's studio. Lakis was wearing dark glasses that were too small and pressed against his temples. Or was it the veins thudding there? Sakis had stuck on a drooping false mustache, which he kept fingering as if it itched. Both wore wigs. Unrecognizable. They'd let themselves in at eleven-thirty with the duplicate keys. The apartment was all fixed up for the couple, with flowers in the vases. But in the bedroom, Ethel's bags were packed, a bikini dangling out of one of them like a conspiratorial tongue. Some undies were drying in the bathroom. The time agreed on was half an hour past midnight. It was now after that.

There was no sound from the neighboring apartments. Once, in the utter silence that pervaded the building, there came a faint echo of the muzzled music of Theodorakis. We must have friends here, thought Lakis, gesturing to Sakis to listen. Sakis, holding the harpoon gun at the ready, wanted to go to the toilet but restrained himself. The suspense and the darkness were killing him. He would have liked to speak but couldn't. Lakis had a fake revolver; their man always went about armed.

"A big fish?"

"Yes."

"Everyone'll be talking about it by tomorrow."

"We share the glory fifty-fifty, that's settled. Not like with Glézos in 1941 . . ."

"Ancient history."

"In court, say I dragged you into it. I almost joined the Lambrakis movement. You didn't know about anything but basketball!"

"*Ssh!* What was that?"

"Nothing."

Outside in the street a couple stopped by the window, kissed, then strolled on under the stars. Then a group went by singing:

As heavy as Hades your loaded gun—
Spread out, so they'll think we're a hundred and one.

"That's what we're doing," said Sakis.

The noises from the ring road streamed into the room. Some passers-by were talking about football, others about the movies. A shadow glided among the bushes. Policeman or Peeping Tom? Holy night, Attic night, conspire with us and muffle every sound!

"It's July thirteenth. We chose the right day."

"The girl had her period. No choice."

"On August thirteenth, Panagoulis came to grief. On December thirteenth, it was the king. On July thirteenth . . ."

"Shut up, Jonah. One crowded hour of glorious life! . . ."

"I've a feeling they're on to us already."

"How? Shut up, can't you?"

His luminous watch said one-fifteen.

"They must have had a blowout. No other explanation."

They were startled by a sudden screech of brakes. Lakis looked out and recognized the American Mission car. He didn't tremble.

They were late because George Foster had been getting stoned. They'd dined at an outdoor restaurant in Kifissia and gone on to dance in a night club. He was the only middle-aged man on the floor. It was while he was kissing the hollows of her neck with his dry lips that Ethel felt the ground disappear from under her feet; the bar, disguised as a fisherman's hut but with psychedelic lights, seemed to go down like a sinking ship. Nets, lanterns, life buoys—all merged into one when she caught sight of him holding a redhead close in his arms, more handsome than ever, a real Apollo. She'd forgotten how handsome he was, with his tapering waist and legs strong and supple as a dancer's. Yes, it was her former lover, the actor now famous under the name of Tzékos. George went on dancing clumsily, clutching her to him, carried away by the whisky, looking forward eagerly to the pleasure he'd soon be having in bed at the foot of the hill, while the first cocks outcrowed one another in the distance on Tourkovounia. Goddamnit, Hélène had come back looking marvelous from the three days she'd spent on the island. She'd sunbathed, and her skin shone now like an emerald in the half-light. And she knew more tricks in bed than ten American women put together; the veterans who'd been in Paris at the Liberation were right when they said French women were real hot stuff. Then he suddenly noticed Hélène wasn't dancing in time with him any more, and he looked around. Spotting the young man among a group at a table, he asked if she'd been looking at him all this time.

Hélène said she felt ill, giddy, and that she wanted him to

take her out of here and home right away. If the light had been better, George would have seen she'd gone white as a sheet with panic lest Tzékos should recognize her. If he did, it would be good-by to the colonel and wreck the whole plan. But the actor scarcely glanced at her any more than a cockerel inspecting a poultry yard—he knew he could have any woman he liked for the asking. No, not a gleam of recognition. That reassured her a little, but she was afraid her own movements might betray her. Bodies that have known one another in bed can read one another too easily dancing, and that was why, though she did her best to play Mata Hari and to remember ploys from the movies, she insisted on their leaving at once. George was preoccupied driving back. Jealousy had hit him for the first time. He hated all Greeks, every two-bit Alcibiades who could so easily take her away from him. That was why he decided not to go back to his own place tonight; they'd see dawn break together, lying side by side.

He parked the car in a space that was too small, so the rear stuck out a couple of yards into the road. Ethel insisted it would cause an accident if he didn't straighten it up.

"They'll see the 'Foreign Mission' plates and understand how it is," he said.

He slammed the door shut without locking it and followed her in. They went down the steps, across the catwalk over the gully, up a few more steps and on to the kitchen door. Ethel turned the key in the lock. She was trembling.

Lakis had watched them coming as far as the service stairs. He saw the "fish" stagger across the bridge and signaled to Sakis to charge. Sakis released the safety catch of the harpoon gun. If a shot was fired from it now, it would be fatal. The door creaked open. A wedge of light cut into the darkness. Ethel entered first, almost running. The colonel tottered after her. But no sooner was he through the door than Sakis' ringing "Hands up!" froze him to the spot. The barrel of the fake pistol was sticking in his back, aimed along the imaginary axis of his heart.

The first reaction of Colonel George Foster was to think that both he and Hélène had fallen into the hands of burglars. The city was overrun with them. There'd been an embassy circular about them, with a special warning on the danger of open windows during the summer. They'd take his money and some of Hélène's jewelry, and then they'd go. He didn't have more than forty dollars on him in cash, plus a nontransferable American Express card, his identity papers, and less than a hundred drachmas. But he realized with surprise that they were looking not for his wallet but for his gun, which was under his armpit. They grabbed it and made him kneel with his head down. Meanwhile, one of them covered Hélène with the harpoon gun.

Then the other, who now had two revolvers, said to him in his Institute English, "We go now. You go first and keep smiling. Nothing is going to happen to you if you do what we tell you. Understand? You'll be let free tomorrow."

He could feel the tears coming into his eyes. His hatred for the natives, reawakened by the young man in the bar, was turning now into self-pity. He obeyed like a child. And, for the first time, there came into his mind a bleak picture of his wife, all disheveled, strangling her children one by one with a nylon stocking. As long as it was only a question of staying with the girl, such thoughts would never have entered his head. But now that he'd been captured by gangsters, the baneful image of his predecessor flashed like lightning across the darkness of his remorse and regret.

What was going on? This wasn't Vietnam. It wasn't Cambodia. They weren't in Amman. This was Greece, and the Greeks, from what he knew of them, were a nation of sheep, pro-Americans every one, with at least one relative in the States, beggars at the mess. He knew them. He'd known them for five years, from experience, inside out, through and through. All crooks, troublemakers, bootlickers. Not even the bitter pride of a gypsy or the intelligence of a Jew. They'd sell their souls for a tin of Maxwell House coffee. So what was going on?

"Keep smiling," one of his two guards whispered in his ear, shoving him into the Volkswagen. His lips froze into an awkward smile until they reached a deserted spot where they blindfolded him and threw him into the back.

Sakis had a hideout in Kaningos Square just behind Solon Street, in the house of one of his aunts. The aunt had died intestate, and the house was empty, awaiting a court decision. It was a two-story building standing by itself next to a garage that closed at night. Fifty yards away there was an apartment building under construction, where men were at work during the day. And as they drove up, he saw a man, who'd apparently been stealing bricks, sneaking away with a sack. Sakis couldn't be sure he wasn't skulking behind a wall somewhere waiting for them to leave. So he and Lakis exchanged glances and decided they'd better go on to their hideout number two.

Number two was a villa in South Kifissia, to which Lakis had the keys. He had lived there for a month once. The house had been occupied by an elderly poet kept by a wealthy patroness of the arts. That is to say, she paid his rent; after the poet's death the house was supposed to become a "rest home for artists and intellectuals." But, unfortunately, the lady was not in a position to save the poet's manuscripts, a whole life's research into popular songs. The day of his funeral, she was with her fortuneteller in the suburbs, having her future read in coffee grounds, so duns and creditors were free to come and swarm all over the place and sell the work of a lifetime by the hundredweight. They kept the old man's little collection of peasant curios to pay his debts. But that's another story. And so, since the lady was afraid the house might be haunted, she let anyone who wanted it have it, to try to give it back some semblance of life; as the poet says, even objects have a soul. The wily Lakis had had the keys copied and kept them carefully ever since.

The coup found the lady on the Côte d'Azur, and there, since she was a Communist, she stayed. Lakis had only once made use of the house, reputed to be haunted and uninhabitable, and that was when he'd had to hide a member of the underground and could find nowhere else. This would be the second time. The man next door was a salami merchant, so the neglected garden was always hung with sausage casings, like condoms or the sloughed-off skins of young serpents. Fortunately, the neighbor and his family were away on vacation, so there was no danger of anyone's hearing them go in. The only drawback was that a couple of hundred yards down the road there was a branch of the highway patrol. But Lakis thought it was better to be right in the lion's jaws. The garden was a jungle. Buried in it was a bust by Aperghis of the dead poet's idol, Angelos Sikelianos.

George Foster was all at sea. The faces behind the masks were a mystery. All he'd seen was a scratch on the driver's determined chin, which only added to the virility of his appearance.

Sitting between them with his fixed grin, he'd tried to transmit his terror by telepathy to the few cars they passed. Now, lying blindfolded in the back, he vainly tried to make out what direction they were going in. He hadn't been able to keep track of all the twists and turns no doubt intended to confuse him. All he could make out when they finally stopped was the rustle of leaves and fragrant air that seemed like the air he'd been breathing earlier that evening at Kifissia. The fact that he couldn't hear the noise of any aircraft didn't necessarily mean he was far from home; planes rarely took off or landed at this hour. He did hear a heavy door creak. Then they crossed what must have been a garden; he could feel spider's webs brushing across his face, twigs hitting his legs. The ground was uneven, suggesting the place had long been empty and neglected. Finally, he went through a door that clanged shut behind him. The rancid air nearly made him faint. Was he in a cellar?

"So I've been kidnapped?" he said falteringly as he was being tied to a marble throne.

"Right the first time."

"But I don't know any military secrets. I'm in the Commissariat."

"So keep quiet," snapped Sakis, tickling the back of his charge's head with the barrel of his revolver on the bump that's supposed to be most vulnerable.

Lakis went to the phone in another room. He flicked off the prehistoric dust and let the phone ring twice at the other end. The contact, hearing it, would know all was well and they were in hideout number two. Naturally, they'd had a third and a fourth in reserve in case they needed them. And now everything depended on the reactions of the junta.

Next morning, like a blameless bourgeois, the contact called in at the Church of the Metamorphosis on his way to the store. There, in the right-hand poor box, he deposited an envelope containing the *Tou îpa paré méros* ultimatum with the list of the twenty-one political prisoners to be liberated in the next forty-eight hours. If there was no satisfactory answer, the execution of Colonel George Foster, officer in charge of the PX at Hellenikon base, would take place exactly forty-eight hours and one minute from the preceding midnight. Then, after lighting a candle and crossing himself in front of the magic ikon of the Saints Anargeros, he left the church, went into a phone booth and dialed the headquarters of the foreign press.

The reporter on duty was drowsing. It was going to be another hot day. For five years he'd been going rusty in this country, where not so much as a leaf stirred. Now his paper was going to transfer him and had already appointed someone to replace him. His successor was an Englishman. He was Irish, once full of revolutionary solidarity and admiration for the Greeks—until he came and saw for himself. He'd never have dreamed they were so spineless. He was being recalled anyway, but he asked nothing better than to go. He'd had enough. Nothing to write about except international conferences at the Hilton and movie stars here for the summer. He sent even that stuff, not to London, but to a local rag in Canada, which did, however, pay more than his own respectable journal. Yes, he'd had enough. Before, at least, there were elections, demonstrations, speeches, strikes, agitation. Now, on the other hand, apart from those bombs at the beginning, everything seemed to have come to a standstill. He only threw a sleepy glance at the TelePrompter once every half hour. He was a Catholic and took an interest in the Pope's visit to South America. That was where things were happening, that was where he'd like to go—run risks, write a story that would shake the world. But here . . . The phone rang. He picked it up languidly. They were calling very early today to announce the official receptions. He heard a voice at the other end—serious, tense. At first he didn't take it in, thought it was a practical joker. But the voice repeated it: in the Church of the Metamorphosis in Ioulianou Street, in the poor box on the right as you go in . . . And suddenly he came to life. This kidnapping would give him something to write about; maybe he'd even get paid on time this month. He could scarcely keep himself from congratulating the man at the other end. Then he alerted the police. But not before he'd xeroxed the ultimatum and sent copies to all the foreign press agencies.

"Forward to Set the Sun in the Sky . . ."

The day dawned disagreeable for the three sequestered in South Kifissia. First the birds in the garden started singing; then the dry leaves rustled in the morning breeze. Two cats fought over a dead sparrow, and the spiders in the old mansion were panic-stricken at the sight of human beings. Cupboards unopened for years shook at the touch of a hand. Through the closed shutters Sakis could see the statue of Sikelianos in the garden: a bird dropping like a tear on one cheek, the nose broken, but the face the lofty visage of a poet. As a once prospective member of the Lambrakis movement, Sakis knew it was he who'd written "Forward to set the sun in the sky over Greece." Sakis felt a secret communication between them, for the sun was rising at least over Athens today.

The colonel was dying of thirst. The ten glasses of whiskey he'd downed last night were burning up his throat now. Sakis went to get him a drink. When he turned on the tap, the water ran cloudy and red, and he had to let it run at least ten minutes before it cleared. For breakfast they gave him a feta sandwich, some coffee out of a flask and a cheese pastry. But he found the cheese too salty and couldn't eat it. He said it was the first time he'd tasted it. Sakis and Lakis were astonished.

"And how long have you been in our country?"

"Five years. With a year in Izmir in between."

"And you've never eaten feta, our national cheese?"

"No. My wife . . ."

"Leave her out of it, Buster. Confess why you've never tasted feta. It'll be charged against you when you're tried by the revolutionary court."

"We're supposed to avoid local products."

" 'Local' yourself, pig."

"That's what we're told at the school—to be careful about them."

"And what else did they tell you?"

"Nothing."

"And now tell us what it is you like about Greece. What have you seen of it in these five years? Come on, let's have it."

"What can I say? Put yourself in my place. If you let me go, we'll get to know each other. And you and your friends can have free entry into the mess. What do you expect me to say? It's the good of Greece we want. . . . Once some young boys stole my car at Glyphada, and I went myself and asked the judge to let them go. I said it wasn't their fault; all boys their age want a car. You see? I understand your people very well. No comparison between you and the Turks. What I suffered in Izmir! My wife and I both used to call on Allah to ask when we were going to get back to Athens. *Ouch!*"

"What's the matter?" said Lakis.

"The trots."

They untied him and led him to the john, his eyes still bandaged. And there he was seized with an acute attack of diarrhea, complete with electronic whistles and salvoes just like the *Pueblo*. It gave Sakis inexpressible pleasure to watch him groping around for toilet paper. Then they took him back to the room and tied him again to the marble throne on which the poet used to declaim his verses.

"Go on."

"What are you going to do to me?"

"We'll tell you that later. Tell us what you've learned about Greece in five years."

"My wife and I have adopted a whole village in Epirus— through the AAW. My name's even carved on the fountain. That's the kind of thing we do. . . ."

"If you behave sensibly," said Lakis, "you'll be free in a few hours. And you can go back to your little wife and family. And remember, this is only the first blow our organization has struck. When we set you free, you're to say how good we were to you. You haven't been slapped in the face or kicked in the crotch, have you?"

"Okay, okay."

"Otherwise, you and your family and your whole colony at Glyphada and the whole lot of you in Greece will pay for every word you say. Understand? There are two, three, a thousand and three million of us."

"Yes, I promise."

"And you're going to forget you heard any birds singing."

"I'll do all I can to put them off the scent."

"The junta's so much in the pay of you and your fleet, they'll lose no time setting the prisoners free. Who do you love most in all the world?"

"My dog, Dick. Why?"

"We'd like to know what your last wish would be if things go wrong. You'll have a painful end—first the harpoon through the heart, then a bullet through the head."

He was crying now. Like a child. How was he to blame, he said through his sobs. Was this all the thanks they got from Greece, which they'd saved by the Truman Doctrine, rebuilt through the Marshall Plan, on which they'd lavished money and food and scholarships. And, since his tears had wet the bandage and made it hurt his eyes, Sakis had to take

him into the next room, sunless as a darkroom, and change
the blindfold. Lakis was already regretting they'd got hold
of such a wet sock. If only it'd been some pig from the base
who'd lose his temper and get excited . . .

"Just one thing," the colonel said. "Was Hélène in on all
this?"

"Of course. Our organization is international. We've got
members everywhere. But it won't do you any good to squeal
on her. Her name's not Hélène, she's not French, and she
doesn't look at all like that really."

This hurt him so much that they'd have done better to kill
him outright.

Monsieur Fambrou

Monsieur Fambrou leafed ironically through the *Tou îpa paré
méros* ultimatum. Among other things, it said, ". . . After
exhausting all legal means and trying in vain to alert international opinion to the tragedy of the political prisoners, we
have turned to kidnapping as a last resort. The puppet government of the colonels has no alternative but to give way to
our demands and set free at once the following twenty-one
prisoners . . ." He skipped some insulting phrases about the
torturers of Bouboulina Street and police spies, together with
a list of "those who would be next to pay for their crimes." He
skimmed through the economic diatribes denouncing the
junta for handing over the national wealth to international
financiers and turning the Greek people into "a nation of
waiters and bellhops." The ultimatum ended with well-known
slogans like "Foreign locusts go home" and "Down with
NATO and the U.S." But suddenly a postscript brought him
up with a scowl: "This proclamation is to be printed word for
word in all the newspapers. Any omission, alteration, or dis-

tortion will constitute a breach of the contract whereby we undertake to free the hostage."

He took a sip of Turkish coffee; it had never tasted so bitter. He shook the ash off his cigarette and ordered his assistant to get Colonel George Foster's address immediately through the American police at Hellenikon.

Putting on his jacket, he reflected that at least these swine had made a good choice in the names on their list. Though the rest of the operation was more like a practical joke, he was disturbed by their list, which showed there was a brain behind it all. The names had been selected from the whole political spectrum, from the royalists to the pro-Chinese, from every prison in the country, and from virtually every region. What bothered him personally was that there were three people on the list he'd tortured himself, and if they ever managed to escape abroad, the terrible fuss journalists make about broken bodies and broken hearts would start up again worse than ever. He'd thought he'd blown all the resistance networks. He'd become an international authority. Other countries, mainly the developing ones, asked him to lecture at their security training schools. He'd even been invited to a seminar in the United States on "methods of research and of collating intelligence." And now was he, who'd never let a Red escape him, to be made a laughingstock by these swine? He let out a curse.

Mrs. Foster had been kept awake all night by heat and jealousy. She wasn't really worried about her husband. All she could think of was that he was sleeping in someone else's arms, and though she didn't love him herself, the idea of that was too much. Her parents would soon be arriving from Asheville, and what sort of mess were they going to find her in? The dog barked in an odd way towards morning, around six, just as she'd begun to drop off. It was ten o'clock when the secret police woke her up and told her about the kidnapping. Soon after that, the ambassador himself phoned to say there was no cause for alarm. The prime minister had promised categorically that the twenty-one prisoners would be released in the course of the day. Special orders had already been sent out to the prisons farthest away. In all this the prime minister was acting with the approval of the Council of the Revolution. Mrs. Foster calmed down.

Then came a glum-looking, disagreeable man who introduced himself as Monsieur Fambrou, accompanied by a man from the FBI.

"How long have you lived in Greece?" he began. He had an inquisitorial manner overlaid with petty-bourgeois politeness because he was addressing not only a lady, but also a foreigner.

His dark suit gave him a funereal look.

"Who is this gentleman?" said Mrs. Foster to the man from the FBI.

"The chief of national security. You must be co-operative and help him as much as you can."

Mrs. Foster put Greek security in the same category as poisoned eggs. Everything indigenous was suspect.

"Since 1965," she said.

"And have you always lived in this house?"

"Until 1967, we lived in Kifissia. Then we spent a year in Izmir. When we came back we rented this villa."

"Whereabouts did you live in Kifissia?"

"Where all the Americans live."

"Where exactly?"

"Don't you know the American colony? We have our own market, our own church, our own school—everything. George even wanted to buy a house in Greece, but I didn't. I've always wanted to get away. I can't stand the heat."

"When exactly did you meet your predecessor, Mrs. John Willis?"

"Are you crazy?" said Mrs. Foster, spluttering with rage. "My Lord! What a question, Mr. . . . What did you say your name was?"

"Fambrou."

"Mr. Fambrou. She was a psychopath. A murderess. I don't see what she has to do with this."

"I didn't ask what she had to do with this, Mrs. Foster," said the hawk affably. "I'm just trying to untangle the threads that may connect us with infinity."

"Infinity?"

"Chaos. We've got to locate your husband in twenty-four hours at most."

"But if you locate him they'll execute him."

"Trust us. We know our own people. They mean well. Our politicians aren't murderers. The kidnappers are probably left-wing idealists—professors, most likely. Don't worry, they won't hurt him. He'll tell you so himself tomorrow. But if he's to be here tomorrow I have to know all about your relations with the Greeks."

"We've never had any relations with the natives. They've always looked on us as a traveling grocery store. It was getting beyond everything. You couldn't tell which they preferred, us or the PX."

"And yet the Greek people mean well, Mrs. Foster. They have great virtues. It would be worth your while to get to know us better. Have you noticed if your husband's movements were at all unusual lately?"

"Yes. He had a mistress."

"Was he often unfaithful to you? You can speak as freely to me as if I were your dentist."

"Psychiatrist, you mean."

"We don't have psychiatrists in Greece, madam. We're a healthy, religious, Western-oriented country."

"Western-oriented! What a contradiction in terms. . . ." She laughed.

"I beg your pardon?"

"Mr. . . . Pipino, American men are like children. They prefer forbidden fruit."

"Have you any idea what sort of person it was?"

"Of course I tried to find out. She was a foreigner, as far as I could make out. A tourist."

The hawk picked up the phone and ordered the airports to be closed to all foreigners.

"Anything else?" she said.

He thanked her, bowed, and left.

Meanwhile, his bloodhounds combed Athens.

Although . . .

Although the highway patrol was in theory independent, that day its whole motorized unit had been ordered to join in the search for the kidnappers. The latter, two hundred yards away from the post at South Kifissia, watched sarcastically from behind the shutters as motorcycles, jeeps, and small trucks rushed to and fro and cops jabbered feverishly into their walkie-talkies. The field that separated the house from the police station, with its barred ground-floor windows, was full of thistles and long grass. Cats used to go there in the spring to have their kittens. The only way through it was a little beaten track, a short cut. The hideout was screened from the police post by a fig tree, a plum tree, a peach tree and an orange tree, as well as by the thick ivy growing over the walls. Inside, the colonel, still tied to this throne, was talking to his guard.

"No, that's all I know. We were taught a little history at the
school before we came out here, but I've forgotten it all.
Recent history, I mean. I know quite a lot about ancient
Greece. It's difficult, you know, always changing countries.
Before I came here, I was in Brazil. Developing countries get
to be alike for us in the end. Fortunately, in two years' time
I'm retiring, and then I can get some peace in Boston. But I'll
go to Kentucky first."

"If you live that long!"

And he turned up the volume of his transistor radio. It was
the news broadcast from the American station at the Hellenikon base. The kidnapping was, of course, the chief item. The
colonel heard himself being talked about as if he were already
dead and gone. The radio informed the kidnappers that the
government would release the twenty-one political prisoners
as soon as the last of them arrived from the prisons farthest
away. Sweden had officially agreed to give the prisoners political asylum. Onassis' Olympic Airways had immediately offered a plane to fly them before midnight to Stockholm, where,
said the announcer, it would still be daylight.

The contact demurely opened his shop at the usual time.
Sakis and Lakis, his assistants, were supposed to have been
on vacation for over a week now. He was just poring over the
accounts he kept for income tax when an old friend who had
a printing press next to the Tower of the Winds came in beam-
ing and shut the door carefully behind him.

"Have you heard?"

"What?"

"They've done it! As good as Paraguay!"

"What do you mean?"

The friend came closer.

"Haven't you heard the radio, the American radio? Some

resistance commandos have kidnapped—do you hear that? kidnapped!—a general from NATO."

The popular imagination's got the bit between its teeth already, thought the contact. Well, it's a good sign—it'll encourage everyone.

"Apparently the Council of the Revolution has gone wild. The hawks and the doves, the Papadopoulists and the Lekanspeditists, are at daggers drawn. The first lot wants to release the twenty-one prisoners, and the others want them executed immediately to make the kidnappers into murderers."

"Where did you find out all this?"

"The retired general whose book on military astrology I'm printing stopped by just now and told me. At last we've got our own Fedayin! The American ambassador has threatened to cut off food supplies if the hawks get their way. He sat in in person at the Council of the Revolution."

The contact listened as if in amazement, inwardly bubbling over with delight. He crossed his fingers to make everything go well right to the end.

"It's going to be even more of a scorcher today than yesterday," he said.

Fambrou's men found the colonel's car badly parked on the ring road at Lycabettus just past the Doxiadis Institute. After questioning the janitor, they forced their way into Ethel's apartment. All they found were the flowers in the vase, some Delphi cigarette ends in the ash trays and a razor blade in the bathroom. They went straight to the agency that rented the studio and were given the name of Hélène Mac-Gibbon, sculptress, and details of her appearance. These they sent in code to all exits from the country at the very moment that Ethel, who'd just landed in an Alitalia Boeing 707, was going through passport control in Rome under her own name.

From Fiumicino Airport she took a taxi straight to Thanassis' place.

The arrests started at eleven on Fambrou's personal orders. The groups infiltrated by the security police and under constant observation were dismantled in less than an hour. The cellars of the police stations were full of men who, up to that moment, had thought themselves quite safe. The prisoners were brutally treated, also on Fambrou's orders. Those who'd been in prison before hadn't seen such fury for five years. Roadblocks were set up everywhere. Innocent tourists began to realize for the first time that something was rotten in the state of Greece. All Attica was combed, then Parnassus, Hymettus and Helicon. Innocent shepherds who didn't even know what government they were living under found themselves answering questions in the village police station.

At one in the afternoon the prime minister in a radio and television broadcast made a last appeal to the kidnappers to release the colonel, a law-abiding father and quartermaster. Otherwise, said he, the sword of justice would fall remorselessly right and left. The guiltless would have to suffer to insure that the guilty were destroyed. They'd all be sent to Leros! The honor of Greece as a civilized Western nation was at stake. If such crimes were allowed, Greece would soon degenerate into the same condition as the underdeveloped countries of Latin America, would regress to the era of barbarians and brigands which Greece had happily long left behind. The days of Tsakidzis were over for good. Greece was on the road to union with the European Common Market despite all the efforts of the enemies of the people to prevent it. He added that the kidnapping had been organized, financed and directed entirely from abroad, that the security police were already on the tracks of the foreigners responsible, and that these foreigners would soon be arrested by Interpol. He refused to believe Greeks would so dishonor their ancient traditions of hospitality, et cetera.

At three o'clock, the vice-chairman of the Council was present at a service held by Archbishop Hieronymos in the church of Saint Demetrios Lombardaris at the foot of the Hill of Philopapou. Prayers were offered for the health and safety of Regular Army Colonel George Foster, heroic fighter in the Korean war, twice wounded, now a great admirer of Hellenic culture, whose two infants pitifully implored the Most High to save their papa.

The answer was two bomb explosions right in the center of Athens. The resistance organizations, stirred by the success of the unknown kidnappers, took courage, came out of hiding and filled the vacuum left behind them by the police with dynamite.

At three-fifteen the first boats began to arrive from Aegina and Leros. The prisoners from Itzedin and Corfu were being flown in by military aircraft. They were awaited in Stockholm with songs and garlands. "They" included, among others, Glezos, Panagoulis, Filinis, Iordanidis, Filias, Notaras, Farakos, Anghelos Pneumatikos, Zannas, Baras, Nestor, Kyrkos and many unknown companions in arms.

In the evening news bulletins of foreign radio and television networks, they even overshadowed the shelling of Pnompenh and Soyuz's record-breaking ninetieth orbit.

The young army officers were infuriated. That day the cadets in the training school on Tourkovounia were allowed to use live ammunition. The smell of powder was a sort of consolation, like the smell of tobacco smoke to someone who's given up cigarettes.

A tape recorder set up by the Patriotic Front in Omonia Square started playing "The Kidnap," the song by Theodorakis that won a prize at the Thessalonica Festival. The passers-by smiled. It took the police a quarter of an hour to locate and silence it.

And when evening came, everyone tuned in to the foreign broadcasts to Greece: Cologne, the BBC, the Voice of Truth from Moscow. Those who listened to the Voice of Truth after the other two noticed it didn't mention the kidnapping. All it had was an interview with "pioneer" workers in Siberia who sent toys and caviar to the children of the political prisoners. Then came a message from the Komsomols to the International Youth Movement, exhorting them to read a book by Comrade Brezhnev on the problems of the young Communist. And that was all. Everyone was back home by ten o'clock because of the curfew ordered by the general commanding the plain of Attica. Shutting the stable door after the horse has bolted, people thought.

For Sakis and Lakis it was a long night. Fortunately, the colonel's diarrhea had stopped and they didn't have to keep taking him to the toilet. They heard on the radio that the twenty-one prisoners had arrived safe and sound in Stockholm, where they'd had a triumphal reception. Then, after giving the contact a prearranged signal on the telephone, they switched on a tape of recorded footsteps moving about and crept silently out of the house. An hour later the contact would inform the archbishop's palace where the colonel could be found. Sakis took the harpoon gun with him and threw George's gun among the dense weeds in the garden. Lakis bestowed a kiss on the bust of Sikelianos, silent under the ivy, enigmatic as Delphi. He wiped the bird droppings off the poet's cheek. At eight that morning, in sports jackets, rubber sandals and blue jeans, with the harpoon gun and a small haversack, they took the first boat to Hydra.

August 1970

2

THE WANDERING SALESMAN AND OTHERS

The Stewardess

Definitely a difficult job, almost impossible. Asked about it, she would give a sad, enigmatic smile. Maria kept telling her it was time she got married and had a home of her own —time to land, in short. "Girls who fly age quicker," she said. "They get wrinkles." Tassia just listened.

She was small and supple, with a face like a cat's and a flat voice, as if all those Boeings had bereft it of tone. Her clothes accorded with the climate of the country she'd just left. When she adjusted her watch, she adjusted her habits and language, so in the end everything came to be the same to her. People and places were all alike, one continent merged with another, and all she knew of any city was a few shops, a few streets, a few theaters, and the hotel where the airline put its staff up. She was just like someone who lives in the provinces and knows only his own tedious little streets and the people stuck in them.

Maria often used to meet her in the studio of a girl friend who was a hairdresser. Tassia would arrive straight from the airport with her bags, full of stories of what had happened last night in Rio de Janeiro or Tel Aviv or Montevideo. "I was picked up by a guy with a Bentley. A gigolo, obviously. He took me to a house in the suburbs where he lived with a woman old enough to be his mother." And she giggled, putting her little fingers over her little mouth to make sure no one jumped to wrong conclusions. Maria and the friend would then open her bags and exclaim over her latest spoils.

Kostas, Maria's husband and a civil engineer, had once introduced Tassia to a friend of his who was an architect. The idyll had lasted a few months, then suddenly ended. Tassia, always traveling about, soon tired of people. Then Maria, who worked at the Social Research Center, introduced her to a group of young graduates whose favorite topic was travel. Tassia was bored with them, too. She'd go to sleep in her chair or start crying for no reason at all if she'd had a drink too many. She had noticed that for Greeks of the younger generation, contact with something abroad, where most of them had been to study, was indispensable. But for her these conversations about travel were more tiring than travel itself.

Her tragedy, if she had one and if it was really decisive, was that ever since her childhood she'd wanted to be a dancer. She'd even been to the Zozo Nikoloudi School, but adverse circumstances—parents separated, a brother in the navy, a first love affair that went wrong because the fellow left her for a Swedish blonde—had forced her to become independent when she was still quite young. So first she got a job on the ground, and then she graduated to flying. But dancing was still her passion, and wherever she found herself, if she was not completely knocked out by "death from the air" and the pills she took to make her sleep, she spent her evenings at the ballet.

The group of which Maria and Kostas were the nucleus, heterogeneous though it was, had in common youth and a tendency towards a "European" society. In other words, they weren't backward or underdeveloped. Thanks to the Boeing culture, whose victim Tassia was, it was a society that might have come to be more or less representative of Greece. If . . .

If, of course, there'd been no dictatorship. The group broke up. The first to go abroad was Maria. A month later,

Kostas joined her with a forged passport. The junta had closed down the Social Research Center and seized all its archives—Marxist-oriented studies on the distribution of population in the capital, card-indexed material on how Greek workers lived in West Germany. Kostas couldn't get work any more; though he wasn't a leftist himself, he had problems with the Asphalia because of his father.

So, during the weeks that followed the fatal day, Tassia acted as liaison. Going back and forth between Greece and abroad, she would get in touch with them wherever they happened to be at the time—for after the unhappy event, as they called the dictatorship, Kostas and Maria did not settle in one place right away but trailed around everywhere and nowhere with others like them.

Of course, Tassia was not their only contact with the "interior." They saw other exiles, newcomers, people who came and went. But Tassia belonged to the old group, and it was of that they wanted news.

Whenever she came, she'd bring duty-free whisky or a bottle of ouzo and always packs of cigarettes. She herself neither drank nor smoked. The other two would have a drink and begin to interrogate her.

"How's Lambros?"

"They arrested him and put him in prison, but now he's banished to the provinces."

"What about Ianni?"

"In hiding. I caught sight of him once. A shadow of what he was."

"Philip?"

"When they let him out he took to the bottle. He's grown a paunch and copped out of everything—resistance and everything else."

"Dimis?"

"Couldn't care less. On top of that, he's got an uncle in

the police, and the others don't trust him. It's all gone to hell—don't be getting homesick. It's just like a graveyard. Silence, sorrow and pity. And what's the news here? Anything happening?" Tassia would ask in her turn. "What am I to tell the others? Is there any hope?"

The first summer of their exile, Kostas and Maria would see Tassia arrive from home all sun-tanned, her only news "yesterday we went swimming at Asteria beach," and they'd suddenly be depressed without apparent reason. And Tassia was depressed, too, to see them doing nothing while she had to get up at five in the morning and manage God knows how many fractious passengers on a six-hour flight. Their respective privations more or less balanced out.

Some are born to tell and others to listen. Unfortunately for the two exiles, Tassia belonged to the second category. She answered in monosyllables and couldn't remember anything farther back than the last two days. She'd say, "Yesterday I went to the theater with Doxoula and her new boy friend. He's very good-looking and nice, but she still loves the first one, the one you know."

"Someone told us he was with the junta," Kostas would say.

"Was or is—no one knows. In any case, she still loves him."

"And who's the new one?"

"A Bulgarian. A student."

"Studying in Athens?"

"Yes, a Byzantinologist. He speaks Greek better than we do. He's got a two-year grant."

"They still have cultural exchanges, then," said Kostas in surprise. "The Greek leftists in prison, and Communists from other countries coming as tourists. A fine thing!" He emptied his glass.

"Still, he's a very nice boy."

Tassia told them of a real Greece very different from the

one they had created for themselves in imagination—of an everyday Athens such as they'd known before they left. But inevitably, living abroad, they'd become what you might call "alienated."

Tassia came and went, always with her various accessories, weightless as a butterfly on a branch, subdued, doped, always the same, always with a ballet or theater ticket in her purse.

For Kostas and Maria, each of their encounters was a traumatic experience, and when she left they always took a while to get over it; the sudden apparition of the real Greece there in their midst was too much for them. The Greece of *Le Monde* or the *Guardian* or *Unità*, like a *son et lumière* Parthenon, had nothing to do with this live creature with two eyes, a mouth, and a beauty spot on her upper lip, telling them about the daily lives of the people they used to know. Until they saw her, Greece was an abstraction, a context within which ghosts of the past came and went freely against a background selected by themselves. And Tassia's visits swept all that away.

"Yesterday," she'd say—and always she could remember only yesterday, never last week or last month, as if her journeys were separate pages of her life, never joined together to form one book—"yesterday we all went to the bouzouki tavern. The place was packed. It was fun. You can imagine what kind of fun when . . ."

When everyone knows Pausanias is being tortured and Argyris is at his last gasp and Menios can't get out of doing his military service and, her unfinished sentence implied, you're not there.

"What tavern was it?" asked Kostas.

"Soitiria Bellou's."

As the bottle emptied, the memory grew full.

"What's happening abroad? Now that Andreas Papandreou has got away, people back home are expecting great things."

They told her the news in the foreign papers.

"A bomb in Salonika? Tell me more. I can't write it down, but I'll record it in my head and remember. Back home we don't hear about such things."

She used to bring the Greek papers for Kostas and Maria, to fill out their picture of everyday life.

"And there's a new book out in English on the junta—*The Death of Democracy.* You ought to take it back for the boys."

"Where can I get it?"

"Listen: 'Fascism has struck at the head of the monster of indifference.' That was written by a sociologist."

And Tassia would listen, charging herself with news like a battery. She couldn't hear words like those Kostas had just quoted either in the Greece of the colonels or in the anonymous ionosphere of the Boeings.

Maria always pressed her to stay a while longer and she'd fix her something to eat—it was better not to come at all than to come just for half an hour. Tassia always refused; she felt such a long way away from this sad couple. She was sorry for them, too, always seeing them in a new apartment, dragging themselves and their luggage from one foreign, distant, neutral, unknown country to another. Kostas lacked the smell of sweat, of olive oil, of prison. And Tassia, creature of space, needed, sought refuge in the smells of the earth.

"I always come back to my old opinion," said Maria to her one day. "This job is bad for you. Why don't you get married?"

But Tassia said she'd got so used to moving about that she couldn't stay more than a week in the same town.

Weeks went by, months, years. The earth revolved, and on it men and beasts caught ecstatic snatches of lost paradises.

Only the traditional leftists persisted in the struggle for the victory of primal matter over secondary idealism. And Tassia landed and came to earth with her sleeping pills, bringing them a little Greek sun distilled on her skin. Kostas and Maria drank more and more in order to be at ease with her.

"Theano has had her baby, Jessy has been divorced, Anna's had a breakdown, Georges is well, Toula's well and Lambros is all right, except the day before yesterday he drove into a colonel in Patissiou Street. The colonel got out of his car in a fury, and Lambros yelled back at him, in fear and trembling lest he should be recognized—he was tried and given a suspended sentence recently. That's the news. Nothing happening on the surface. Everyone's busy sleeping around. They do it all the time, wherever they can find a place. It's their only release. The latest pop star is Tolis Voskopoulos; he's even zapped Kokkotas. Dinos writes lyrics with hints between the lines. He says it's his contribution to the resistance. The intellectuals are trying to formulate the epistemology of the dictatorship. On the whole, there's more free speech than there was."

"Would you like a couple of eggs?" said Maria.

"No, thank you."

"But you look so tired."

"What's the weather like back home?" said Kostas.

"Yesterday it was sunny."

"Here it snowed."

"Did you see the astronauts?"

"No, just missed them, alas."

She looked tinier than ever in her miniskirt. She was sleepy. Some details she told them about some new stores in Athens astonished them.

"Life goes on. Living and partly living."

Her visits got rarer and rarer. Once she brought a new boy friend with her—an Argentinian.

"Why?" said Kostas. "Aren't Greeks good enough for you any more?"

"It's all very well for you, abroad. Back home it's hell."

So the years passed by, and the months within the years. More and more planes were hijacked. They were anxious about Tassia. The Tupamaros multiplied. They were anxious about Tassia. And the months passed by, and the weeks within the months, countersidereal. It got dark early. And always the same question: "What's the news?"

In the end, it wasn't really clear whom they were talking about.

The Dinner Party

It was the eighth time they'd discussed it at 357 Amsterdam Avenue, in one of the most fashionable parts of the second capital, in the apartment belonging to Iann Libidowsky, well-known protector of the arts and the Greeks. The subject in question was yet again the film that was to help both themselves—exiled intellectuals, actors, directors, editors, cameramen—and the Greek resistance, which was too poor and powerless to supply the scope necessary for more practical action. Those who represented the Greek resistance abroad were all known and marked. Almost all the young Greeks in exile remained aloof; they weren't going to pour their energy into the same old useless activities.

Naturally, they'd all come for a meal. Libidowsky went everywhere with his dog, big as a horse and elegant as a deer, and with his manservant, said to do double duty as a bodyguard. The other servant served only as cook; because of his master's philhellenism, he specialized in Greek food. The Greek restaurants in the second capital were usually beyond the émigrés' pockets, and the chance of a free Greek meal was one not to be missed. Of course, they also came because of the film. If they really got it set up it would enable them to earn an honest penny and, if they could agree on a subject, render a great service to the cause as well.

The subject—that was the problem. Their host had promised he'd try to raise the money for the film on the condition that the main part be played by a handsome young actor already known for his screen appearances and regarded as a sort of second Lord Byron because he had come out in opposition to the dictatorship. But what was the film to be about?

A documentary unmasking the colonels, a sort of cinéma vérité, was ruled out from the start; no film producer was going to risk his money backing antijunta propaganda.

"We have to remember all producers are sharks," said Libidowsky, "and they won't put up the money unless they smell big profits."

This superficially cynical remark, in fact, defined the limits of the discussion. It was as if he'd said, "Listen, boys, I know your problem, but we've got to be realistic. What ever subject you choose has to be commercial as well. We can use that as camouflage to attack the dictatorship."

The person most deeply affected was a gifted young director who saw this as yet shapeless project, based on the exiles' good intentions rather than anything concrete, as an opportunity for expressing all the anger against the dictatorship that had been accumulating in him for two years without an outlet. His intelligent eyes darted to and fro like twin pearls on one thread. The others were always talking about "the subject, the subject," but they didn't really put themselves out to find one.

It was on the next occasion, the ninth, when they were all once more invited to dinner, that the director arrived with his subject up his sleeve. It had come to him, he said, like an inspiration from the Holy Ghost, as he was drinking his morning coffee before going off to his day's work as third assistant on a film. The job kept body and soul together, but for how long he had no idea. There was no permanence in the profession, and he had so many mouths to feed. He was thinking of the folly of wasting time on such stuff when, over his steaming coffee, just as he was lighting his first cigarette, he suddenly saw that the subject had to be this or nothing.

He'd just finished his introduction and was about to embark on the subject itself when Jorge, the butler-bodyguard, announced that dinner was served and would get cold if the guests didn't sit down right away, and cold *bourrek,* he said, is uneatable.

So they took their places at the round table and fell greedily on the cheese fritters, brought in by the plateful, like French fries. They ate and licked their fingers, and it was only when the main dish arrived and they saw it was their favorite— meatballs in tomato sauce and potatoes all swimming in oil, which would soak up the gravy—that they settled down and wanted to know what the subject was to be.

Jorge passed the serving dish, beginning with the ladies. He balanced it skillfully on his hand, a small base for such a huge dish, tilting it daringly for the guests to help themselves to the gravy. "It's the gravy that makes the stew," he said.

And the exiles, mostly leftists, thanked him, embarrassed to be sitting at the table while he served them. Even when circumstances made them play the masters and him the slave, they didn't forget the class struggle.

The director began, twitching about on his chair like a butterfly with a pin through its middle, waving his arms to illustrate what he meant. For as a director, he saw everything in images—so much so that one of his gestures nearly boxed Jorge on the ear as he circled the table offering second helpings. Everyone served himself greedily execpt the leading man, the hippy, who was dieting to lose four "inexcusable" pounds he'd put on lately. As the director was apologizing to Jorge for almost hitting him, he upset his glass of red wine over the tablecloth, and everyone shouted, *"Guri! Guri! Tha paï cala i tenia mas"* ("It's luck! It's luck! The film will be a hit"), and dabbed the spilled wine behind their ears. By exclaiming in Greek, they were breaking the tacit convention by which they only spoke English or German so that their host's protégé, the young actor, could understand. Libidowsky himself knew some colloquial as well as classical Greek from his many visits to Athens before the dictatorship, but for his friend's sake, he'd asked the rest of the guests to use more international languages, even Spanish or French if they liked. They'd all agreed without protest, not only out of courtesy, but also because they didn't want to displease their prospective patron, the one who might put some gas into their empty tank. (The Neo-Hellene absolutely depends on foreign capital for survival. On his own, he is incapable of breaking through the barriers of language and economic stagnation. Since no society entirely based on foreign capital can still have values of its own, it will always be a foreigner who supplies backward peoples with equipment, reputation and fame. Even the tools of the revolution that enable the slaves to break their chains will be imported tax free from abroad.) But, just as one has a primitive need to use one's native language when swearing or making love, so, spilled at the moment when the director was revealing the subject that had come to him with the steam of his morning coffee, the wine spreading over the patterned cloth made everyone spontaneously shout *"Guri!"*

The director addressed chiefly the hippy and Libidowsky. To spur himself on whenever he felt himself flagging, he glanced occasionally at the others, who listened, trying to make as little noise as possible with their knives and forks.

"As an idea, I think it's marvelous," said the chief of photography as soon as he'd finished. "It's got everything a producer wants."

The servant began to remove the plates, having brought smaller ones for cheese and fruit.

"No, leave them!" two or three of the guests faintly protested. "It isn't as if we'd been eating herring."

The plates had been wiped so clean as the guests mopped up the gravy that they shone like new. But Jorge insisted on having clean plates for the cheese. This evening there were French cheeses famous for their delicacy and the elaborate semantics of their names, each with its own goût, each affected by a different kind of maggot; and to appreciate them, you had to eat them off real porcelain.

"Just as the champagne we're going to open soon has to be drunk from special glasses made of real crystal," said Jorge.

He enjoyed seeing them all gathered around the common table like monks of a strict observance, eating and discussing their plans as he himself had done when he'd left Franco's Spain before being taken in, thirty years ago, by Iann, typical abbot of a less rigorous order, though philanthropic, philhellenic, and fundamentally antifascist.

"Anyway," he said, "no need to worry. We've got a dishwasher."

"Don't forget to take Papadop out to pee," said Iann.

When he heard his name, Papadop, the boxer, thumped his stump of a tail where he lay under a chair. Iann stroked him with his long, expressive hand and threw him a bit of gristle. Dop caught and swallowed it and spent a long time licking his chops.

The squares of mirror completely covering the walls multiplied the guests. The actor kept looking at them as if to reassure himself that he existed.

"And what part is there for me?" he asked. Like all stars, he could see everything only in terms of himself.

"We'll look after that all right," said the director, who hadn't quite expected such a blatant attack. "Don't you worry."

He'd finished now and was breathless and pleased with himself. He'd sketched only the beginning of the film, which was to be a musical with gags, humor and suspense. It would be able to get in all sorts of digs at the dictatorship as it told the adventures of a bouzouki orchestra that had fled abroad after the coup to play the music of the maestro whose work was banned at home. The idea was based on fact. Such an orchestra actually had fled when their maestro was arrested.

"So who shall I be in the orchestra?" the actor insisted.

"Why not the first bouzouki, the leader?" said a film editor.

The actor was highly delighted at this idea, and, therefore, so was Libidowsky. Two or three others cried "Bravo!" Only a writer sat silent, eaten up with jealousy because somebody else had thought up the subject for the film. If it was an American production there'd be a big advance just for the basic idea.

"Perfect," said the actor. "I'll be the first bouzouki then."

Thrasyvoulos, the first bouzouki in the real orchestra, was cursing heaven and earth because the telephone had been cut off and he couldn't call Athens and speak to Pharnezis and Koltsas and Mimis the Goldfinch and all the other friends who implored him to return. He knew what the regular rates were, and they told him his fee would be much more by now because of his successes abroad. The others lived like pashas, while he . . . And it wasn't fear of being interrogated in Bouboulina Street that kept him from going back. The junta was discreet with celebrities. What held him back was something more intimate, more complex: how could he leave the others in the lurch? Without him, the big attraction, the orchestra would go to pieces. And if he went back, wouldn't it be as if he had denied his years abroad, as if he'd suffered for nothing? Yet he couldn't take it any longer. At first things had been difficult, but they hadn't seemed insurmountable. But now he couldn't see any daylight anywhere. The world had other problems. It had forgotten Greece and its music. And he couldn't go on hearing his little boy say he was hungry. No, he'd rather see the earth open and swallow him up. He'd tried; no one could accuse him of deserting. But it just couldn't go on. Hesitating between yes and no, seeking desperately for a solution that seemed not to exist, he watched television without understanding the language, guessing the plot from the actors' expressions, while his wife knitted him a pullover for the winter in their two-room flat in the suburbs. With the phone cut off, he hadn't any real life. He looked at his watch. A quarter to ten. At this hour, he thought, Libidowsky is always back in his mansion. He'd phone him for a small loan, enough to pay the incredible bill he'd been sent for the last couple of months, and get the phone connected again. He couldn't live without it. Whenever he was overcome with homesickness, like tonight, he'd dial Athens to restore his morale.

On the fourth floor in the same building of low-cost flats, there was another Greek, who'd told him not to hesitate to come and use the phone at any hour of the day or night. So he went down to the fourth floor and dialed the number. The butler-bodyguard answered.

"Who's calling, please?"

"Thrasyvoulos, the bouzouki."

"Hold on, I'll see if he's in."

There was a silence, as if the person at the other end had covered the mouthpiece to ask the Maecenas if he wanted to come to the phone.

Then, "Very sorry, Mr. Libidowsky isn't here. Perhaps you'd care to call back later?"

"Why are we still in the dining room?" said Iann. "The sitting room's much more comfortable."

His word was law. Everyone rose.

"Bring some ice for the whisky, please, Jorge."

Jorge had just come in with the dog. The house was on the edge of the park, so he hadn't had far to go.

"First bouzouki," said Iann. "It's a good title, but it doesn't tell us anything about the part. What we have to think about now is what he'll do as first bouzouki. He's the one the producers will put their money on"—and he pointed to the actor, snuggling down in his comfortable armchair. "I find the subject very attractive, a good seed, and an excellent starting point for a package deal, but I can't give you the go-ahead and the advance that goes with it until we've decided what his part is going to be."

At the magic word, "advance," their faces lit up. It was so long since they'd heard it.

"I've an idea," said a very talented ex-director of photography who'd been unable to find work here because the film technicians' union, thought leftist, was afraid foreigners would push up standards. "I mean," he said, calmly peeling an apple and dipping it in the crystal finger bowl he'd brought in from the dining room, "something to give the film a dramatic dimension. The psychological dilemma of the main character. He finds all the thousand and one difficulties of exile unbearable and in the end gives in and returns to Greece."

But Byron grew angry at this.

"We're supposed to encourage people," he said, "not show them our weaknesses. Anyone who sees the film has got to come out with his morale lifted, whether he's Greek or foreign. Through humor and tragedy, we've got to put across a message of optimism. We can't show the rest now. That has to come later."

86

He'd spoken with such passion, bringing into play all the folds of his features and all the hypnotic grace of his hands, that the unfortunate ex-director of photography, whose suggestion had met with no support, was obliged to withdraw.

"Of course," he said. "You don't quite see what I mean. For deserting his post, he'd be punished. For running away, despised. For going back, arrested. The ultimate effect will be positive."

"No, it won't do!" said the actor, sitting up in his chair. He discreetly rolled himself a cigarette in his tobacco pouch. His neighbor gave him a light. Then he looked at himself in the sitting-room mirror he had positioned himself opposite and straightened a revolutionary curl. He was very cross.

Almost eleven o'clock. His wife had gone to bed. The children had been asleep since nine. Alone in the two-room apartment, facing the TV showing the late night news, the same as at eight o'clock, Thrasyvoulos was about to go down and telephone again. He had nothing to turn to. And in this part of the town, everything was closed by ten. If he went out, there was nowhere to go. But back in Aigaleo . . .

He'd been working as a carpenter in that neighborhood when the maestro had discovered him and taken him into his orchestra. The dictatorship had blighted him just as he was beginning to succeed. His brother-in-law had been arrested the first night, and he himself had taken the first opportunity to escape abroad, his instrument under his arm, to act as disciple and herald to the music of the composer he loved.

In Aigaleo, before he had become a star, he used to take his bouzouki at this time of the evening to the Journey's End—what a name for a pub near the cemetery—and stay there until dawn playing prison and junkie songs. He could work off his feelings like that. But where was he to go here?

And if the maestro hadn't still been in prison, he'd have had no scruples about going back. As it was . . .

He tiptoed out of the flat and waited for the elevator, which stopped at his floor, the eighth, to let out a group of young men and women. They were neighbors, nice boys. He'd found nice people everywhere. That wasn't the problem. The problem was an emptiness nothing could fill—the lack of money to pay the phone bill to enable him to talk to his friends, Pharnezis and Koltsas and Mimis the Goldfinch, and hear, like the swell of the ocean, the background noise of the pub they were in. He apologized to his compatriot, who was in his pajamas, and started to dial Libidowsky's number again.

"The first bouzouki mustn't give in," said the actor, exalted, handing around whiskies and soda. "No, he must go and see the workers in Essen and Dusseldorf and Frankfort and breathe life into them."

"Socialist realism," said the ex-director of photography.

"That's not the problem," said the director, to smooth things over. "The film's going to be a musical, and entertainment will sugar the pill of the message."

The phone rang, and the butler hurried to take it. Papadop wagged his tail.

"It's the same one as before," said the butler, covering the mouthpiece with his hand. "He says he wants to talk about something terribly urgent."

"Tell him I'm not in," said the philhellene. "I haven't come home yet."

Jorge gave the message, embroidering it a little. "I'm sorry —something must have held him up. Can I take a message? Who? About money? Of course. I'll tell him."

A deathly silence fell when he'd finished.

"But that was the *real* bouzouki," the director blurted out.

The Reason Why

"It kills retsina to be shaken about," said Dinos. The huge demijohn stood waiting to be ungagged.

"It shouldn't be drunk out of bottles," he went on, driving the corkscrew deeper into the cork. "Only out of the cask."

"Our host is certainly difficult to please," said the fellow —once a coal miner in Belgium, now a steelworker in Germany—who was sitting beside his plump wife on the divan.

At last the cork yielded, and the glasses were stood in a row.

"Who'll be our cupbearer?" said Dinos.

A freind from Yannitsa, now a *Gastarbeiter*, a guest worker, in Karlsruhe, eagerly offered his services.

"Our Ganymede," said Pavlos, the archaeologist from Salonika. He was looking for a printer for his thesis on the amphorae of the geometric period. Since he himself couldn't go to Greece but had to have his thesis published originally in Greek to get it accepted at a foreign university, he'd had the idea of trying in West Germany. Dinos had offered to help him, at least in his own area.

They'd first met the evening before at the Pan-German-Greek congress on the struggle against fascism and found themselves in complete agreement on the need for action. They both thought the old leaders were like an elastic wall. Beat your head against it as much as you liked—you couldn't knock it down, and you couldn't do yourself any harm either;

it just gave, like rubber. So after the meeting, they and several others of the same age decided to see what they could do alone to expel themselves from the party and continue the struggle independently.

"I don't ask that thousands or even hundreds go back clandestinely," said the archaeologist. "But how long is it since there's been even one? And yet the junta's obliged to leave the frontiers open for the thousands of workers to go to and from West Germany all year round."

Dinos was still unhappy after his argument with the orthodox wing at the conference.

"I still think," he said, "the best way of getting things done is to have one foot in the party and the other outside."

At that, they had separated late the previous night, planning to meet again this morning near the sign of the Chinese restaurant in the main square, before going to ask about prices at the printer's. The temperature was just below freezing. While they waited for the streetcar, the archaeologist, who lived in Umeå in southern Lapland, said he was dying of heat; in his part of the world the mercury dropped to twenty below at this time of year.

Dinos looked at him curiously. He'd brought his little girl with him because his wife worked in a bank, it was school vacation, and he couldn't leave her alone in the house. They had no relatives here, and the neighbors were all at work too. It was always a problem to know what to do with the child, especially since there was no central heating in the apartment —only a gas fire. Now, dressed in a hood and miniature boots, she was pleased with her excursion and skipped onto the streetcar, light as a ladybug, holding her father's hand on one side and his friend's on the other.

"Don't bother about tickets," said Dinos. "I've got cards."

He stamped them in the machine; there was no ticket collector.

"If they catch you traveling without a ticket," he said, "they can stop the streetcar and call the police. It happened once to one of ours."

They got off to change streetcars; the printer's was miles away. This time there was a ticket collector, and Dinos showed his cards.

For Pavlos, the printer's was a disappointment. He'd expected the smell of ink, the din of machinery, grime, the noise of the presses, a stuffy underground room with antiquated equipment, the walls covered with pinups from *Romanzo* and *True Love Stories* and photographs of Castro, Bithicotsis and Domazos. But here everything was clean and orderly. There were only two men at work, both young, in spotless overalls, like dentists, screwing the fourth issue of *Spitha* into the press. On the wall was a poster of Xanthopoulos and Ria Kourti, advertising the film forthcoming at the Adolf Cinema the Sunday after next, together with an Olympic Airways poster boasting special fares to Athens and Salonika for emigrant workers in Düsseldorf, Frankfort, Essen, Cologne and West Berlin. Dinos' little girl read "Santa comes by Olympic Airways" and asked her father if it was true. The archaeologist felt completely out of place; nothing was familiar here. But he ran his fingers through the cases of Cyrillic characters that spelled his former world, defining its limits and composing his dreams. He had lost all that once he left Greece. But with the smell of ink, which he now bent to sniff at like a dog its own dirt, his mind flew back to his revolutionary youth when they used to print *Pamfitikiki* in an underground room in Salonika and went on demonstrations in support of the "15 per cent aid for education." Seeing the boss coming out of his office with a German customer made all this seem like a stage set, with the bitter cold and the German boot outside. The customer's self-assurance and firm step showed Pavlos he was on his home ground and that in case of disagreement the customer would always be right. The police and the courts would protect him, not them —the *Gastarbeiter* in the press with its Cyrillic characters, uprooted flowers doomed to wither. Then he picked up a handful of little omicrons, tiny zeros, and let them trickle through his fingers, listening with pleasure to the dull sound of lead on lead like an old moneylender playing with his gold.

Of course, it was better not to talk about the prices. They were exorbitant. And his job at the university brought in just enough to support his wife and child. He couldn't get any money out of Greece. As he said jokingly to the printer, he could only have afforded those prices if he'd been a crook in antiquities instead of an expert on antiquity.

"Ruinous!" said Dinos as they came out. "Didn't I tell you? It would be cheaper to type your thesis and get it photocopied than to pay 650 marks for sixteen pages."

"If it wasn't for the plates, that's what I'd do."

Before they parted, Dinos asked him if he was going anywhere that evening.

He said he wasn't.

"Why don't you come to my place for a drink, then?"

He accepted the invitation, but he wouldn't be able to stay late—he had to leave very early the next day.

Dinos lived in the center of the town near a spare-parts factory where the lights were all burning. It was an old house that had escaped the bombing and was now inhabited by Turkish, Greek and Yugoslav workers from the factory.

As Dinos was putting the little girl to bed in the only other room, his wife came in from work. She was annoyed with her husband for bringing visitors without letting her know. He might at least have called her up at the office so that she could have bought something at the co-op while it was still open. Now what were they going to eat? There was nothing in the house except some spinach risotto from yesterday. And what were they going to drink? Dinos told her not to worry—they'd find something.

This evening wasn't the problem. It was her work that had been getting on her nerves for some time now. Before, she'd done piecework in factories and been a cleaner in hotels and even at the slaughterhouse, wearing boots and an apron spattered with blood. She hadn't minded that. She came home tired but not nervous. But for the last year she'd been sitting working in an office, with just a glimpse through a window of what was going on in the street outside, and surrounded by Germans—reactionary-minded, petty bourgeois. The office was as far from the apartment as the printer's, only in the opposite direction; and after an hour's journey on the U-bahn, she arrived home every evening a wreck. Dinos was not working at the moment. He occupied himself with party business and looking after the house and the little girl when she was not at school. So now she had priority to get worked up, just as Dinos had had it in the days when he worked in the factory and she looked after the child.

She was a nice girl, a leftist who, at the time of the banning of the first peace march, had had some knocks from the Asphalia. These had frightened her at the time, but she'd soon got over that to "dedicate herself," as she said, to the demonstrations of July '65 and later. These had left an indelible mark on her, her friends, her whole generation.

"I'll go down to the grocer's and see if he's got anything," said Dinos.

It was after eight, and the Balkan grocery store in the *Heim* near the entrance was closed. But like all Greek grocery stores, even in the West German Republic, it had a back door that was still open for special customers. To get in, however, you had to have a key—the grocer didn't hear you otherwise —and Dinos wasn't really a regular. So he went down to the second floor to borrow a key from the ex-miner, who opened the door in his pajamas; the Greek broadcast from Munich for immigrant workers had just ended, and he and his wife were going to bed. But he gladly accepted Dinos' invitation to come up for a drink. Then Dinos and the archaeologist let themselves into the shop, which sold fruit and vegetables as well as groceries.

"Welcome, comrade!" cried the grocer, a shrewd type from the Piraeus, who managed to be on good terms with everyone so that everyone would be his customer, but who gave himself away one day when Dinos had cornered him to contribute to a collection by saying "I don't give dough to the Commies."

"You haven't deigned to set foot here for three months and now . . . You want some hors d'oeuvres? That depends what wine you're having."

"Red."

"I don't have any red. But I've got a very good demijohn of retsina. I'll let you have it cheap, and I won't charge you for the bottle. . . ."

"And some salted herring."

"I don't sell herring with retsina. It would be an insult both to the herring and to the retsina. Do you get it? Either learn to drink or else better not drink at all. *I'll* choose your hors d'oeuvres for you."

He chose feta, cucumber, tomatoes, squid, olives and some raw onions.

"Are we being honored this evening by the big boys from the Kremlin?" he said, with a glance at the archaeologist.

"Why don't you come up and join us for a drink too?" said Dinos, paying.

When he got back to the flat, he found the miner and his

94

plump wife already sitting on the edge of the divan. The lad from Yannitsa, Ganymede, filled the row of glasses. A sausage was cooking, and there was a copious mixed salad. They'd also found a tin of octopus in the cupboard.

The miner was telling about his experiences in Belgium— how he got there in 1956, before the labor agreements were signed, and how, out of the five hundred workers who first arrived, only eighty were left after a month. The baptism of *poussière* was enough to send the others back to Greece.

"What *is poussière?*"

"It comes from the French word for dust, coal dust. I worked in the same mine that collapsed on top of two hundred and forty miners and buried them a few months after I left. There were about ten Greeks among the dead. That was the place where the fellow who was working beside me, an Italian, was suddenly buried one day when the roof caved in. I rushed to help him and got cut off, too. Here—you can still see the scar. But I made a mistake in getting out after only three years. If I'd stayed five, according to a law I knew nothing about at the time, I'd have been able to get a permit to drive a taxi, open a pub, all sorts of things, just as if I'd been a Belgian citizen. Five years' work under the earth gives you the right to work however you like on top. Now, I regret it. We came to Germany thinking it would be better, and it's worse."

Suddenly the overloaded bookshelves began to tremble, and books tumbled all over the floor. The little girl in the next room, awakened by the noise, began to cry. Thorez, Togliatti, Mao, Lenin, Marx, Plekhanov, Sarafi, Che, Castro, Velouchiotis, Dimitriou, Pryomaglous, the *Communist Review, New World,* the *Art Review,* Trotsky, *March, Von Tiras Theotokis*—all the books now fell in an avalanche to the table with the typewriter and the sheepskin rug.

"Told you so," said his wife. "I told him, 'Don't buy any

more. There are too many for the shelves already.' But obstinate as a mule . . ."

"Never mind, never mind," said Dinos. "I'll pick them up. They haven't broken anything."

Meanwhile, Ganymede, the miner and the archaeologist increased the confusion by getting up to help.

"Sorry to have given you such a scare," said Dinos' wife.

"It's nothing at all," said the plump neighbor. "If we'd been downstairs, now, we might have been scared. But not here."

And she drained her glass.

"If you don't mind my asking, boy," said the steelworker to the archaeologist, "where do you come from?"

"Thessalonica."

"Ah, he's from Salonika!" exclaimed the other, turning to his wife. "That's the reason we get on so well together."

There and Back

"Who knows?" said the intellectual of the proletariat. "Perhaps the reason why our people don't rise in revolt is that the cells of our race have grown old."

The proletarian of the intellectuals shook his head.

"Compared wtih the Latin Americans, for example," went on the first, "we're terribly backward. The Tupamaros come from young cells which haven't yet passed their prime. But as our ancestors said, the Great School at Constantinople doesn't produce either teachers or students any more. It's in decline. Perhaps it's cellular deficiency?"

They were chatting on the train. The intellectual of the proletariat was a professor of electronic spectrology and the proletarian of the intellectuals was a lecturer in Modern Greek literature. They both belonged to that category of the cultured bourgeoisie whose left-wing sympathies have more to do with sentiment than with class consciousness. At present, they were not only traveling in the same compartment, but were also engaged in the same movement. They were going to a city in West Germany, Lower Bochum, to be precise, to address a meeting of workers and students organized by the three co-operating resistance organizations: the Joint Movement of Students and Workers Abroad, the Students' and Workers' Movement against the Dictatorship, and the Greek Democrats' Resistance. The intellectual of the proletariat was the

97

delegate of the last; the proletarian of the intellectuals, the delegate of the second. The delegate of the first had gone by air and would meet them there.

"This is the last time I take part in this sort of meeting," declared the proletarian of the intellectuals. "The experience of all these years has shown words are useless. We need acts, not words."

"As Karamanlis would say," put in the intellectual of the proletariat. He laughed his crystal laugh, but neither that nor his kindly expression could conceal his bitterness over the "springtime of Athens," when the end of Karamanlis' rule had seemed to foreshadow the return of the "brains," and he himself had gone back, together with dozens of other scientists who'd distinguished themselves abroad, to staff the new University of Patras and the various extramural institutes, research centers and associations. Then came the coup.

In his haste to catch this early train, the professor hadn't had time to buy a ticket, so now he had to keep paying a supplement every time they crossed a frontier.

But the lecturer was even worse off. At the first inspection and the word "police," he jumped like a released prisoner reliving his arrest; he'd forgotten his passport. He'd put on a new jacket for the meeting and omitted to transfer all his papers. In vain he slapped at the pocket it should have been in, as in self-punishment or like a thief caught red-handed trying to demonstrate his innocence. Fortunately, he found a work permit showing he taught at the University of Lyons, but though this satisfied the French cop now, what was going to happen in the other countries?

The professor, too, was submerged in gloom.

"What do they need passports for in the Common Market countries?" he cried. "As far as administrative routine goes, the tyranny is just the same as in the nineteenth century. What does their famous union really amount to?"

"The problem isn't getting out without a passport—it's getting back again," said the lecturer in despair. And he told how one of his female colleagues had been held up two days in Brussels once, while waiting for someone to bring her passport from Paris.

As Brecht said, passports are a fundamental problem for émigrés everywhere. And it wouldn't have been so bad if the lecturer's passport had been out of date, false, or with forged dates, or if he hadn't had one at all because his consul had kept it when he went to renew it. But to think he had a perfectly good one and then went and forgot it! . . . The professor tried to console him by changing the subject to the trial in Athens.

But the lecturer's anxiety about whether he'd be allowed to cross the German border was soon made more acute by the first Belgian customs inspector, a stout fellow in a peaked cap. In his Walloon accent, he told him he ought to get off at Charleroi, the next stop, and take the next train back. But that would mean he wouldn't get to Bochum till after the meeting, and all his journey would have been for nothing.

"Yes," said the intellectual of the proletariat, "but if what he says is true, better to turn back at Charleroi than at Aachen."

"You have to take risks in this life," said the proletarian of the intellectuals.

The professor had rolled up the curtain to rest his head on, and now, his eyes shut, he seemed to see himself and his companion talking not in a railway compartment, but in the prison at Aegina. He started awake. The train, fortunately, wasn't a prison, and ugly as the landscape was, it was constantly changing, unlike the view through the window of a cell, with "the prison tree and the women." He was always thinking of the friends of his who'd recently been arrested; hence the chronic nightmares.

"At least they've put the problem of Greece back on the map," he was saying now to the lecturer. The junta was trying to get death penalties by exploiting an anti-Communist law passed during the civil war.

When they crossed the Belgian frontier again, the customs official was more affable. He seemed to have had bitter experience of fascism himself; as soon as he saw they were Greek, he suggested that the lecturer solve his problem by taking out a *laissez-passer*, valid for forty-eight hours and costing only three marks. He even had a word with his German colleague, who was on the train already and would start his inspection as soon as they had crossed the frontier; neither the intellectual of the proletariat nor the proletarian of the intellectuals knew any German except what they'd picked up as children under the occupation, when they heard *"verboten"* and said *"faflouchten."*

"God helps those who help themselves," said the lecturer.

"Practice makes perfect," replied the professor.

And he opened a new textbook on cybernetic spectroscopy. He read during gaps in the conversation, making notes in the margin. The lecturer had on his lap the *Eighteen Texts,* which had just been published in Greece. Every man to his trade, he thought.

The studious silence was interrupted by the noise of the door suddenly being slid back. It was the ticket inspector. The professor had to take a supplementary ticket from Aachen to Lower Bochum. As he had no marks, he paid in francs, the devaluation of the franc and the revaluation of the mark making him lose a clear 20 per cent on the transaction.

"And they call it a united Europe!" he sighed.

Both men were hungry and went to the bar, which was in the next coach. The proletarian of the intellectuals ordered a cheese omelette; the intellectual of the proletariat, a ham omelette. As they went north, the weather became clearer;

patches of blue appeared among the leaden clouds. The train was now sliding smoothly on German rails. There was no longer the pitching and tossing there'd been in Belgium, where the earth, undermined from within, makes the ties unstable. A thin drizzle was falling in the Ardennes, as always a mist that never resolved itself into real drops, never indulged in a good downpour and then blew over. It was reabsorbed by the clouds, and the clouds dissolved again into drizzle, piercing, tired, tiring, frustrated, an endless short circuit.

The lecturer always felt somber anyway going through Belgium. He'd been down a couple of the coal mines and knew the miners lived in dilapidated hovels, if not actual barracks. He could see some of these through the window as the strapping policemen carried out their inspection. The thought of all this haunted the lecturer as he looked out at the great pipes running parallel to the railroad and the heavy barges, immersed up to the waterline, moving over the black water.

Artificial hills of tailings adorned with almost equally artificial trees, the result of centuries of burrowing in the bowels of the earth, bore witness to the vast expenditure of human life. By daylight the landscape was still endurable. But at night, with lignite flames coming from the chimneys so that men breathed carbon dioxide instead of oxygen, the livid emanations were like the remains of some ancient hell. All this was quite different from such ultramodern installations as those on the outskirts of Cologne, which they were now approaching. Here the entire great Bayer complex sent up only one blue-and-yellow flame, the final quintessence of experiments leading up to the definitive formula for aspirin. It made him think of the experiments conducted during the war on Jews destined for the gas chambers.

When the professor and the lecturer got back to their

compartment, they found a couple of Germans there, typical ex-Nazi faces. One had a scar on his cheek like the mark left by the ricochet of a bullet. The other had a stick and looked as if he'd been wounded in the war. They were over sixty and so must have been in the bloom of youth during the war.

"How many people do you reckon he exterminated?" said the proletarian of the intellectuals, looking at the man opposite him. He had a harsh, ruthless face, the red mouth still twisted from giving orders in concentration camps.

"About a thousand," answered the intellectual of the proletariat. "Dead souls," he added.

The German looked at them, not realizing they were talking about him. They went on speculating aloud, perhaps hoping to provoke him, but of course not succeeding.

One town followed another at intervals of about a minute, with the mathematical precision of the timetable they'd been given at Aachen. They checked the punctuality of their arrival and departure by each station clock. There had been other periods in history when the trains ran on time.

Cold drinks and coffee came around, handed out by an elegant fellow with glasses and the gestures of a headwaiter in a fashionable restaurant. The tray of bottles hung from the neck of a sturdy peasant with a pleasant face. The heavy load of orangeade, lemonade, beer, and Coca-Cola forced him to balance himself by leaning back like a bucking steer. His chief selected whatever bottle was asked for, opened it, poured the contents into a plastic cup and gave the customer his change. Meanwhile, the other stood by, silent, without even perspiring, a bastion of the consumer society. The lecturer remembered his childhood, and the same master-slave relationship between the German officers and their batmen. He thought of the batman who used to polish the officer's shoes in his family's house in Salonika, after it had been requisitioned by the Nazis. It made him shudder to see that thirty years later, in peacetime, the same relationship of idiot soldier to sensitive officer could still exist.

"What time do we get in to Bochum?" asked the professor.

The lecturer consulted the printed timetable.

"Six-twelve Upper Bochum," he said. "Six-twenty-one Lower Bochum."

At six-twenty-one exactly, they were getting off the train.

A delegation of workers and students welcomed them with flowers. The party split up among various cars and met at the home of one of the workers.

"Well, what news from Paris?" a student asked the intellectual of the proletariat, who at once began to describe the situation in full. The proletarian of the intellectuals was impatient; he wanted to hear what the others had to say.

A little boy kept saying tearfully, "Where's Zorze?" His mother had no one to leave him with, so she'd brought him with her to the station. On the way back he'd sat on the lap of someone called George, from whom he'd got separated; and now he blamed his loss on the visitors, whose thick glasses made them look different from all the rest.

There was one worker who wore glasses, but in his case they did not mark him off from everyone else. They seemed to be incorporated into his face; their frames seemed to have merged into the flesh. The proletarian of the intellectuals reflected that they were like the glasses of political prisoners, embedded in the face of the wearer. Intellectuals' glasses mist on the outside, as when you come out of the cold into a warm room. Workers' glasses mist on the inside, from the sweat of their labor at the machines.

"Where do you work?" he asked the man sitting next to him on the sofa.

"At Volkswagen. Spare parts."

The host's wife, after scolding the little boy for driving

everyone mad with his "Where's Zorze?," took the professor's jacket on her lap and started to sew a button on it. It had come off on the train, probably when he was paying for one of his tickets. The intellectual of the proletariat, whose wife couldn't get out of Greece, said with his crystal laugh that he still hadn't got used to being a bachelor. At that, the worn jacket of the professor in the hands of the worker's wife took on a symbolic value; a friendly relationship suddenly came into being. What mightn't have happened so easily back home, because of the division of classes into hermetically sealed compartments, came about in exile, where they were all in the same boat. With skilled fingers used to machinery and roughened by housework as well (for emigrants' wives not only worked a full day in the factory, but also looked after house and children and did the cooking and washing up before falling dead tired into bed only to get up again at six the next morning), she finished sewing the button, bit off the thread, and handed the coat back to its owner, hoping he would not be a bachelor much longer. Then, full of energy, she got out the ouzo and liqueurs and went into the kitchen to make some sandwiches.

Since it was Good Friday, the proletarian of the intellectuals asked if they were going to church.

"Not to the junta's church with the junta's priest," said a worker who seemed to have difficulty raising a smile. His face looked as if it had taken on the ash-gray color of the city and was as inflexible as if the northern cold had frozen its once mobile features. "My mother died here," he went on, "and the junta's priest, knowing my democratic views, didn't come to the funeral. I had to send to Hamburg for another priest. I'd brought my mother here for the winter because I couldn't go back there. And she never went back either—we buried her here."

The hostess tried to give a more cheerful turn to the conversation by putting on some bouzouki records. Then she brought in the sandwiches.

"Ham and cheese on Good Friday?" cried the proletarian of the intellectuals, his mouth watering. The omelette he'd had on the train had long since evaporated.

"It's no sin for travelers and those who are sick," quoted the pretty earth mother, setting down the tray on the table.

Meanwhile, the intellectual of the proletariat had discovered he came from the same part of the world as another worker at Volkswagen. They were both from Thassos, though from different villages.

"Are there many emigrants from Thassos in West Germany?"

"Thassos isn't there any more—it's here," said the man.

"How long is it since you've gone back?"

"I went last year, but I didn't like it any more. Lousy with bungalows. They've ruined the beach."

"And you didn't have any trouble?"

"The spies hadn't got to work yet," he said meaningfully.

"He means," explained another, "things have changed since the consulate's been staffed with army people in civilian clothes. Until then, no one bothered you except for some definite reason, even if you were seen taking part in a demonstration."

"And where are you going for your vacation this year?" the lecturer asked another man, who'd been silent all this time, not smoking or eating or drinking.

"For the last five years, we've vacationed at home, under the trees of Bochum campus, swimming in the chlorinated swimming pool. But we heard it was quite cheap in Yugoslavia, so we're taking the family there this year. Let's hope we find a bit of . . ."

"Greece," he was obviously going to say, but didn't.

It would soon be time for the meeting, which was due to

start at eight. It was being held in the assembly room of the German unions, "only a pistol shot away," as the man from Thassos said. Someone suggested walking there since the speakers must be stiff from sitting in the train, and everyone agreed. They all thanked their hostess and set out.

They divided up into little groups. The worker whose mother had died suggested they call in at the club, which was on their way, "so that our friends can see our refuge." The town was dreary, like most towns in West Germany. After twenty-five years, it still seemed not to have got over the Allied bombing. Huge blocks of houses stretched along sidewalks wide enough for cars to drive on. Posters on the walls announced a forthcoming world exhibition of agricultural machinery. Before setting, the sun managed to find a little break in the clouds, and these few rays were like the exiles' hope of a change or a new phase or an amnesty, which revived every now and then, when politicians or international organizations denounced the junta, or some foreign power held out promises. But the only permanent outlook for a long way ahead was cloudy. All other forecasts had proved false.

A young man was standing at the door of the Workers' Club carrying two milk-fed lambs in his arms for Easter.

"The Germans don't know how to cook lamb," explained one of their companions. "Before we came, their butchers used to throw away the head—can you imagine that? But since 1960, there's been more demand and the price of the heads has gone up. The Germans eat only pork."

Inside the club there was the warmth and intimacy of an Orthodox church. Ikons of Lambrakis, Petroulas, Papandreou, Mandilaras, Yalis, Beloyannis, Velouchiotis and Mavroyenis hung on the rood screen. On the altar of the bar were the body and blood of the Lord, red wine and wholewheat bread. The choir stalls were the booths, and the gospel, the *Complete Works of Lenin* in the thirty-two volumes of the *Editions politiques.*

In smaller frames were pictures of prisoners—women, like saints not yet canonized. And the priest was the bartender, without a beard, certainly, but with a white apron for a cassock, which didn't conceal a sizeable paunch. He purified them with a glass of ouzo instead of holy water.

"Well," said the visitors, "isn't there any split among the left here?"

"We leave splits at the church door," said a curate, a young waiter from Kalamata.

Dissension might not trouble the left there, but it put in an appearance at the Center Party. Hardly had they arrived at the hall where the meeting was to be held when they saw a group from the Greek Democrats' Resistance coming up to their delegate.

"What's the matter?" the lecturer asked some of the Joint Movement members who were plotting together in a corner.

"The Resistance delegate's a spy," they answered with one voice.

The lecturer was flabbergasted.

"The professor of spectrology, a spy? Who says so?"

"Our delegate."

"Who's he? Just let me talk to him."

Two or three people barred the way. The Joint Movement delegate was concealed behind the scenes until the matter could be cleared up. *Verboten.*

"How can you possibly say he's a spy?" shouted the Students' and Workers' delegate furiously. He was pleased, nevertheless, that such divisions were not confined to the left. "He was sentenced to ten years' imprisonment *in absentia.* He's a loyal party member who does honor to the resistance and a distinguished scientist."

"We have orders from high up," said a member of the Joint Movement, with the false respectfulness of bourgeois parties trying to copy the impeccable organizational techniques of the left.

"You need evidence before making such serious charges against anyone," growled the lecturer. "Otherwise, you're just playing the junta's game."

"You're right, comrade," said one of them. "But that's what we've been told, and that's what we say."

"I want to see your delegate," the lecturer insisted.

In the end, he was allowed to. The delegate was a tall fellow who seemed to have an inferiority complex and exploited the dissension between the two groups to acquire power. Over whom?

"We've nothing against you," he told the lecturer. "But the other one—no."

"But this is unthinkable," said the lecturer. "I simply don't understand. Your attitude strikes me as unreasonable, to say the very least."

"Unfortunately, sir, that's all I can tell you now," said the delegate, like a general in the hour of battle. "One day you'll find out, and then you'll see I'm right. For the present . . ."

"In that case, I won't speak either, and the meeting will be down the drain," said the lecturer.

Meanwhile, the audience were getting restive. Some were Greeks, but there were also many Germans, most of them students, "long-hairs," as the workers called them, who had an innate distaste for authority without necessarily having definite political views. They were warmhearted and kind, and their disinterestedness had been of great help to the movement.

"Can you hear them? They'll all go home," said the Students' and Workers' delegate. "It's eight-thirty, and we've only got the place till ten."

The intellectual of the proletariat, surrounded by his supporters, was fuming. The proletarian of the intellectuals implored him to keep as cool as possible so that the audience wouldn't guess what was going on behind the scenes. The professor promised, in the name of their friendship and the day they'd spent together on the train, not to make a row in public.

So all three mounted the platform. As they'd agreed, the Joint Movement delegate spoke first. The Students' and Workers' delegate was supposed to speak second, but he was going to give way immediately to the Resistance delegate, so that the Joint Movement objector would find himself presented with a *fait accompli*. But this was decided without the third thief himself, who simply went on talking till ten minutes before the meeting was due to close. He spoke slowly, bending the microphone over in a curve like a swan's neck, with figures of speech and restrained gestures, like an Englishman addressing the House of Lords. This, together with the German translation which followed each sentence, put the audience into a daze; such platitudes didn't justify his monopolizing the mike. Meanwhile, the other two speakers were becoming more and more enraged. To keep themselves within bounds they tapped clenched fists on the table or made swastikas out of used matches.

"Peanut politics!" whispered the intellectual of the proletariat to the proletarian of the intellectuals. "Provincial trivia! Not a word about the prisoners. People are rotting in jail, and he treats us to his micropolicy of exile."

Finally, without undue haste, the speaker put his notes into his briefcase, descended from the platform and walked out of the hall. Then, like a herring darting from the net back into the sea or an escaped tiger fleeing the zookeepers, the professor leapt to the rostrum. He grabbed the microphone, forcing his teeth into its slits and pressing his mouth as close as he could in a mortal kiss, like someone biting the pin out of a grenade. He spoke with passion, without notes, without a translator, and electrified the audience that his predecessor had lulled into lethargy. He was horrified, he said, by the deplorable attitude of some people, trying to turn the great resistance of our people into a personal thing of their own. A storm of applause broke out at the back of the hall. Even the Germans who didn't understand the language felt a thrill go through them, for this speaker corresponded much more closely to their concept of Zorba, the typical passionate Greek, than had the previous speaker, with his phlegmatic filibustering.

The man in charge of the hall had already started to switch off the lights when it was the turn of the third speaker of the evening, the proletarian of the intellectuals. In a couple of words he simply asked the audience to disperse quietly, without the torchlight procession to the consulate that the intellectual of the proletariat had suggested to them in the enthusiasm of the moment. They didn't have police permission, he said.

At the door, several members of the Students' and Workers' Movement came up to their delegate. They said they all worked at the local rubber factory, legendary for the number of hands that had been eaten up by its machinery.

"And is that what happened to you?" the lecturer asked one of them.

"Yes," said the man.

"Will you come somewhere for a bite?" asked a middle-aged man from Vermio. "So that we can talk. We don't often have the pleasure of seeing fellow countrymen who are intellectuals, and we'd like . . . Wouldn't we, boys?" He turned to the others as if for their approval. He was too moved to be able to finish the sentence.

"Ask the organizing committee," said the proletarian of the intellectuals.

And he began to walk away. But suddenly the bandage on the workman's hand riveted him to the spot like a magnet. He couldn't take his eyes off it. It became blindingly white in the darkness, like the supernatural light that appears to mystics in ecstasy. A white wound in the dark. The man stood there, his hat pulled down, his coat drawn in the waist, looking at him, his arm in its cast and a sling round his neck. The lecturer couldn't tear himself away.

"We're waiting for you," called the professor from inside a car. "We're going to the station buffet—it's the only place open at this hour."

The other moved over to the car like a sleepwalker. He didn't know why the bandage wounded his sight so. It wasn't the first he'd seen, and it wouldn't be the last. So why did it affect him like this?

"I don't know what's the matter with us Greeks," said the professor as they were undressing by their couchettes. "This evening was just one more proof of the curse that's on us as a race."

"You were marvelous, anyway," said the lecturer, already stretched out on his bunk. "I wish I'd had a tape recorder. You wouldn't have recognized yourself."

"I know what's wrong," the professor went on, talking to himself. "It's worn-out cells, a biological falling-off. We have to admit that races grow old just as individuals do. Our cells were at their peak two thousand years ago. Now it's the turn of other people in other places. The Tupamaros are the Alcibiades of Latin America. They have youthful cells that are still intact. Don't you think I'm right?" he said as he lay down.

"Maybe," said the lecturer. "I don't know about anybody else, but *I'm* tired. Good night."

Maids and Mistresses

And a time came when mistresses found out about political developments from their minds. The maids' boy friends were police spies, primitive, virile brutes who had free access to the various ministries as bodyguards to the big shots and went around armed, watching the movements of the "opposition" after bombs started to explode more and more often at central points in the capital. When they came off duty in the evening, they would recount the incidents of the day to their Dulcineas in the employ of important families. And next morning, duster in hand, the maids would tell their mistresses that such and such a minister had said the price of bread would not go up, or that "when my boy friend went into his boss's office, he found him talking to a high-ranking American officer about the bases at Souda." And the ladies would call one another up on the telephone, amazed that they, who used to pick up political news at suppers and galas amidst champagne and crème caramel, should now be beholden to their domestics. In the old days, a mistress used to forbid her maid to entertain her boy friend in the mistress's absence. But now the maid could have him in at any hour of the day or night. If he was free to come and go in the office of the prime minister, he was free to do the same in the house of a lady who was nothing in comparison with the first lady in the land.

"But what future can there be in an affair with that big oaf?" madame would say to her maid, Maria. The girl's sobs didn't help clarify matters. "Where will it get you? Spies don't get promoted unless they're educated. Your boy friend might have gotten somewhere if he'd ever been to high school, but what future is there for him with his three years in primary school? At best, he'll get a raise from two thousand to twenty-five hundred. And then what? What sort of a life can you have on that?"

Now if Maria had only got to know someone in the post office, say, with a real future . . .

"Yes, madame, but I like him," the girl would say. "He's got . . . I don't know . . . I hardly like—" she laughed and sobbed at the same time—"a long thingummy that goes right in me."

"I can quite appreciate that," said the lady, "but you're still very young, and you haven't yet learned that love, feelings, don't last. If you stay with him, you'll always be doing other people's washing, you'll be a menial all your life. Is that what you want?"

"Oh, no, madame, of course not!"

The lady had to fix it so that she could hide a member of the resistance. The bourgeoisie tended toward the left as the proletariat inclined toward the right. She'd been playing cards and gossiping with her friends, saying they really ought to do something about the "situation"—what had things come to, ruled by the king's horses instead of the king's court?—when, as the game ended and she was getting ready to leave, a young dentist's wife came up to her and whispered that if she really wanted to help, she could take in someone who was living underground and hadn't anywhere else to go. She agreed to do so but explained that for the moment it wasn't possible because her maid's boy friend was a spy who worked on behalf of the "situation."

That was why she was now trying to persuade the girl to send him packing.

The maid listened to what she had to say. She'd been with the family for years and was attached to it. How lively things had been when the master sat for Parliament! People came from all over the province with chickens and turkeys and honeycombs. She'd been hard put to supply them all with cups of coffee. Then there was the summer vacation, when her employers took her with them to their seaside villa in Crete. She liked that. But now she also liked Panagis, her fiancé, a nice outgoing boy, on good terms with the police. And then where she was going to find anything better? When the master had a finger in every pie—he'd been a deputy and once a minister—people were always coming to the house asking favors, and then she'd gotten to know several nice boys, but she hadn't had the sense to hold onto one. Now you'd think the place had mildew. The master hadn't been re-elected; there hadn't been any elections. Not a soul in the house. Others were in command now, and these others had no dealings with her employers.

There could be no question of firing her, thought madame. There was no plausible reason for doing so. She wasn't lazy, she didn't steal. Maybe she helped herself to the groceries sometimes, but only within reasonable limits. Besides, madame liked the girl and had spent years training her! How could she start all over again with someone else? People don't realize how difficult it is to tailor a maid to fit the needs of a household exactly. And madame didn't hand over the maid's wages. She put them away in gold sovereigns for her, so she'd have a little cash dowry when she decided to be married.

But madame's friend, the dentist's wife, stuck like a leech. She telephoned every Wednesday and Friday.

"Any developments about the business I mentioned to you?"

"No."

The friend wanted them to meet, so they arranged to have tea at Flocas' one afternoon.

After making sure they weren't being overheard, the friend asked bluntly, "Well, do you know another house he could go to?"

The lady thought for a moment and suggested one.

"The poor fellow takes it so hard, living at our expense, he refuses to eat anything. The day before yesterday we gave a party, and he stayed locked in the closet all night, listening to what we said. 'I'm delighted to see the dictatorship doesn't have popular support,' he said afterwards. We had to give a party, have people in, to throw them off the scent. And he's pining away. He's afraid for us. The houses that used to be open to people like him are closing one after the other. It's even said they're trailed there by the secret police, though they deliberately don't arrest them. So, of course, people in hiding try to avoid such places. And," she added, fitting a long double-tipped cigarette into her even longer holder, "they haven't any money. The party abroad doesn't send them any. The poor wretch explained it to me one day: his party's broken off with the Russians, apparently—I didn't quite follow, but he seemed pleased about it. Now, he said, they'd be able to build up a new party like the one they'd always dreamed of. He's a saint. But the fact of the matter is they haven't a penny to get around on. . . . I don't like the look of that man sitting opposite at all. . . . Oh, yes, Depy's going to Nice this summer on her husband's yacht—lucky creature! She hasn't any worries." Then she added, in a low voice, "So be as quick as you can."

"I'll try the other place."

"I'd feel much better about it if he went to you."

"But darling, do you realize how difficult it is to break up an affair that's based on sex?"

"How long have they known each other?"

"About six months."

"How did they meet?"

"At her brother-in-law's on her Sunday off."

"And she doesn't suspect anything?"

"She doesn't understand that sort of thing. And, of course, he gave her a big line. The next Sunday he picked her up and took her for a drive in a Buick belonging to the Asphalia. You can imagine what sort of reputation we're going to get in our building!"

"Perhaps he's supposed to be watching your husband?"

"My husband hasn't any secrets, except . . ." She meant affairs with women, but she didn't say it; the former deputy was regarded as a symbol of marital fidelity. They both laughed bitterly.

"The best way to get rid of her would be to send her back to her village."

"She doesn't go back there any more. She likes Athens. She says 'Always improve yourself' is her motto. From the village to the town, from the town to the capital, and from the capital to Europe and abroad."

"That's an idea. Send her to Australia!"

"But the ambassador we used to know has gone. Everyone's gone, everything's changed. We're ruled by our servants nowadays!"

"Oh, well, if it's impossible, just drop it!"

Each paid her share of the bill, while an elderly lady with blue-rinsed hair scanned all the customers through her lorgnette, the waiter waited in terror for the next bomb to go off, and the tourists, mostly Americans, chattered away noisily under the roof that was formerly the floor of the American military mission.

"I forgot to ask you—how do you manage with your own maid?"

"My dear, you can't have a maid and someone who's in hiding both in the same house. It's like putting a candle near a powder keg. Haven't you noticed my hands? I use rubber gloves to do the dishes, but I can't play cards any more. The washing and scrubbing make them unfit to be seen. I feel like Pontius Pilate—as if everybody's looking at them. Of course, my guest helps as much as he can, even if it's only for something to do. But . . ."

They'd come out of the tearoom, and the lady had just put on her white gloves when the giant confronted her. As he bowed, she felt the varicose vein in her right leg throb. She returned his greeting politely, hastily getting out her dark glasses to hide her embarrassment. But he meant to speak to her at all costs.

The sidewalk was crowded. A nearby traffic light had just let a flood of pedestrians across, and they were all slowed down by the outdoor tables of the tearoom. A waiter carrying a tray with at least ten orders on it had got caught in the crowd. At the same time, the lines of cars started up again. The noise seemed to increase the impossibility of throwing the man off.

"What's the matter?" asked her friend.

The man was right beside her, and she could see the bulge in his jacket made by his revolver. With most people, the bulge would have been a wallet. The two objects were equally lethal.

"Why has Maria been avoiding me?" he asked. "It looks as if she doesn't want to see me any more. Is there somebody else hanging round?"

"I don't know, I know nothing about it," said the lady. "I don't meddle in anyone's affairs, not even those of my dog."

"She's been acting funny lately," continued Panagis. "And I'm not the sort of guy to let himself be taken for a ride."

"What do you want *me* to do?"

"Tell me what's really going on, lady. I'm sorry to bother you, but I love Maria and I want to marry her."

"But what are you doing here at this hour?"

"I'm on duty. Tomorrow I'm on in the morning. Tell her I'll call in the afternoon."

"All right."

Her friend was waiting for her farther on.

"It was he. My maid's famous boy friend. He's on duty here."

"I can see why she doesn't want to give him up," said the friend.

"Yes, but what about the practical side—how would they manage? The police only pay a pittance. The demand for jobs exceeds the supply. Maria's told me all about it. They get a fixed wage of two thousand and a bonus of fifty drachmas for each person they nab. Of course, he can get free tickets to the theater and the local movies, but what do you suppose a dolt like him understands about art?"

As they separated she added, "When I've found out about the other place, I'll let you know."

When madame got home, Maria was spreading out noodles to dry in the sun on the veranda. They were freshly made— the recipe they used in her own village. Underneath, she'd spread a couple of old sheets.

Time went by, and one day Maria found herself pregnant. It was his child she was carrying, and she married him. The bride's matron of honor was Madame Despina, the prime minister's wife. Maria's name appeared in the papers. A local paper in Kalamata, where her husband came from, even printed a picture of them exchanging rings in the column "Society Weddings." They rented a little apartment at Kory- dalla. The money madame had saved for Maria was a great help getting them started. They made the first payment on the flat and bought a refrigerator and some furniture. Panagis got a state loan for their major expenses.

So the lady was at last able to hide the fugitive. And later she took in many more. She'd forgotten Maria and her encounter with the spy. Now and then Maria would visit, curious to know what changes there'd been in the house. But her mistress was always in a hurry and took her along to do the shopping.

One day, a year and a half later, when her little boy was just twelve months old, Maria arrived dressed in black and weeping. Her husband had been killed in a car accident. It was a strange affair: the police car itself was hardly damaged, but Panagis was found stone dead. She wept and sobbed and said she couldn't bring up her orphan son alone unless madame would take her back again.

How could she be unkind to a faithful servant? And, after all, what harm had the poor girl done, just getting mixed up with a spy? It was the time when most of the original members of the resistance had already been arrested and their successors had no contacts with the aristocracy. So the lady took in Maria and the baby. But she always wondered: was Panagis really killed in an accident, or was his death an act of the new resistance that was starting to materialize?

"Ça ne Peut pas Durer"

It was sultry, and when they got to the house they realized they didn't even know their hostess's name. So the concierge, a Polish émigré woman, couldn't tell them which staircase to take. They knew it was the fourth floor; it was to avoid climbing up all those stairs for nothing that they asked.

"But don't you even know her Christian name?" said the concierge. "Or her job?"

"Her sister has a bakery."

That was all they could tell her. In fact, it was how they had come to be invited. They'd been buying some pastries when the manageress of the shop, a shrewd, lively woman whose head always looked as if it had just emerged from the hairdresser's hands and who was always full of newspaper headlines, had invited them to dinner at her sister's. A friend of her sister's lived with a Greek political exile like them, she had said. They asked his name. Stavros. They'd lost touch with him for six months, and they accepted eagerly. Besides, a free meal is not to be sniffed at when you're an émigré. They had exchanged phone numbers and later fixed the day.

"All right, then! Tuesday at eight-thirty. At that address, fourth floor, on the right as you go in."

But on the right as you went in there were two possibilities: the staircase immediately to the right after the entrance and the one to the right through the inner courtyard. Which was it? The concierge couldn't help them without any indication

of name or occupation. They could just vaguely remember something about "immediately after the door."

The spiral staircase made them more hot and bothered than ever. His wife stopped on the second floor and waited for him to call down. But instead, she heard him coming back, shaking the stairs to their foundations. So there was no doubt about it; their hostess lived on the other staircase, beyond the courtyard. . . . They paused on each landing to catch their breath. It was heavy, thundery weather, and because the evening brought no cooling breeze, it got them down. It was hot in Greece, too, at this time of year, they remembered, but the climate was different—dry, Attic and always cool in the evening. Here the damp air choked you; there was no escape from the heat. It alternated with torrential rain, which the tarred streets drank up like parched earth. Strange.

They were the first to arrive. Stavros and his girl hadn't come yet. Their hostess was young and pretty. Her husband, a magistrate and an elegant example of the typical Frenchman, was talking to his brother-in-law, the baker, a pleasant, fat, easygoing man of about fifty with a red rosette in his lapel, won fighting for his country. Two cherubs of children in pajamas said hello to the visitors and then went back to bed to discuss them. A poetess friend was in charge of the dinner. She was all nerves and smoked one cigarette after another.

"What's the latest from Greece?" she asked.

"Nothing new." He was puffing like a locomotive.

"An apéritif? Whisky? Port? Gin?"

"Whisky—with ice, if I may."

"The situation there can't go on like that," said the baker. "Such a beautiful country. *Ça ne peut pas durer.*"

He'd been hearing that for the past four years. "It can't go on." But it did go on and on and on.

"We love Greece, my wife and I. We've been there."

121

"When?"

"When was it, now? Five years ago, or six?"

He sighed again. He was always uneasy asking when, because the answer revealed the political attitude of whomever he was talking to. If the person had gone there immediately after the dictatorship or the following year, he put him on his black list and brought the conversation to an end. But if it was before the coup d'état, he went on and would even cap the other's praises of Greece because they referred to a time when he himself had lived there and was part of it.

"I wasn't all that crazy about the islands, to tell you the truth. What's that white one called?"

"Mykonos."

"That's right. Mykonos. Besides, I'm a bad sailor and stayed in my cabin the whole voyage. But my wife was on deck and got talking to some Greeks. They gave her a little ouzo, and she had a fine time. Didn't you, dear?"

"Yes, sure. We got along marvelously, even though we didn't speak the same language."

"I preferred Delphi and the Peloponnese—and Athens. Such a beautiful country! The situation there can't go on like that."

It was also a way of avoiding "the main issue." The other more reliable way, as he had discovered in the course of many similar evenings with well-disposed foreigners, was to talk about their own problems. He always began with politics.

"Are you a member of the party?" asked his hostess.

"No," he answered.

She was pleased. As she explained later, she considered the Communist Party responsible for the failure of the May '68 revolution. She herself supported the Krivinists, an extreme leftist group that opposed the party.

At this time, in the Paris of 1970, it was fashionable for the

petty bourgeosie living "within the walls" to have "advanced" political views, opposed to both capitalism and Communism, the two "establishments," as they called them, that had betrayed them. In a country with a political tradition like that of France, where the silken thread of natural continuity has never been broken, it was natural that the criticism that no longer came from the outmoded and aged right should come from the extreme left of the left.

The hostess was studying philosophy at Vincennes and so was entitled to have ideas of her own. Besides, among bourgeois couples, an intellectual wife is an ornament and object of pride.

"My best friend is a Communist," said the baker just to show he wasn't narrow-minded. "He's been a member of the party since 1926. We don't see eye to eye about everything, but he's my closest friend. You can talk to him. But *I* work twenty-four hours a day. A capitalist is someone who works like a slave. And these hands work." He held them out. "I live by them. I stir and knead and decorate with them. And it hasn't always been my job. I used to be an officer in submarines."

His wife, with the well-groomed head full of headlines, put a stop to his bourgeois monologue by making a brisk survey through the periscope.

"Peru," she said, "earthquakes. I'm going to send a crucifix to the relief fund—they're very religious. Brazil: things are going from bad to worse. Soviet Union: they've put more intellectuals in mental homes. Paraguay: they've found the skeleton of a prehistoric mammoth."

"But how do you know all this?" the guest cried; he'd stopped sweating by now.

"My wife takes an interest in everything," said the shopkeeper, with obvious pride. "She can talk to you on any subject you like. The job broadens the mind, you know. Every customer has his or her problem, and you need a solution for each. You have to know how to talk to them."

"What's your opinion about Garaudy?" asked the hostess. "My son did a sketch of Le Dantec this evening. . . . But they'll never dare arrest Sartre. . . . Do you like Nietzsche?"

At this point, Stavros and his girl arrived. He was in his prime, strong, handsome. The two Greeks greeted each other, but not in Greek; one of the typical symptoms of exile is to feel it's discourteous to speak your own language in the presence of foreigners. So they found themselves asking in halting French, "How's Paul?" and "Have you seen Androclis?"—banal phrases bridging the half year in which they hadn't met.

Stavros had just begun to make a life for himself in Greece after twenty years of prison, camps, and banishment to the provinces, when the steamroller of the dictatorship came and flattened everything. And he found himself adrift abroad, past the age when you can take things lightly and start all over again. The first few years were difficult. The French comrades were not as hospitable as he'd expected; their party hadn't foreseen there would be so many émigrés. It had managed all right with the Spaniards and the Portuguese, but when the Greeks came along, too, and didn't even use the Latin alphabet, they didn't know what to do with them. The party machine could absorb only 3 per cent of all the Greek exiles, and even this 3 per cent were soon rejected, like grit that hampered that highly perfected machine's perpetual motion. But Stavros was made of stern stuff and didn't easily give in. He was in favor of a union between the two opposing factions of the Greek left but saw his efforts shipwrecked when he wrote a "manifesto" and sent it to various militants for their support. Though it came back to him with flattering comments about how excellent and historic a document it was, it came back without any signatures. So he didn't belong to either side; he was straddling the fence.

Two Greeks meeting after a long time in a foreign environment constitute a chemical reaction: their tongues may stumble over foreign alphabets, but they speak with their eyes. Each mysteriously takes courage from the sight of the other's face, as if something inside him has said, "I'm not alone—he's in the same boat as I am." Each serves as a mirror, enabling the other to see himself as a third person. And memory works in its own fashion, speechlessly, the face of each a conductor for the other's past. A secret communication unperceived by any but themselves.

The poetess-cum-cook announced dinner was ready, and they sat down. The bouillabaisse awaited them in a deep tureen, the fish arranged on two separate plates as if just emerged from a bath. A huge crab on its back occupied a dish of its own, though it had been cooked with the common herd.

"What's the name of that wine you have in Greece?"

"Retsina."

"What does that mean?"

"They use pine resin to make it ferment."

"I like it."

"I can't stand it."

They opened the French wines, one after another. They talked about Nietzsche and Garaudy and the high cost of living in France. The fish were reduced to bones; the soup dwindled in the tureen. After the bouillabaisse came the cheeses, and after the cheeses, the wood strawberries. It was hot—hotter than ever now, after the steaming fish soup. They opened two windows to make a draught, but there was no breeze as there would have been in Athens.

"I see you've got some gray hairs," Stavros said to him in Greek.

"I'll start to dye it soon, too," he answered.

"*Ça ne peut pas durer,*" said the baker. "It *can't* last much longer." He hadn't understood what they'd been saying, but he'd hit exactly on what they were thinking.

Parallel Lives

Suddenly one of the voices nearby caught his ear. The two Persians were speaking Greek! He didn't betray this to his interviewer, who was speaking in a low voice and leaving an enormous pause after each question. Until this moment, the man had got on his nerves, but now that he'd become an involuntary eavesdropper he was grateful to him for this opportunity to listen.

So the men he'd thought were Persians were Greeks. One seemed to be a ship's engineer, and the other appeared to be a sailor also. He'd taken them for Persians at first because they were very dark. Not unusually so, but here in the north, where he was used to the fair coloring of the local residents, dark people stood out in relief, and he always assigned a swarthy skin to Persians, Armenians, Iraqis or Turks, rather than Greeks. He was always surprised when he found himself mistaken. He'd never have been wrong at home, but abroad they all looked alike. The white Aryan screen onto which they were projected abolished all nuances of brown, just like the Karagiozis shadow show; he himself never bothered to find out whether its origin was Persian, Armenian, Iraqi, Turkish or Greek.

These two Greeks weren't talking like other Greeks he used to run into at stations or in public squares. He'd overhear the others saying such things as "I sure gave her something to take away" or "Blond as an angel and hot as a bitch"

127

or "I came eight times running" or "Get lost, you lousy queer"—phrases revealing the sexual frustrations of Greekness, of emigrants in a hurry to shake off the restrictions of village life even before they found a job, who spoke like this in stations or in public squares because they thought no one could understand them. But the two Greeks at the next table drinking Heineken beer had been talking all this time about ships.

They weren't talking quietly or at all conspiratorially, but there was quite a distance between the two tables, and it was only when they raised their voices slightly that he could catch a phrase or two as he sat back and waited for his interlocutor's next question.

"What do you think about armed struggle in Greece?" asked the interviewer in English—he himself was uttering silent prayers that the fellow wouldn't mention such words as Greece, Papandreou, the colonels or the dictatorship lest it alert the men at the next table and drive them back into their shell.

"I mean," the other went on, "is armed struggle inevitable because the students imitate the young revolutionaries in the West, or is it bound to come because of the nature of the junta itself?"

"And we started up the engine without damaging a single bolt. . . ."

The phrase floated across from the next table, mild and consoling as the touch of a breeze at dawn in a valley.

"Let's hope it never happens," said the other man, adding something else that was inaudible.

"Do Andreas Papandreou and the PAK agree, in general, with the line taken by Theodorakis and the PAM?"

"They're meeting about now in Rome," he answered.

"It's said some right-wing opponents of the junta are going

to be there, too. How many royalist hostages have the junta taken?"

"I don't know exactly how many."

"How do you think the colonels will be overthrown if there isn't armed struggle?"

"Muller scored two goals. . . ."

Again he caught the voice nearby. He supposed they must be talking about soccer now. He wanted to get up and go over to them and say, "I'm Greek. What's the news?" But what if they thought he was a spy from the embassy, paid to report the political opinions of Greeks passing through? And what if they themselves supported the junta? He turned cautiously and looked at them. No, impossible—their faces ruled that out. They were Papandreist faces, he thought, without quite knowing why. But they looked like tried and lifelong democrats.

"And it's then it starts to have no end . . . ," said the second man, answering something which couldn't be about soccer now.

"When you say the whole Greek people took part in the national resistance against the Germans and Italians, do you mean they were all with the left?"

"Not all, of course. But the EAM had the situation in hand."

"So how do you explain the civil war?"

"The right wasn't content just to have power handed to it on a platter. It had to persecute the members of the left as well. So they had no alternative but to take to the maquis again."

The blond interviewer hunted through his papers for the next question. He wasn't a professional journalist, he explained, apologizing for being so inexpert. In fact, this was the first interview he'd ever done in his life, and he was scared stiff. But he was interested in Greece. He'd gone there twice, and his sister had recently spent two years there. She'd even written a few articles for the papers. Ah, here they were!

Fortunately, the men at the next table suspected nothing and went on calmly with their conversation.

"I told him at Piraeus that if he didn't refit . . . ."

They talked away mildly; the level of the beer sank in their glasses. From time to time a word wafted over to him, and he was as delighted as he had been when he had come across the word "wheatear" for the first time after many years, in an otherwise unmemorable novel. Wheatear, a bird of the plains, slightly bigger than a sparrow but not as plump as a quail. Its name sent a thrill through him, bringing back boyhood memories of going hunting with his grandfather in the Sari Saban plain near Nea Karvali and shooting at larks that he "mistook for quail," as they say in Thassos. The wheatear was a charming bird the color of wheat, always pecking about near the sheaves—a lost bird he'd neither seen nor heard of for twenty years.

Thirty-two thousand ships came or went in the port of Rotterdam each year, and there were many Greeks. He'd been amazed the previous evening at all the Greek words he'd heard as he strolled through the streets. Whole families were out shopping; the city, destroyed in the bombing, was proud of its new shopping center. The port served mainly the neighboring *Bundesrepublik*, just as Salonika might have served the hinterland of Yugoslavia, Bulgaria and Rumania if Greece hadn't been handed over to the British by Stalin after the war. If that hadn't happened, it would have been a living port instead of the no man's land he knew, with its idle cranes. So Rotterdam always had a lot of people passing through, especially sailors and merchants traveling with their goods. And although the Dutch in general considered it a place without culture, the port itself thirsted for art, like *nouveaux riches* wanting to ornament their houses with pictures and fill their shelves with bindings. So the wandering salesman found himself here for an international book fair.

But the Greek consulate was a viper's nest of hoodlums, temporarily recruited seamen who were sent for a pittance whenever there was an antifascist meeting anywhere in Holland to put on a show as the "indignant citizens" of the old days. And so, as he had no like-minded companions to protect him (the fair had no direct connection with politics), the wandering salesman had to be careful not to call attention to himself in the street. For there's a fraternity between things; they hunt in packs. But inwardly he cursed the horrible "situation" that twisted and distorted human relationships. Especially abroad. Especially here, where all he wanted to do was say hello in his own language.

The interviewer, scrabbling through his papers—for as a beginner, he explained, he'd prepared the interview—at last found the question he was looking for.

"What's your opinion of the Greek people's apathy?"

"What do you mean, apathy?"

"Most foreigners can't understand why such a lively people put up with things so quietly."

"What do you suggest?"

"I'm a bit of an expert on Iran," he said. "They've got the same sort of regime there. And, more or less, in Turkey. So why don't you join all your resistance organizations together and make a common front?"

"We can't even agree among ourselves," said the book salesman, taken aback. "How do you expect us to agree with Turks and Iranians?"

"But why? Why?"

"The cloth goes through without paying duty. . . ."

Now a woman of about forty had come in, with fat white bare legs. She was asking her husband for more money. She'd found a shop selling material at what she called fabulous prices. Her husband opened his wallet and handed over a hundred guilders, and she went off again, holding a child by the hand. Alone once more, the two men went on with their conversation. The voice of the first broke the sound barrier and entered the salesman's ear like a ray piercing the clouds at sunset.

"And you talked like that in front of a dozen people. Be careful. How do you know who they . . ."

He guessed the rest. The other man, whose back had been turned since his wife came in, must have said something in public against the junta, and his friend was warning him to be more cautious. What else could he have meant by "be careful"? So he'd been right when he assumed they were democrats. The realization made him regret even more that he couldn't talk to them, offer them a glass of beer.

"The first one who planted a bomb was a professor, wasn't he?" said the interviewer. "I can't remember his name."

"He wasn't either the first or the last," the wandering salesman answered in a low voice, looking to see if anyone had heard.

"Maybe. If a man in his position gets to that point . . ."

"He's not back from Boyati. His motorbike broke down, and he hasn't been able to get the spare parts. . . ."

Suddenly he saw the absurdity of the situation. The two men over there had an ordinary life back home like everybody else's, one that hadn't been sliced in two by the knife of the dictatorship. Their wives were shopping. That meant they were going back, they weren't "wanted." But it didn't mean they were on the other side, either. They were merely going on living, while for the exiles like him, life had stopped the day of the coup d'état. They'd gone on with a sort of supernumerary life lacking the natural link of the cocoon with the silk, a tie that cannot be broken however much it's stretched. All the efforts made abroad for Greece—meetings, demonstrations, speeches, plays, concerts—reached a consummation in a foreign organization, in a foreign country, by foreign youth. All of it was absorbed into foreign cells. It didn't really affect Greece or the people there. And foreign societies like Holland had sufficient economic resources to help others—Biafra, Greece, Vietnam—even though, in the final analysis, it was themselves their aid really helped the most. And the contradiction that had been gnawing at the wandering salesman struck him clearly for the first time during this parallel conversation. On the one hand were the two Greeks waiting for their wives to come back from the stores and peacefully finishing their beer. On the other were himself and his foreign interviewer, talking about the civil war of the past and the armed struggle of the future, the latter at least as abstract as the former for those who didn't fight in it. And between the shadowy Scylla and Charybdis of past and future there slipped, like a solid wedge, the present.

The wives came back laden with parcels, the husbands paid their bill, and they all went out through the quadruple swinging door. The child wanted to buy ice cream from the vendor on the street corner. The wandering salesman was left with the would-be journalist, hunting through his notes again for the next question. Suddenly the place seemed terribly empty now that the voices had gone—the voices of the sailors, sirens, ship's whistles, the singing of shells, the creaking of cables that tomorrow would be tying up at a Greek jetty.

The Vegetable Garden

"Our village is Xehasmeni. You'll remember it, of course. It's a tourist spot. My wife and I both come from there, and so do some of the other emigrants here. I'm a carpenter. Or, to be precise, a coffinmaker. Restful sort of work."

"We all have to die some day," said Yelastos, the philosopher of the group.

"Of course, of course," agreed the party representative, though his little brain with its blunt logic really thought it was a rather pessimistic occupation.

"I've worked for every firm in the district," Petros went on. "I must know a couple of hundred people. I respect them, and they respect me. I've never given anyone cause for complaint. But as for going back, it's out of the question. I wouldn't get away with it."

They were eating a braised chicken which Paraskevi, Petros' wife, had prepared on short notice. Four of them had found themselves stranded in the city without a train home or a hotel, and since it was August nearly all the emigrant workers were away on leave or vacation. So Yelastos, who'd been with them, had looked in at the club. The lights had been on there, and before he'd gone up, he had said, "If I nab them playing dice, there'll be a row." But fortunately, he had found them playing cards, not for money, so he'd invited the others up for a beer. There wasn't anywhere else to go, he had told them; everything closed at ten and it was half past twelve.

So when the wandering salesman had said, "If only there was somewhere we could get a sandwich," Petros, well known for his hospitality, had gone on ahead to tell Paraskevi to thaw a chicken, the modern version of killing a hen for an unexpected guest.

The empty club looked like a bourgeois drawing room that had seen better days or a Lambrakis Youth Club at Kaisariani, with its tables and easy chairs and photographs on the walls. After Petros had gone, Yelastos, who combined the functions of club secretary, Greek teacher to the children in the district, and instructor in the antifascist struggle, had walked over to the card table. As soon as they had seen the strangers come in, the four workers had got rid of their cards and prepared to leave. They had faces like extras in *The Battleship Potemkin* —weary Macedonian faces of no particular age. Suffering doesn't have any age. They were men born old in their villages, deprived of everything except perhaps goat's milk. The youngest, also the most recent arrival, wasn't yet worn out like the others, who looked like ruins.

The party representative, with his light suit and tie and white shirt, seemed from an entirely different world, even though his was the "labor" party. But these workers didn't belong to it; as the visitors' guide explained, two were uninterested in politics, one belonged to the center, and the fourth to the "moderate right." The wandering salesman, though he claimed to be with the masses, didn't seem to belong in their world either, in his fashionable gray-green jacket with gilt buttons. The student, ill-shaven and untidy, didn't look all that different from the workers, except for a slight paunch which he attributed to the sedentary life of the scholar. His wife sat a little apart; she always felt awkward about being the only woman there. That was why she greeted Paraskevi with a big smile of unwritten alliance when they arrived at Petros'.

To get to the rest of the flat, you had to go through the kitchen, and as they did so, they saw Paraskevi coping with the potatoes. The braised chicken wasn't visible. The student's wife told her not to go to any trouble—they didn't want to be a nuisance at one o'clock in the morning. She asked to be allowed to help, but Paraskevi said everything was done and she'd soon have a "bite" ready for them. A "bite," coming from a working-class housewife, means a good deal more than it says.

Petros pressed them to go on through into the living room. Opposite a big tiled stove, dating from the time of the Czars and reaching from floor to ceiling, was a doll from Brindisi, its white-lace dress billowing out like a parachute and presenting a glimpse of plastic legs. Two cheap prints of pheasant shooting and a soccer calendar completed the décor.

The party representative was sitting on the comfortable divan beside Yelastos. The wandering salesman was opposite the student's wife, and the student was beside Petros. The student asked if they ought to speak softly so as not to wake the children. "They sleep in another wing," said Petros, as if it were a palace. Then he got some ouzo and beer out of the refrigerator. The salad of cucumber, tomato, and olives "imported from Greece," tossed in "pure olive oil," was soon no more to be seen. "All we need is some feta."

"Would anyone like some raw onion?" asked Petros. "I can get you some from the vegetable garden."

They couldn't believe it, and the wandering salesman and the party representative went down with him to see. Sure enough, there was a little garden containing a selection of vegetables. Petros, armed with a torch, named them: beans, tomatoes, pimentos, basil, baby squash, lettuce and onions.

"Want one? Here!"

And he pulled one up, shook the earth off it and showed it in the light of the torch.

Through the leaves of the tree that shaded the garden, they could see the stars coming out at last. The wind had begun to blow the clouds away.

"It's going to be a fine day tomorrow," said Petros.

The party representative inspected the garden as if it were a nursery of future party members, and the plants recruits gained by the movement. The wandering salesman was chiefly interested in the names of the plants; buried there in the soil, they made him think of frail creatures exposed to the Siberian winter.

They went back upstairs, and Petros raised his glass and proposed a toast. "To freedom!" They all drank it.

"Well," said Yelastos, "tell us how it happened—why you can't go back."

"Last time, I wrote and asked my brother if he thought it was all right for me to go. He said in theory yes, but he couldn't be responsible. So my godfather said he'd sponsor me. He's mayor of a village. At the frontier, the Evzones stripped me naked as the day I was born. They went over me with a fine-tooth comb. I had some leaflets and other papers with me, but I hid them in the engine when I spotted them searching the cars in front.

"I intended to stay a month, but I left after two weeks. Why? Because I talked. My friends asked me, 'What's it like in Sweden, Petros?' I told them workers were insured in Sweden, and you get work without having to produce a 'loyalty statement.' I spoke quite openly, and everyone tried to shut me up. But why should I be quiet? We're the most important family in the village, we're known all over the district, and anyone you mention a Scordomylias to will tell you he's an honest man. Then one evening at a village dance in Sidero-castro, the record I'd asked for broke off in the middle. I yelled out, 'Who's the lousy pig who did that?' The lousy pig turned out to be the police captain.

"From then on, things started getting difficult. And one evening my godfather, the mayor, stopped by and told me to get going, he couldn't answer for my safety any more. Next day at dawn we set off in the car for the frontier. And there, though I didn't have anything to hide this time, they searched me even more thoroughly than before. They even put me in the guard room. Before I went, I told Paraskevi I might not come out again, and in that case, she'd have to manage as well as she could.

"The walls of the guard room were covered with photographs of people to be arrested as soon as they slip over the frontier. There were so many of them, large and small, they overlapped like foreign papers and magazines on a bookstall. 'Wanted!' Just like a Western! I didn't dare look at the walls in case I saw a picture of myself taken at a meeting here in Sweden. Once the *Dagens Nyheter* had a picture of me carrying a banner. Then I said to myself, Don't worry—if they've spotted you, you've had it anyhow, and if they haven't, you'll be all right. So I looked. And I wasn't there. But I did see two other fellows from my village. And"—he turned suddenly to the party representative, who was trying to spear a Kalamata olive—"I think I saw you, too."

"Me?"

"I think so. Unless I'm getting it mixed up, and you've been here before."

"It *might* have been me," said the other, puzzled. He traveled strictly incognito, and no one outside the party was supposed to know who he was. Even in democratic countries like Sweden. The spirit of conspiracy makes professionals of the left preserve complete anonymity and use different pseudonyms as if they were engaged in guerrilla warfare on enemy territory. Anyone who doesn't observe the rules of the underground even when not living underground is regarded by the left as unreliable. This attitude derives from the theory that though local conditions may change, the enemy remains fundamentally the same. But in most cases, the cloak of anonymity is used to conceal not the existence, but the non-existence of personality, as with people who are silent only because they have nothing to say. Silence isn't golden, because gold's articulate. Only lead and tin don't talk. Gold and silver and diamonds cry out all the time, even from the catacombs of Swiss banks. Whoever possesses power is always garrulous. So silence can never be golden.

"Anyhow, after they'd stripped me, they let me go. But I don't think I could go back. The children go, my wife can go. But for me, it's all or nothing from now on. Either the height or the abyss."

The chicken was getting cold on their plates.

"Let someone else get a word in," said Paraskevi. Her pink cheeks, still redolent of the forest, were flaming. Like all wives when guests are present, she thought her husband was boring them.

"I've finished," answered Petros. "I was only answering Yelastos' question."

And he filled the glasses with ouzo. Then total silence fell as they dug in. Everything was devoured. The chicken grew wings again and vanished; they gnawed the bones and licked their fingers. All this was a great compliment to her cooking, but Paraskevi would have preferred them to say something. They seemed to be people who'd traveled, not workers like themselves. All she asked in return for her efforts was the story of their lives to give her something to think about at night.

"Anyone like some more salad?" asked Petros, quite willing to go down to the garden again.

"No, thank you."

Someone praised the potatoes, fried in oil, someone else the ouzo, which he said hadn't existed "before the revolution."

Someone else praised the olive oil; someone else, the home-baked bread, so different from what you bought in the shops here.

"It tastes sweet," said Petros. "And if you squeeze a loaf in your hand, all you get is a handful of dough."

"We bake ours ourselves in the electric oven," Paraskevi told the student's wife.

After the feast, they opened the beer, but anyone who preferred could go on drinking ouzo. Nicely replete, they were now ready to talk about other people's troubles.

"With the money I've made here, I've bought twenty acres of land between Xehasmeni and Alli Meria," said Petros. "My brothers get three crops a year off it—wheat, corn, and clover."

"Has the junta helped the peasants?" asked the wandering salesman with a belch.

"Yes, of course. They hand out credits right and left. But to get a loan, you have to be on their side. They won't give one to my brother. We have a past, you see. One night the guerrillas came to our place and took bread and provisions and went away again with our blessing. Next day the national guard arrived, and one of the neighbors sent for their officer and told him my father had given them supplies. My father insisted they'd just taken them, but the neighbor swore he'd given them the stuff because he sympathized with them. The neighbor had always been jealous of my father because he was an honest man and had one of the finest houses in the village. So they took my father and beat him up. He never got over the shock. He was in bed, paralyzed, for fifteen years. They'd bashed his ribs in. He died a few years ago."

The party representative leaned back, sated, in his chair. Yelastos and the wandering salesman were still drinking, finishing off the ouzo. The student was talking to Petros about

140

people and things in the area. The two women were telling each other what they thought of Swedish women.

There was a photograph on a shelf, taken at a dance at the club. Everyone seemed bubbling over. Petros, slim and dark, and Paraskevi, all round and pink, were dancing the hully-gully.

It was Yelastos who broke up the party. He took with him the party representative, who thanked the workers for feeding the intellectuals who were fighting on their behalf. The other three were to sleep there. The host and hostess gave up their double bed to the student and his wife. They left water and a glass and cigarettes on the bedside table. The wandering salesman and Petros were to sleep on the divan, which converted into another double bed. Paraskevi went in with the children.

It was three in the morning, and dawn was already showing in the east. It looked like a cool, cloudless day. Before getting into bed, the wandering salesman looked out once more at the vegetable garden. Through the leaves of the tree, you could just make out, against the dark earth, the beans and tomatoes and pimento and basil and baby squash and lettuce and onions, growing on a patch of ground just big enough for the family to lie in, if necessary.

The Suitcase

The couple were finishing their meal, sitting facing one another in the window seats. The compartment was divided in two by a wooden partition, and when they first entered, the wandering salesman and his local assistant sat down beside a Swedish girl traveling with her baby, blond offspring of a blond mother. But since the couple on the other side of the partition were speaking Greek, they kept quiet to listen. They could tell from their accent that they were country folk. They talked about the food, about someone who "sucked his wife's blood." And then their voices were drowned by the blast of the engine starting up. Blood again, thought the salesman. That was Mediterraneans for you. Then they abandoned the Swedish girl and her baby, moved to the other side of the partition, and struck up a conversation.

The man was older than his wife, who'd put the leftovers from the meal into a plastic bag and was stowing away her things one by one in her carryall. Protruding out of the luggage rack above, like the tail of a fish sticking out of the frying pan, was a battered cardboard suitcase, one of its metal locks raised like a supercilious eyebrow. It formed a striking contrast beside gleaming Swedish leather or plastic suitcases. It smelled of Greek poverty, its bitterness and its poisons; and its straps were tight as garters. It was a suitcase, thought the wandering salesman, filled to bursting with the dream of going back.

The man looked headstrong. The glitter of his baldness was dulled by a few gray hairs. His big workman's hands had all ten fingers intact.

The wife looked younger in comparison, though she must have been over forty-five. Her grim smile softened only when she was teasing her husband. Her face was wrinkled; her body, in its worn brown dress, seemed to move all in one piece. She kept rubbing her right kidney, as if the discomfort of the journey was tiring her, and at one point said to her husband, "You sling me on these trains like a sack of manure."

They were returning from their vacation. They'd just spent two weeks at Kalmar with some relatives they'd taken in years before when the relatives had first come to this country and had nowhere to go. The hotels were so expensive—ten to nineteen crowns a night—that the newcomers would have spent all the savings they'd brought with them from Greece. So the couple had taken them in, and now it was their turn to stay with them.

This couple themselves had been in Sweden a long time— since 1964. They worked in the metal factory. Before they emigrated, they'd been shepherds in a village near Grevena.

"Are there others here from your part of the world?" asked the wandering salesman.

"Yes. More and more of them. If there weren't any restrictions on visas and the frontiers were left open, everyone would leave."

They said they were working to give their children an education "back home."

"*We* stayed ignorant," said the man, "but we want the children to have a better chance. You can't develop the mind without education. And it's through the mind that man makes progress."

"The system's different in Sweden," said the woman. "Children become independent of their parents quite young.

143

They have to work for their pocket money. Whereas we're still feeding and clothing ours when they're grown up."

"Did you go swimming in Kalmar?" asked the wandering salesman's companion, the local representative.

"The sea's like ice there in July. Give you pneumonia just to go in."

Beyond the train windows, lake after lake went by, pine forest after pine forest.

"Pretty country," said the wandering salesman.

"Yes—plenty of green."

In the six years they'd been here, they'd got used to the landscape. It hardly impressed them any more.

"Do you like it here?"

"Yes. How could we not like it? If you get sick here, you can stay home for a week and no questions asked. Then you go to the doctor, and you can get paid for six months at the same rate as if you were working. The workers are insured. Everything's for the workers. How could we not like it here?"

His wife shook her head doubtfully.

"You're not telling the truth. Do you call it a life here? From home to the factory and back again? No amusement? In Greece you take a walk on Sunday, or see a movie, or go to the pastry shop together."

"Yes, but in Greece there isn't any money," he answered. Then, turning to the others, "Of course, the best thing would be factories in our own country. In Grevena, where I come from, there's a population of 180,000. If 30,000 of them worked in factories, they could easily support the other 150,000. But we were there for six months last year, and we saw for ourselves: the people haven't any money. With the money we'd saved here, we opened a café in the village square. But we had to close down because we lost so much giving credit. Someone would come in and offer a friend a glass of wine, and the other one would have to refuse because he hadn't a drachma in his pocket to offer a round himself. That's why I say it's better here. I won't go back."

"Ah," sighed his wife, "but there isn't another country like our Greece."

"I don't deny it," said the man. "A good climate and a good life—if you've got the wherewithal. But if not, you've had it."

"They just don't know how to live here," she repeated. "They only work to get a pension. The women are the only ones who do well out of it. They work, but they keep the money they earn instead of handing it over to their husbands as we do. *You* take all the money I earn at the factory. And then when you get home, you take off your shoes and stretch out your legs, and it's 'Fetch me a glass of water' and 'What have you got for dinner?' A wife's a slave. If I could just keep what I earn, at least! But I don't have enough to buy myself a popsicle. I have to ask you every time. Go through your pockets. A Swedish husband helps his wife in the kitchen, even does the dishes sometimes. Ah, lucky Greek women who marry foreigners!"

"What's your work at the factory like?"

"What do you think? At least it's sitting down. But with the house to look after as well, I never go out. I get caught up between the two. You marry us to do everything for you— we can never do anything for ourselves."

The former shepherd shook his head sympathetically. He wasn't annoyed. Obviously, he'd heard it all thousands of times before.

"And why should I have you on my neck all my life?" she went on. Then, turning to their fellow travelers, "Isn't that right?" And then, to him again, "Do I have to wait till you're dead to be rid of you?"

The Harpoon Gun

"You don't know which of us will die first," he said.

"In the normal course of events, you will," she said, worked up, but not angry, "because you're older than I am. And then I'll get the insurance."

"No one knows who'll be taken first."

The dialogue was like a one-act play they were performing mainly for the sake of the audience.

"How would *you* like to have someone on top of you all your life? Eh? Answer. It's a good thing we came abroad; it's opened my eyes a bit. We see how other women live. Women see farther than men. And better."

"You talk like a representative of the women's liberation movement," said the wandering salesman. "It's spreading now. Especially in the States."

The woman didn't know anything about either women's lib or the States, but she was sure she was absolutely right.

"Anyhow," she concluded, "a woman can live without a man, but a man can't live without a woman."

They offered each other cigarettes.

"Go on, take one," said the wandering salesman's friend to the wife. "You have the same right to smoke as your husband."

On the flap that formed a table by the window, Mema Stathopoulos, wearing a swimsuit, was smoking on the cover of *Romanzo*.

"How about the church?"

"A priest from Stockholm now and again."

The train pressed on. They all had to change at the same station, one pair to go northward, the other to continue south. The wandering salesman threw his cigarette end on the floor and crushed it out with his foot, a typically Greek gesture. At first the shepherd said nothing; but after a moment, he bent down, picked up the butt and put it in the ash tray.

146

"I can't bear to see butts all over the floor," he explained. "That's why I closed down the café. And don't tell me I didn't provide enough ash trays! But they'd just empty them on the floor. And they'd tear up empty matchboxes and scatter the bits. As soon as I saw an empty one, I used to rush over and snatch it off the table. We're a very backward people. It'll take decades for us to become civilized. You don't see litter in the streets here. You feel ashamed. They make you feel so ashamed."

"And in their churches," added his wife, "you could hear a pin drop. And nothing but hymns. Not like us—we go to church for a gossip."

"Back home they ask you what it's like in Sweden, and when you tell them they stare at you openmouthed. But they'll go on in just the same way as ever."

"But it's beautiful—Greece," sighed his wife.

"Yes, Greece is beautiful," said the man. "It's we who are no good. We've even spoiled Sweden. At first the Swedes used to weep at the sound of the word 'Greeks.' But now there are so many of us . . . And we're always taking sick leave without a certificate. We abuse the rights the laws give us. The Swedes use them. But don't talk to me about going back. It's just darkness there now, with that bunch in power. They throw you in jail for the least thing. And the less important you are, the harder they are on you. The big shots and the rich don't get beaten up, at least. They may lock them up, but they treat them decently. But if you're a worker or a peasant . . . The people have to pay for everything. My name's Papangelou, and everyone at the factory calls me Papandreou. Even in Kalmar, when we went strawberry picking just for fun, they called me Papandreou."

"If *they* knew back home," said his wife, "a fine time our son would have doing his military service!"

"That's why we lie low," said the man. "We have three children back home. We came away to be able to bring them up and educate them. If we got ourselves talked about here, it would be them who paid. Did we leave to help them or to get them into trouble? If we got ourselves talked about here, we might just as well have stopped where we were. And there are lots of people like us—most, in fact. They're afraid of reprisals on their families back home. But *they*—that bunch ought to die the way Patilis did. They ought to be tortured and suffer first, then die the way he did."

His wife was silent. The shepherd spoke out boldly, clenching his great fist on the table. When it came to politics, his wife didn't interrupt. She compressed her lips, and for the first time you could see they were faded. She hung her head.

"And what do *you* do? How much do you earn?"

"I sell books. Do you speak Swedish?"

"A few words. At work. If people don't understand, I say the same thing two or three times."

"Where do you live?"

"In a rambling old place—quite comfortable, but no hot water. But we're on the list for a government apartment. That'll be better. New, all modern conveniences."

"Isn't it a question of pulling strings?"

"No, everything's done according to the rules here."

The train was approaching the station. The couple were delighted to have met them. The wandering salesman and his friend saw them afterwards on the opposite platform, the huge suitcase at their feet like a faithful hound. All around them were blond Swedes, girls straight out of canned dreams, little dogs, cripples, raisinlike old women; and the shepherd and his wife stood there among them, their equals, waiting. "As long as there are Greeks, there'll be a Greece," said the salesman. He could still hear their last words, "Please excuse the way we speak—we were brought up as peasants."

The Suitcase

The battered old cardboard suitcase, in striking contrast to the gleaming Swedish suitcases made of leather or plastic, waited beside them, with its straps like garters, filled to bursting with clothes, and, in spite of everything, with the dream of going home.

Sarandapikhou Street

He waited, sunk in his seat, for the speeches to be over and the films to begin. It was a series of short documentaries made before the dictatorship by young film directors just starting to try their wings in the seventh heaven. The last speaker made a few remarks about this other "lost" generation. Then the lights went out and the program began.

The first film was about Greek miners in Belgium. He was annoyed to see again on the screen the place he'd just come from. He'd been a practicing lawyer before he had moved to Belgium and opened a Greek kebab restaurant in Namur. He was in Paris for his summer vacation when he'd heard about this program. He reached the theater early and was one of the first in, expecting the films to give him a glimpse of Greece, a glimpse of his beloved Athens that he missed so much. He was depressed to find himself confronted with the gray, monotonous towns of Belgium. And he knew a lot more about the problems of Greek emigrants than the director did. But he consoled himself by thinking that the film had been made before the coup, which proved that even then, artists had been concerned with this topic.

"If the others are like this one, though," he said to himself, "we'll have been had."

Fortunately, the second film showed him what he wanted to see, what he'd gone to such trouble for, changing twice in the stifling labyrinths of the Métro: a glimpse of Athens, a fragment, showing just the Monastiraki district. He prayed for the camera to point upward a little and show a bit of his Lycabettus or the Acropolis, but the director focused only on the actors. Only once, when the "hero" sprang into the air, did the camera go up with him and show a general view of the city. But he saw with joy how distinctly, unmistakably, the light and shade registered on the screen, articulated on the sidewalks in verticals and horizontals, absolutely clear. After living for three years in the twilight of the gods, the divorce of sun and shade, he thrilled to see the light of his native country, even though he couldn't feel its warmth. If only this had been an "aromascope," perhaps he would have been able to smell the sweaty armpits of the men in short-sleeved shirts, hauling home the shopping.

What a poor lot we are, he thought, looking past the main character to the marginal poverty in the background: poor people such as lottery-ticket dealers and peddlers, well-known but forgotten faces who passed by quickly with only an almost imperceptible glance at the camera. The confrontation between the reality of ordinary life and the theoretical talk of exile was like a refreshing shower. He felt cleansed. Yes, he thought, that's how it is.

Next to him, two fellows were whispering. A Greek was explaining the commentary of the film to a Frenchman. He was annoyed by the intrusion of a foreign tongue into the purely Greek atmosphere that had made him forget where he was. "Pipe down, can't you?" he growled toward them, just as he would have done before in the Rosiclair in Omonia Square, to some youth spelling out the Greek subtitles of a foreign movie to his grandmother or girl friend. He couldn't stand people making noise at the movies. In the old days, he used to change his seat if anyone fiddled with his worry beads or shelled peanuts, and the same with cellophane wrappers and the toasted almonds so many people had the deplorable habit of munching at the cinema.

The third film, luckily, more than compensated him. Here, at last, was the Athens he knew, his Athens: tall apartment buildings, cars, crowds, winding stairs, ice-cream vendors, cheese-pastry and *donner-kebab* peddlers, priests, soldiers, streetcars, trolleys, three-wheeled motorcycles. The director had composed a skillful montage of the city, which took him, unprepared as he was, by surprise. He scarcely followed the plot; he was too absorbed by the names and street signs. He was moved by a couple of close-ups of newspapers: the front page of *Kathimerini* with its small, heavy type; *Avghi* announcing a Soviet conquest of space in enormous headlines. Now he was happy; now he was alive.

And his euphoria reached its peak with the fourth and last film. He saw the shop in Aeolus Street where he used to buy his shoes; the bar where he used to have a beer during the noon break; the Central Post Office, where all the people looked familiar. Then suddenly the camera, as if he himself had been handling it, rose to Mount Lycabettus, showed the guns and the church there, and began to descend the other side toward Strephis, where he used to have a house, a one-story building in Sarandapikhou Street, from which he could see the whole of Athens as if it were being offered him on a platter. The camera came to rest on what used to be his balcony, with its pots of basil and jasmine. He could see his own initials on the sheet hung out to air. "And you became completely tender to me. . . ."

The lights came on. The audience drifted out, disappointed at not having been shown tanks and torture and the other paraphernalia of dictatorship. Obviously they hadn't understood the man who'd introduced the films, who'd said they were made before the coup. But even as examples of the renaissance of the Greek cinema, the films weren't up to par;

they were considered academic and thin, like the first attempts of Film Institute students.

At the exit, he asked who had made the last film on the program. He was shown a man of his own age with long hair. He went over to him.

"Congratulations on your film," he said. "I liked it very much. So much I'd like to see it again."

"Did you really like it?" asked the other, not sure whether he meant it or was making fun of him.

"Yes, really," he repeated. "I can hardly tell you. When could I see it again?"

"That's not up to me," said the director. "A private showing is very expensive."

"How much?"

"At least fifty francs for twelve minutes. But give me your address," he said, smiling at some people who were congratulating him, "and the next time it's shown, I'll send you an invitation, if you really . . ."

He was going to say "if you really liked it."

"Unfortunately, I don't live in Paris."

"Where do you live?"

"Namur, in Belgium. I'm just passing through. What moved me most—it's ridiculous, of course—but what moved me most was when you showed . . . Fifty francs for a private showing, did you say?"

Jingle Bells

They called him that because one day he was stupid enough to tell them a story about himself.

He lived in a city full of old men, with faces chiseled by the crimes of an age, harsh as the concentration camps where most of them, mentally at least, had served. The camps were still there like scars, like cruel incisions on the skin of the earth; the new growth that covered them each spring could no more hide them than a beard can hide the mark of the knife. The buried camps could still be seen through the growing corn, the spring sea of uncut wheat, just as the faces, camouflaged by the present, spoke of their past—the faces of old men and old women he used to meet on the bus, and in the factory, street, and supermarket, before his accident.

An iron bar had dropped on his head from a crane, driving his safety helmet into his skull and making him an invalid for life. Just a poor, ordinary, unknown emigrant, come here in search of a better life and to help his seven brothers and sisters back home in the village—this had to happen to him! It turned him into a cripple. But the doctors, who were paid by the union, which in turn was paid by the bosses, still refused to declare him entirely unfit for work, so that the doctors' bosses, management, wouldn't have to pay him maximum compensation. They sent him from one office to another, to fill in forms in a language he didn't understand; he'd known just enough words to get by in his job on the scaffolding, as a

construction worker. They did dole out small sums, but what
he wanted was outright compensation as the victim of an industrial accident for which the crane operator, not he, was responsible.

The worst of it was he couldn't even go back to his village
and rest under the plane tree in the garden. When he was
still able-bodied, he'd gotten into a fight with some thugs one
Saturday night at a bouzouki dance. In this town full of old
men, Saturday was the only night of the week when the
bouzoukis made their appearance, as if by spontaneous generation. One word had led to another, then to blows, and the
thug had pulled a knife. He had seized the hoodlum by the
wrist, twisted it till he dropped the knife, then, as the thug
had bent down to pick it up, had given him the kick in the
pants he'd dearly have loved to give the dictators. The poor
devil who did get it was just a worker like himself, except that
the consulate greased this worker's palm from time to time
with a fifty-mark bill, for throwing his weight around among
the democrats. So after that incident, the informer had re-
ported him, and when he went to the consulate to renew his
passport, they had kicked him out—an added incentive to
pursue the struggle against fascism. And that was why he
couldn't go back home.

He had suffered from partial amnesia after the accident;
and since he couldn't do anything and couldn't bear just
staying home, he used to wander all day through the streets
of this inhospitable city, an island from which all the young
people had emigrated, leaving only the old men with marked
faces, like attendants in a war museum.

Then came the day when, just by chance, he told his
friends about this incident. It was in their usual café, where
they used to meet upstairs every evening at six o'clock after
work. Here, he'd listen to the news and the gossip and the
disquisitions of the "brains" who happened to be passing

through. Here, copies of *Makedonia* and *Acropolis* would pass from one horny hand to another, the ink, instead of paling, growing stronger from the thirst with which it was drunk up, the exaggerated headlines boring into the readers' memories. This upstairs room could hold all the students and workers who lived here and were unable to go home to Greece. Unlike the other emigrants, who preferred to meet in suburban cafés, the Greeks, with a belated sense of the metropolis, always chose those in the center of the town. One would imagine himself in Omonia, another in Fouat Square, another in Ichtyoscala. In the last analysis, what distinguishes the Greek from Turks, Persians, Iraqis and orientals in general is the sense of *Demos,* the civic sense, which makes citizens gather at the foot of the Acropolis to decide whether to demonstrate or go on strike.

So it was here he made the blunder, in the midst of both friends and class enemies, as he called the members of the Center Party. They'd all stopped feeling sorry for him about the accident and no longer asked him which doctor he'd been sent to see that day. His adventures at the dispensary for foreign workers had become legendary even beyond the frontiers of the city. The wound had scarred over; the bit of bone they'd removed had been replaced by a metal plate; his memory had gradually returned. Everyone regarded him with the resigned sympathy bestowed upon those who've always been known as invalids—as if they'd never been anything else. He took notice of this, and so one evening, when there wasn't any particularly sensational news and everyone else was talking about betting or broads, he told them. What a blunder!

He was walking along a side street, he said, when he noticed a shop window with a can of dolmas in it, imported from Turkey. Even though it was written in Latin characters, he couldn't fail to recognize "Dolmas Yalandgi." He knew the handful of shops in the town that sold Greek things, but it was the first time he'd seen this one, and it looked different. He went in. As he opened the door, he was greeted by the pleasant sound of mountain and forest bells such as he used to hear in the village in the evening when the goats and sheep were returning from pasture. He didn't pay much attention—in any case, he was bowled over by the pretty girl who had come forward to meet him as if he were a customer. She was wearing tight velvet pants which did ample justice to the elegant curve of her leg from thigh to ankle, not to mention the gentle feminine "cambering" of the knee, as a pal of his in the building trade used to say, and the buxom quivering bottom, set off by the hem of panties pressing against the velvet. Then her bust, unconstrained by any bra under her blouse and still full of virgin milk awaiting relief from an infant's lips—all this left him no attention to spare for the gentle tinkling that announced his entrance.

The shop dealt chiefly in oriental goods—"exotic, aromatic, langorous." There were bags and shepherd rugs from Macedonia and Arakhova; Persian carpets; tiles from Iran; hand embroidery from countries where girls still make their own trousseaux, until some Royal Providence takes them over for export; cheese from Bulgaria; and, in addition to the Turkish dolmas in the window, halvah from Istanbul. He noticed the only thing the merchandise had in common was the shop assistant's ignorance of it. What connection had there ever been, anyway, between shepherd rugs of genuine Greek sheepskin and embroidered carpets from Baghdad?

Six months of living abroad had taught him that foreigners lumped all underdeveloped countries together, just as he himself put employers all in the same category whether they were French, Belgian, Dutch or German. He wandered around the shop trying to find something else that was Greek and not too expensive. Since he was in no hurry—where was he to go?—he amused himself playing Peeping Tom. In addition to the girl who had met him as he entered, several others now emerged from the fitting rooms, trying on the sheepskin coats and vests popular with long-hairs. He couldn't make out whether they were customers or assistants—this sort of shop was often staffed by girls who couldn't afford to buy the things they so enthusiastically sold.

But his Greek face and look betrayed him at every step. He couldn't pass himself off as a serious customer. Just as he was leaving, full of apologies, he found himself face to face with the bells that had tinkled so musically when he had come in. They were of all dimensions and hung in a row on a strip of leather, arranged in diminishing order. So they all rang together, sheep bells and goat bells, whenever the door was opened and closed, with a sound like that of the flocks as they used to pass his house in the evening, their soft tinkle mingling with the dust raised by the hoofs. As he stood with his hand on the door, about to leave, he was carried away for a fraction of a second by the sound, sweet and intoxicating as honeycomb, beloved as the years of his childhood, before he left the village to be a stonemason in the town, when he still guarded the herds in the winter pasture and led them to drink at the pond. Scenes from the past unfolded before his eyes with clockwork precision: the soft horns on the brow of a kid; the dewlaps of a ewe angry because her ram has been killed; the sheepfold; the scorpion; the milk that attracted snakes; the trusty sheep dogs; the sun as it sank and made the shadows grow long. The sound, like memory's alarm clock, brought all the old life back before him—a great field of clover with quail hidden in it, clumps of spiky reeds where the animals would sleep on their feet with hanging heads. Overcome by all this sweetness, he took the row of bells gently in his roughened fingers, as he used to play with his grandmother's braid, sitting on her lap as a child. The girl stood behind him, waiting for him to go. All he could think of, to cover up his falling into this ambush of memory, was to ask how much the bells cost. "They're not for sale," she said in her own language. "They're part of the shop." And ever since, for three days running, he'd been back there every afternoon pretending he wanted to buy something—either a can of Dolmas Yalandgi, or some Bulgarian cheese, or some halvah from Constantinople, or some pickled eggplant—just to hear the sound of the bells as he opened the door.

"You mean you're stuck on the little lamb?" said someone when he'd finished.

"Come off it!" said another. "Anyone would think sheepskins are hard to find."

"Why don't you write your brother to send you a dozen?" asked a third.

"A white rug's the best place there is for laying a girl," said one scapegrace.

"Why white and not red?"

They teased him mercilessly. And when he suggested that perhaps, as a result of his accident, he'd developed some new sense enabling him to communicate with the past through the sound of the bells, they tried to shut him up by calling him "Jingle Bells." And the description stuck, like ice accumulating in the freezing compartment of a refrigerator until you can't melt it, until you can only get rid of it by disconnecting the whole thing, forcing it to go quite silent.

The Maid and I

When she opened the door, her face lit up.

"You're he, Greco?" she said, in her highly Hispanic French.

I said I was. My French was decidedly Balkan.

"Come in, come in," she said. She didn't know what to do with her hands, which were covered with strings from the beans she'd been preparing in the kitchen. They looked like bits of darning thread.

She'd always been very friendly whenever I'd asked to speak to her mistress on the telephone, but seeing her like this for the first time in the flesh, incarnate in her wrinkled skin, I realized she had something particular to say to me. Then I concluded she probably welcomed every guest like this, with a great show of warmth, so that he would feel enveloped in the good will of the house. I was grateful for the pretense. That's how a good maid ought to be, I thought to myself. Make you feel you're in a place where everyone is fond of you as soon as you step through the door.

She helped me off with my coat and consigned my wet umbrella with care to the umbrella stand. As I adjusted my irreproachable tie before the mirror, I noticed again that she was embarrassed at not knowing what to do with her hands. I was just finishing an essay, which I was going to send to *Cimaise,* on hands in painting from Rembrandt to Velázquez. Depicting hands was the masters' biggest problem. Even geniuses like Rembrandt had difficulty making them lie down peacefully in the graveyard of the picture. Most painters merged them into the material of the model's clothes, hid them behind a chair or ignored them altogether. (I considered this last solution the best.) Hands as represented in works of art had become my secret passion. Friends who were actors had told me there was the same problem in the theater: what to do with their hands in a scene when they didn't have to greet someone or weep or move around. For hands are not like feet, which you can put into a pair of shoes and forget about. Hands are twin tongues with their own voice, the inaudible speech of the body. The fins of the flying fish, wings, hands, fingers are the great problem of the figurative arts. And as often happens when I'm writing something, I was so preoccupied with my subject that I could see the maid only as a portrait set in the frame of the hall.

I lingered there for a moment, thinking my glasses were wet from the rain. But when I wiped them with the end of my tie, I realized they were just misted over from the sudden change of temperature, the central heating after the cold street. With my glasses off I could see her outline only vaguely when she approached me, as in the field of a badly focused camera; but I felt the warmth of her hand, still damp from the beans, on my arm, and heard her say in her Catalan accent, "I understand. I was just like that when I was first living in exile here in Toulouse. I'm on your side. It's just recent for you. We've been having to pay for a long time. Courage! *Vincerremos!*"

I lost my head and hurried into the sitting room, bestowing on the old servant a smile of what purported to be sympathy.

The discussion on neostructuralism seemed to have reached its height when I entered. Two diametrically opposed theories were at it tooth and nail: Marxist structuralism versus structuralism pure and simple. The champion of the first was a young woman intellectual in a micromini, who was saying that just as geological strata change, though man cannot identify himself with the earth, so pre-existing structure is liable to change. "Take language in your country," she cried, looking at me. "Hasn't that changed since the days of antiquity, while preserving its original structure?" The advocate of pure structuralism, as opposed to the dialectical theory of change, was a charming middle-aged man so absorbed in the argument, or, I thought maliciously, in the micromini, that he didn't even notice me come in. Only the hostess, my friend and colleague at the center, rose and, in the Slav manner, planted three smacking, scarlet kisses on my cheeks. Still warm from the discussion, she asked me what I'd have to drink.

"A Campari with plenty of soda," I said. My doctor had recently forbidden liquor because it was bad for my kidneys.

"What a marvelous maid you've got," I said, nodding meaningfully toward the door, now closed. "What a treasure!"

"A wonderful person," said the lady. "And when I say person, I mean with a capital *P*. She's been with me thirteen years. A tragic case. All her people were killed in the civil war. When she first came to Toulouse, she didn't know a soul. I think she's still connected with the underground Communist Party."

The hostess was a left-wing intellectual, open and frank, divorced, with two children away at boarding school. She'd taken me under her wing as a victim of the dictatorship, with whose bloody history she was well acquainted. And I'd liked her salon on the two occasions I'd visited her before, without encountering the maid. I'd had plenty of good things to eat and drink there—that was when I was still allowed to drink—and, above all, I knew I was sure to meet extremely interesting people, like the two presently dissecting, with the accuracy of entomologists, the father of structuralism. Lévi-Strauss, the miniskirt was saying, was like Freud, bound to be outstripped in his old age by his own best disciples.

The following day, at three-thirty, Martha told me on the telephone that madame was at the dentist's and wouldn't be back until six.

"I didn't call to speak to your mistress," I said. "I knew she wouldn't be in. She told me yesterday. I just wanted to say how touched I was by your kindness yesterday evening."

"What are you saying? *Alma mía!*"

"When you were passing around your excellent stew and the others just helped themselves without even glancing up, I was looking at you."

"*Alma mía!*" she repeated. "I hope we shall be seeing you more often. Greece is like Spain. The people are warm-hearted."

"Can I come and see you now?" I asked.

"But—madame won't be back till six."

"I said to see *you*. For us to talk. Tell each other our troubles."

"But madame isn't here. She's at the dentist's, and she won't be back till . . ."

"That's why I suggested coming *now*."

"Now?"

"Yes. So that we can talk."

"But the house without her is a house without . . ."

She hesitated.

"Right," I said.

And hung up. I called a taxi. It was still raining.

With the same mechanical gestures as the evening before, she took my coat and wet umbrella and led me into the sitting room. The air was still vibrating, for toward the end, the miniskirt and the middle-aged fellow had almost come to blows. Everything had been put in order—the ash trays emptied, the cushions plumped up and arranged in the armchairs like swords restored to their sheaths—but something of the previous evening's cyclone still hovered in the atmosphere.

Martha was completely at a loss. She didn't know what to do with a visitor who'd come just to see her. All the friends of the family, whom she liked and treated as solicitously as if they were her own, were, in fact, simply by-products of her mistress; and in her mistress's absence, she had no idea how she herself should treat me. She was roasting some lamb for this evening's guests, and when I suggested she sit down so we could talk about our two countries, she excused herself, saying she had a tart in the oven and must see it didn't burn. I lit a cigarette and helped myself to a drink while I waited for her to come back. But when she had been gone for quite a while, I went out to the kitchen myself.

"What are you doing in here?" she asked, tears springing to her eyes. "Don't you know if madame were to come in and find us . . ."

"There's no harm in it," I told her. "I'm here because you told me yesterday as I came in that—that you were on my side. I came to swap experiences—because our tragedies are related. I felt at home with you. . . ."

I could see she was suffering. Everything had been turned topsy-turvy. She saw, perhaps for the first time, that the house she'd been living in for thirteen years didn't belong to her. And who knows? Maybe she was glad, maybe she didn't really want to have a house of her own. But perhaps she had been feeling like a bird in its cozy nest and just now realized she was only a maid who was fond of her mistress's friends in order to fill the void left by her own, who were dead, killed.

"Do you have any time off?" I asked, switching suddenly to the familiar *tu*.

"Once a week," she said. "It'd be better if I didn't."

"Why? Nowhere to go? Haven't you got any of your own people you can visit?"

"I go to see my sister, who's married to a Frenchman. But I don't like that sort of atmosphere. Madame and I, now—we get on like a couple of real sisters."

Smoke was coming out of the oven.

"I told you so!" she cried. "It's burned!"

She opened the oven, bent down, grabbed the cake tin with her bare hands, let out a yell, rushed to get the insulated gloves and finally pulled out the jam tart. The top was burned to a cinder.

"Now what am I going to do?" she said, crying. "It's the first time that's happened to me in thirteen years."

"It was my fault," I said. "I'll help you make another one."

"No, please—do go," she said. "You've no business to be here when madame's out. You're her friend, not mine."

Her wounded pride expressed itself in a hardening of her heart.

"But what about the Spanish civil war? We had a civil war in Greece, too, ten years later, in 1947. My father was killed in it. That's why I came—so we could talk about it quietly. Because yesterday, in the hall, you opened your heart to me."

"I can open my heart only when madame's here."

I was ashamed of the blunder I'd made. I hadn't known—how should I?—that the deepest wounds feed on their own flesh, and that perhaps I myself would, a few years hence, refuse to accept such crude, ill-considered and unforgivable intrusions as mine had been.

She came out after me with my umbrella as I was looking for a taxi. I hadn't left it behind on purpose.

I never went back there, though the lady of the house telephoned to press me to come and said that even if I wouldn't do so for her, I must come to please Martha, who adored me.

But, unknown to the mistress, the maid and I had contracted a secret agreement.

Departure

He looked at his friend Aris, unable to believe he was such a wreck. There was only a shadow of him left. And it had been scarcely two weeks since he'd met him in Tours, where Aris and a girl friend had hitchhiked to dance in a club run by a Greek. But it happened that the club owner was going through a bad phase and was closing down after a fight with his partner in which they'd all but taken knives to each other. So Aris and the girl were left high and dry; they'd hoped to earn at least enough for the journey back. And to think he'd taught her the syrtaki specially, this nice brunette from Marseilles who was also on distant terms with her family, or, in other words, penniless. Aris also had his pride. It didn't suit him at all to live at the expense of women who loved him. Of course, that wasn't the case now. He loved her idiotically, absurdly perhaps—it was a gift he had. He was inconsolable that it should be at this moment that for the first time in his life he didn't have a sou.

"But you knew I was in Tours," Aris' friend reproached him. "Why didn't you look me up?"

"I didn't want to impose on you."

"That's a consideration between acquaintances, not between friends. And see where it's got you. You look terrible."

"The doctors say it's general debility and I need a couple of months' rest. I'll go back home to Greece. I won't get mixed up in anything at first. What do you think? Will they bother me?"

"How should I know?"

"But I must see you and talk to you. What about late this evening?"

"Okay."

"Midnight at the Apatrium?"

"Right."

They had been standing, and the waiter came over to ask if they were going or staying, because they were in the other customers' way, positioned there in the middle of the café. If they ordered something, however, they could stay right where they were. Otherwise . . . They said they were leaving.

"Anyway, before you go you'll have to get your hair cut. A mop that length is in itself reason enough for them to march you straight off to jail."

Then they separated. It was a mild evening. The spring had finally arrived, late, in that part of the world. The cafés had put their tables out on the sidewalks, and the terraces were full of people. This season was always a nightmare for the Greeks. Winter and cold had no connection with their own country. But as soon as the weather had gotten warmer, both last year and the year before that, a strange nostalgia had gripped them, the spring had gone to their heads, and they had all longed to go back, to be again in the narrow streets where once, on nights like this . . .

Today Aris and his girl from Marseilles were particularly sad because they'd just heard on the radio that Panagoulis had been recaptured. He'd escaped with a warder from some unspecified prison, and the incident had been creating a world-wide stir since the day before yesterday. All the front pages ran a recent photo taken when journalists had visited him in prison a month before. It showed him walking with bowed head, weighed down by his mustache, in the prison yard. In the background you could see a warder, perhaps the one who'd escaped with him three days ago. Aris remembered having heard at first that he'd got away with five warders, the whole shift on duty, and he talked to Keremis about how a full-scale raid would be needed for such a break. Keremis knew the area and said there was no military prison at Boyatis —unless the junta had built one there. He must have got away by air; there were two airports nearby, one at Tatoï and one at Tanagra. This sort of thing isn't at all easy to pull off, he said. You need a solid organization behind it. And if he hadn't got away by air, where could he hide? The nearest coast was seventy-five miles away. Unless—nothing could be ruled out—his body had been found by innocent fishermen, like that of Mandilaras. A well-known tactic.

They had made all these speculations the first and second days, when there was still no sign of Panagoulis. Then they began to share the opinion of Panagoulis' brother, living in exile in Rome, who said he'd probably been liquidated, and the reward of 500,000 drachmas was just to pretend he was alive and throw dust in people's eyes. But what if he *was* still alive? Suppose he was underground in Athens? What did it mean if the dictator put a price on his head like a sheriff in Texas, offering a reward of half a million to encourage informers, state squealers instead of state scholars? Perhaps they'd recaptured him already but went on putting up roadblocks to harass everyone and nab others in hiding who hadn't yet been caught. Public opinion all over the world was concerned about what had become of the fugitive. Why? Weren't there other and worse manhunts in Greece and elsewhere? Hadn't sixty Vietcong been killed the same day the news of his escape had broken and his heavy, sweet face had appeared in the papers? Hadn't at least six patriots been tortured the same day by the Asphalia? What was all this business of making a hero out of one man and ignoring whole masses of the oppressed lying in the dark? Why these Western spotlights, trained on one individual as if he were a movie star? Yet another privilege of the Western free world! But to hell with it anyway! Aris was glad if, because of Panagoulis, the world was taking an interest again in his country. And he hoped it would all end well, that there had been a real plan behind it, that Alekos would escape abroad and tell about how horribly he'd been tortured. And now, after three days in which none of the resistance organizations had claimed responsibility for his escape—which according to Aris and his friends meant the affair was even more serious and secret than they'd thought—he and his girl friend heard on the French radio, France Inter, that he'd suddenly been caught. All the details were supplied. It was in Patissiôn Street, right in the middle of Athens, in a modern apartment. The janitor happened to work for the police. The same evening, the announcer concluded, they were going to show the captive to journalists, like a trapped beast, the way head-hunters in the jungle have themselves photographed smiling proudly before rare quarry. And all this, added to their fatigue and lack of money, increased their melancholy.

They went into an underground garage, the kind they had seen in the movies, where the criminal, fugitive or hero, hides from the police—the long dark galleries and pillars make a more interesting background for a manhunt. When the girl had dried her tears, they came out again.

The foliage swelled out to fill the space over the boulevard. The surface of the street itself was packed with cars. It was sultry. The humidity, in contrast to the dry climate of Attica, retained the heat and reduced them to jelly. They ran into some people they knew on a bench outside a café. They, too, were suffering from the sadness of events and the sudden upsurge of spring.

"A strange business," said the tall fellow with the little beard. "Why did he have to hide in the middle of Athens?

Why not somewhere else—Mount Helicon, say? What do you think, Aris?"

He had no comment.

"The whole business smells fishy to me," said another. He had a little beard, too, but was shorter and more assured than the other. "They must have set it all up beforehand. They knew all his movements in advance. The warder must have been planted."

"What would be the point?"

"To throw dust in people's eyes."

They seemed to have been discussing it for some time. They'd only just heard he'd been caught. The whole group always met after four in the afternoon, in order to give themselves time to read the latest edition of *Le Monde* and have something to talk about.

It was windy. Girls kept going by dressed like hippies, with Cretan head scarves, Sarakatsenika boleros and various exotic getups, all baggy at the knees and elbows. The country boy from Laka Souli kept turning around and saying "Look!" The identical human fauna circulated at night; only then, more palpitating, stoned. Aris observed the dreary procession of the same young people who were making a great revolution the previous May, trying to find a way out of the stifling atmosphere of the consumer society. And last May, he and the friends now sitting on the bench had risen up and taken an active part in the students' revolt, believing it really was a solution. Having started out with one dictatorship around their necks, they found themselves with two afterwards: their own and a foreign one as well.

Aris and his girl said good-by to their friends and walked on with heavy hearts, lungs half choked by exhaust fumes. A few yards farther on, Aris caught a sentence in his own language, "If I don't think in French, I can speak Greek better." It was a man to a woman. A tree had separated them for a moment, then they could hold arms again. Depersonalization syndrome, thought Aris. He didn't say anything to the girl. She wouldn't know what he meant anyway.

The crazy guy with the plastic rat was in his usual place outside the Saint-Claude, an old fellow of the *clochard* type, though with nothing really in common with that noble species. He looked like a reformed alcoholic and appeared every spring when people started to stroll around the streets and sit on the sidewalks. His act was to startle women by suddenly producing the plastic rat from the crook of his ragged sleeve. Some would instinctively recoil; others screamed; others clung to their escort's arm for protection; some knew him and walked on disdainfully without taking any notice. In any case, the people sitting in the cafés were always highly amused by the women's reactions, and the horrible old Quasimodo would pass the hat every quarter of an hour for them to show their appreciation.

Walls, scaffolding and hoardings—an underground parking lot was under construction in the square by the church of Saint-Germain-des-Prés—were all covered with posters for the runoff of the presidential elections. Someone had penciled on four identical photographs of Pompidou, converting them into four different portraits: Hitler, his hair plastered over his forehead; Nixon, with a jutting, aggressive chin; Dayan, a patch over one eye; and Stalin, with walrus mustache and tunic. And so they walked on along the wide streets below the posters.

At midnight exactly, Aris went to the Apatrium to meet his friend. His girl was tired and had gone to bed. The café had chairs of plastic made to look like leather, individual jukebox selectors on the walls, and couples kissing as if they hadn't anywhere else to go. It wasn't long before the friend came in with his girl.

"Well, what do you say—do you think we'll have any trouble? They say the police don't just come down on people at random—without evidence. They haven't got anything on me. I'm not a celebrity. And I intend to lie low to begin with, until I see how things are."

His eyes were moist at the idea of going.

"Have you ever been in any photographs?"

"I was in one ages ago, carrying a banner. You can only see half my face."

"If anyone asks you about it, which I doubt very much, say it's someone else, and, for good measure, say it's caused you a lot of inconvenience."

"Yes, okay. I'm ashamed, but I can't stick it out here any longer. I need a good rest. The doctors said so."

"Why are you making apologies?"

"I'm making them to myself, not you."

"Even supposing they ask you to recant—we need people like you, people who are not in prison."

"Recant? Out of the question. I don't know what I'll say, but if they have any sense they won't ask me."

"Is there a file on you?"

"Yes. And I was called in by the Asphalia in the early days of the dictatorship. But a friend got me out of it—he was a cop and voted for Brilakis. But they must have fired him by now."

"What if they ask you what you've been doing abroad?"

"I've got papers saying I work in a television film unit."

"But your hair—you must get it cut not later than tomorrow, so it has a chance to grow in a little and won't look like you had it cut specially."

"Jacqueline will cut it for me tonight with a bowl."

Time passed. They smoked cigarette after cigarette. All three were extremely nervous.

"How shall we write to one another?"

"Let's make up a secret code," said the friend's girl.

She got out a pencil and paper.

"We'll call Papadopoulos 'Panayota.' "

"That's my sister's name."

"And we'll call the situation 'Sidra.' "

"Everyone does that. Greece, these days, is full of Sidras who are sick."

"Let's try to think of something more original."

"The best thing would be for your girl to write to us in French. In any case, you'll be back in September."

"Let's hope so."

"How are you going? Via Brindisi?"

"No. The fellow whose car we're going in says it's cheaper to go through Yugoslavia and then via Salonika and Athens."

"Why don't you take the boat at Ancona?"

"It depends on how much gas we use."

"It'll be terribly tiring otherwise."

"True."

"And if you go to Mykonos, go and see Argyris. He's got a big place there, and he'll put you up for nothing—both of you."

"I'll go to some island or other, but I don't know whether it'll be Mykonos or Leros."

They got up to leave. The couple were taking a taxi.

"Châtelet's on our way—we'll drop you."

"Do you mind if I ask what language you're speaking?" asked the cabdriver when they were settled in the pneumatic bliss of the Citroën.

"Greek."

"That's what I thought. Beautiful country, Greece. I went to the islands five years ago, and I'm going back again this year. . . . Of course, they say the situation's not so good there. But where is it any better? Take France . . ." Stop-

174

ping at a light, he pointed at the twin posters of Poher and Pompidou.

Aris got out at his hotel. As he said good-by, he took off his red scarf and gave it to the girl.

"To remember me by," he said.

Then he hurried off into the darkness.

February 1969—September 1970

3

SELF-SLAUGHTER

On November 9, 1968, the body of K. X. was found in the forest of Grundenbach near Koper, capital of Norland. Age 37, unmarried, Greek citizen, member of the Orthodox Church. Cause of death: revolver shot in right temple.

—Press Release

1

"Who found him?"

"A Norlander."

"What type?"

"An early bird—the type who takes his dog out first thing, in slacks, with a stick. Records bird calls on tape, maybe. Anyway, he happened to be walking through the woods when suddenly . . ."

"He saw the body."

"Yes."

"It was probably the dog that found it first. It would have been off the leash, bounding around after squirrels and moles, when it came upon the corpse. Then it started to bark, and its master came over and—"

"Yes, something like that. They say he ran back to his car. The dog wouldn't follow. He drove to the nearest service station and called the police."

"Did you ever meet this 'early bird'?"

"No. No one else did, either. There wasn't even a picture of him in the papers. Nothing. But a rumor reached us, at the time, that this mysterious Norlander said in his first statement that there was a revolver lying a certain distance away from the body. If so, there could be no question of suicide. But he was supposed to have altered his statement later."

"Did anyone have a chance to read it?"

"No. The cops have hushed up the whole affair."

"Why would they do that?"

"To avoid scandal. The Norland government—the Social Democrats—had a majority of only two. They were afraid if there was a public outcry it would give the Christian Democrats an opening."

"Could the death of a foreigner have such major political repercussions?"

"Norland's problem is that it's more concerned about other people's problems than its own. Biafra, Vietnam, South Africa, Greece, Czechoslovakia . . ."

"Is the explanation really as simple as that?"

"Of course not. But we have to make do with whatever clues we've got. If we tried anything else we wouldn't get anywhere. And it would give them an excuse to expel us as undesirables within twenty-four hours."

"I smelled a rat just from reading the reports in the Italian papers. Why did he go so far into the forest? Anyone who wants to end his life does it on the fringes of life. I mean, he chooses somewhere he'll be found. Otherwise, he doesn't leave a farewell note. A lot of people have died in the Alps, but I've never heard of anyone committing suicide there. See what I mean?"

"Go on."

"So I tried, from what little I knew of him, to imagine his 'suicide.' And I couldn't."

"What do you mean?"

"It was like trying to paint a picture and not being able to. You know—you make two or three attempts, but you can't get anywhere. There's something wrong somewhere. Well, it's the same with K. Suppose we admit he decided to do away with himself? Right? And he chose the forest because it's romantic. Like Iannopoulos riding into the sea at Salamis on a white charger. So. He must have stopped somewhere to write the note. And farther on he would have stopped again. Looked at the trees. Listened to the birds . . ."

"It was night. He was found in the morning, but it was at night he killed himself."

"It makes no difference. He'd have seen the stars. Gazed at the Big Dipper. Made a wish—his last wish—on a falling star. Then pulled the trigger . . . But again, it just isn't convincing. You know as well as I do how he suffered at the thought of his friends in prison—tortured to confess to non-existent acts of sabotage. You know how he went into action when they asked for the death penalty against Panagoulis. How he felt it every time the dictators made another deal with a foreign company. How he denounced the sale of beaches in the Peloponnese. How could someone who felt like that just collapse?"

"Maybe all that political activity was just to prop himself up. Perhaps for him it was a last resort—the only escape from total despair."

"Of course, you knew him much better than I did. But still . . ."

"Perhaps he was disappointed in love. We ought to examine all the possibilities. Maybe he'd been to his girl friend's that evening and couldn't make it."

"I don't approve of mixing sex and politics. Freud can't always be used as a lining for Marxism. There's too much material, and the suit won't lie right. That's where Marcuse came unglued. But enough about that—it's too ridiculous. The problem is who killed him and why. Not to intimidate the rest of us—no question of that. But I can think of another possibility. What's your opinion of the interpreter?"

"I haven't seen him for over a year."

"I mean as a person?"

"Very pleasant."

"What if he was an agent for some organization you and I don't know about?"

"Impossible."

"I don't say he is. I just put it forward as a hypothesis."

"Like the Greeks here. That's what they said at the time."

"Well, we're Greeks too, even if we don't belong to this particular minority. And why shouldn't we dislike the Norlanders as much as they dislike us? According to the old saying, all foreigners are barbarians. *I* say all foreigners are suspects."

"Yes. But the interpreter's different—very sensitive. He was so shaken he's severed all relations with the Greeks here. No. His mind doesn't work like that."

"All foreigners' minds are peculiar."

"I don't see what you're getting at."

"Just that whoever killed him must have been someone close to him."

"Why not you, then? Or . . ."

"Why not? Nothing's impossible."

2

She couldn't bring herself to go over. Or to look. The forest was savage in its late splendor. She stifled a cry with her green scarf. The plain-clothes men who held her, one by each arm, respected her grief. She could see a dark patch through the trees: the public prosecutor, the police surgeon, the security chief and the photographers. The vultures, she thought. She'd put on high heels, never dreaming—how could she?—they'd bring her to the very forest he and she had walked in one Sunday afternoon three years before, when they'd met. But then, she remembered, they'd gone to an area where lovers took rowboats out on lakes. This was still part of the forest of Grundenbach, but it seemed primeval, almost like a jungle in these northern latitudes.

When she got out of the patrol car, her feet sank into the leaves as into a swamp. She'd had nightmares like this as a child. The farther she walked, the deeper she sank. She had screamed and woke herself up. But this was a nightmare from which she couldn't awake. A good thing it's been so long since we were together, she thought.

Someone broke from the group and came over to her. She saw him push through or vault over the low branches. Then, in the light filtering through the dense foliage, she recognized the interpreter, K.'s blood brother and inseparable friend, partner in his travel agency before the coup. People called them "the twins" because they shared all their secrets, like two men living with the same woman. Now he put his arms around her, lavishing on her all the pity he had denied himself. She could no longer doubt who the dead man was. She sank into his arms, almost fainting.

As her head lay on his shoulder he wiped away her tears with the green scarf. Her pale face hadn't recovered from the first shock; the brutes of policemen, no doubt wanting to finish their work as quickly as possible, had made no attempt to break it to her gently. And they say, or we say, whatever wakes you is stamped indelibly on your face, made malleable by sleep, just as the body is marked by creases in the sheets or springs in the mattress. As he dried her tears he whispered in a language the police couldn't understand, "They're trying to make it look like suicide."

It flashed through her consciousness, until then lethargic in the arms of the interpreter, who'd been her lover before K. And they say, or we say, old embraces keep their magnetism, and bodies have only to meet again for a moment for everything to start up again. Human warmth has its own logic, as matter has its own time. So, drowsy still, she'd found a strange consolation in those protecting arms, and an inexplicable pleasure had numbed her limbs. But at the words "they're trying to make it look like suicide," she collected herself with a sudden courage born of anger and broke away.

Then, stooping to move a branch aside, she went forward, almost tottering, to where she was loath to go.

The interpreter held her hand. The wind was tearing the leaves one by one from the eternal trees. Undergrowth, dead branches, saplings blocked the way. He could K. have walked alone at night through this deciduous jungle, without a torch, without moonlight, in order to "commit suicide"? *She* had to weave her way through, like a fox or a weasel or a snake.

The voices fell silent at her approach. The men were a wall between her and the body. When they stood aside she saw the beloved form lying under a fawn blanket on a stretcher. She took a step forward. A rabbit fleeing among the bracken startled her. On a topmost branch a bird applauded. She watched the fiery leaves fall on the softer red-brown of the blanket. From beneath it protruded the Cretan boots K. always wore. A camera flashed. Whispers merged in the sound of the wind. Turning, she saw the consul trying to hide behind a cop in a plastic raincoat. If she'd had the strength, she'd have shouted "Murderer!" When they drew back the blanket and she saw the dried blood on what looked more like a shattered wheel now than a face, she noticed, through a mist, that though K. had been left-handed he was holding the revolver in his right hand.

3

"He'd had this handicap since he was a child. An operation had only made it worse. He tried to conquer what had become almost an inferiority complex. He always used his left hand for target practice—he supported it with his right, like they do in cowboy films."

"Where did he practice?"

"On top of the building he was converting into offices for the New Resistance. I worked there too. For five years I'd been abroad, earning a living in factories, and that was the first time I was able to work as a carpenter again. And I was glad because I was helping the movement at the same time.

"It was one Monday noon, I remember—one of those Norland noons when night's already creeping up from the next corner. The street lights were on. Day fought in vain.

"I was making some built-in cupboards when he started to shoot with his air gun. The darts got nearer and nearer the target, and K. was pleased his aim was improving. Then, like a fencer exhausted after a bout, he came and sat beside me on the bench where I kept my tools. 'Any more news?' he said. My brother-in-law had just been arrested. I said, 'Information goes back from Koper all the time. We must watch out.' He shook his head drowsily. Sign of ill omen? He asked me, 'Do you think there's an informer among us?' That was the last thing I remember him saying to me. Every time I talk about it I go cold."

"Why did he practice shooting?"

"He believed in urban guerrillas."

"With an air gun?"

"Of course not. Two months before they got him he bought some guns that had been smuggled from East Europe. He always went around armed. In my opinion it's impossible he committed suicide. I'll tell you why. According to the official version he shot himself in the right temple with the left hand. Just try, and see if you can do it. Like that—put your hand over your head and try to hold it at a distance from the temple —four inches, according to the police surgeon. That's right —there. Now try to hold it still. You see how difficult it is! Now try to pull the trigger with your right hand. You see? The answer is the murderers didn't know he was left-handed and blasted him from the wrong side. And the people who

.ried to camouflage the murder put the wrong gun in his hand."

"You mean put the gun in the wrong hand."

"No. K. had a Czech revolver, and the one they found was a Beretta. The interpreter saw it when they pulled back the blanket for him to identify the body."

"What's the difference?"

"Enormous. A Beretta's flat, holds six bullets, is made of plastic and doesn't look real. The other's cylindrical, fires eight shots, is automatic and does look real. It was a Czech revolver he used to carry around at that time. He liked it because it was always accurate. A Beretta's almost an inch off at more than twenty yards."

"Couldn't he have had two revolvers?"

"Impossible."

"So?"

"So the murderers weren't people who were very close to him. Or even fairly close. You only had to see him once to notice how he wrote, how he used the telephone. He always hid his right hand under the table or in his pocket. You see what I mean—he was ashamed of it. So what I think is, the murderers may have turned up at a rendezvous he'd made with someone else—even if I knew who, I wouldn't say. Since then, we've all gone numb. The movement here nose-dived. Even if K. didn't belong to the left, in Koper he was the heart and soul of the struggle."

4

The news of his untimely death broke before the evening papers. As soon as they were off work, the Greek colony gathered at the club. The first to arrive was the doctor, also chairman of the Committee for the Restoration of Democracy in Greece.

The doctor had lived in Koper for many years—as a leftist he'd fled from Greece after the defeat in 1949. Poor, hunted, alone in a war-ravaged Europe, he had been changing trains one day at a station in South Norland when he met a woman who'd been a partisan in the Greek resistance, a victim, like him, of the civil war. They married. At first life had been difficult, but gradually they had grafted themselves onto that vigorous foreign stem, and eventually, by unflagging hard work, made a lot of money. Some people said they'd found the money buried in jerry cans in the cellar of a house they had bought, which used to belong to some Jews.

Little by little the doctor and his wife had become so assimilated they began to forget their origins. In any case, during those years Greece hadn't given them any particular reason to be proud of it. They had had children, and the children too had been assimilated into the sturdy structures of the foreign society they'd grown up in. The doctor and his wife had worked, grown richer and richer, bought houses all over. They'd learned from bitter experience that bank notes were just scraps of paper, that even gold could depreciate, that only real estate was safe. They'd almost forgotten their origins, and no one could blame them when, with the coup d'état, they had suddenly found themselves, like many of their compatriots, in the forefront of the opposition. On the morning they had read in the papers and heard on the radio that "fascism had reared its head again in Greece," all the buried past suddenly emerged from the decades of involuntary oblivion, like an old coin that has lingered useless in a pocket and by some unexpected turn of events recovers its original value, its former brilliance. Inevitably they were soon in direct contact with K., the first to "raise the standard of revolt" in Norland.

Naturally there were many things they disagreed about. Everyone reacted differently to the challenge of the dictatorship. The oldest among the expatriates saw it as their last chance to eliminate what for years had been rotten in the state of Greece. Others saw their country as a ship in distress that had to be saved from final wreck. Some younger people used the coup as an excuse for copping out of politics for good, the I-told-you-so brigade. And finally, there were a few who felt the usurpation of power by a pack of frustrated colonels as a personal blow. K. was one of these. Which was why the resistance policy he advocated was diametrically opposed to that of the doctor.

The next to arrive was the lawyer, chairman of the Committee against the Dictatorship and vice-chairman of the Norland branch of Amnesty International. Unlike the doctor, he had come to Koper as a student before the Second World War, married a Norlander and settled there. As a former anti-royalist he now found himself in the front line of the fighting. He was submerged in work; every day he had phone calls from the frontier from people with false papers, no money, unable to speak any language but Greek. He had to spend all his time looking after them. The dictatorship was a poison the country had to spew up. And this exodus was the vomit of the mother country—all these refugees, outlaws, emigrants without invitation or contract, driven in hundreds to the one frontier where a Greek political exile would not be turned away. The Committee against the Dictatorship, whose offices were in the club building, was originally a body for co-ordinating the struggle in Greece with the informing of public opinion abroad. It had now dwindled to a relief center for refugees, with the lawyer at its head.

The club was on the third floor of a building scheduled for demolition—that meant the rent was low—looking out over the town. There was a bar, a reading room, a Ping-Pong table, and chess and backgammon boards. Workers and students could get Greek food there. Today they flocked to the club, outraged at the news. Suddenly they had all found themselves drawn together. Karamanlists and Papandreists, Partsalidists and Colliyannists, Andreists and Edinists, Trotskyites, Maoists, Guevarists, anarchists, Marxist-Leninists— all the thousand and one particles fused into the only unity possible among such incorrigible individualists. All they wanted was an opportunity to explode. So much frustration had built up in a year and a half of totalitarian action and democratic inertia. That the oppressors should have dared to extend their hand abroad—the suicide theory wasn't entertained for a moment—was the last straw.

After the coup the Greeks of Koper, most of them still politically uncommitted until then, had rallied around the personality of K. Most were villagers proletarianized abroad under particularly harsh conditions. In K.'s instinctive reaction they had found the image of their own. The left as a whole had maintained a benevolent neutrality towards K. A few dogmatists feared "bourgeois influences," but those who were really politically aware thought that a bourgeois enlightened by experience should be given a chance to play his role in the process of revolution. So they had supported him discreetly. His character was sufficient guarantee of his integrity.

They soon decided to act against the Greek consulate—the crime against K. could have originated only from there. Ever since the *Putsch*, the consulate, instead of being run by career diplomats, had been full of spies from the Asphalia—sergeants, captains, thugs metamorphosed into commercial attachés when their only qualifications were for drug traffic.

They started out in a group, anger their only directive, armed with stones, moldy tomatoes and rotten eggs.

Theodoris, the club bartender, a stonemason from the island of Alonissos, wished he could have gone with them, but someone had to stay behind. When he'd locked the door after the last comrade, he began cleaning up; they'd left the place in a real mess. He went around methodically crushing out the cigarette butts setting light to each other in the ash trays. As he opened the window to clear the smoke he saw the others down in the street, splitting up determinedly so as to converge on the consulate from different directions.

But there the mounted police were waiting for them; the would-be storm troopers were the ones taken by storm. The consul, nearly out of his mind—he would be crucified for this business whatever happened—had ordered the sergeant specially sent from Athens to organize the thugs to tell the fake student acting as lookout to phone for police protection; "Greek and foreign anarcho-Communists are preparing to attack the consulate." The policeman at the other end must have shaken his head and smiled. "These Greeks! Only a handful of them, and always in our hair. One half calls the other half fascists, and the second half calls the first half Communists." So when the consul saw the demonstrators arriving with their banners—"Down with the junta," "Death to the murderers," "Consul, your last day has come"—he was glad his word to the chief of police was being made good. Beside him the captain, the sergeant, the bouncer, the thugs, all stood with clenched fists watching the demonstration from behind barred windows. The athletic-looking "student," once undisputed leader of the "parallel" police, now editor of *Ideas,* a review sponsored by the colonels, took pictures with a telephoto lens until a couple of rocks smashed the window and made him withdraw to safety. The voices were faint, the slogans almost inaudible. The police, night sticks in hand, kept the crowd at a respectful distance from the baroque building in which the Greek consulate occupied the first floor.

Though its government was openly hostile to the junta, Norland's democratic intentions were somewhat compromised by the fact that it belonged to the North Atlantic Treaty Organization. Of course, NATO was invisible here. It's only in underdeveloped countries like Greece, Turkey and southern Italy that it exhibits itself shamelessly. As K. once wrote in a letter, "I can see their bases here on the Tyrrhenian Sea near Pisa. Big cars. Women torn between hysteria and alcoholism. Men without charm. The town converted to fit the base. It all reminds me of Salonika when the Sixth Fleet came ashore. Or the intersection of University and Bucharest streets in Athens, just past the Zonar, with its everlasting sponge peddler, where you'd see the gruesome staff of the Foreign Mission waiting for the black shuttle to take them home. Some with their briefcases and the guilty air of the occupier; others with their decorations—at least not as ostentatious as ours. The most barefaced talked and joked among themselves; the others hung around like mutes waiting for a hearse. And the waves of passers-by paid no attention. We were used to them, the affront to our country's dignity had become a part of us, and that section of town looked like Saigon before the Têt offensive." In industrialized countries like Norland, NATO hides behind a smoke screen of factories and banks. The occupiers are given away only by their wives, who betray themselves with their dollars and their extravagance with traveler's checks in boutiques of Eskimo art.

That was why, once the protest had been taped by TV, the doctor and the lawyer moved among the demonstrators saying quietly, "Now break it up—that's enough for today," to avoid giving the police an excuse to intervene. But to some

hot-blooded students the Norland police were just as odious
as the Greek consulate itself. What they were fighting was the
system, not one particular dictatorship. Though Greeks, and
studying abroad at their papas' expense, they were cosmopolitan enough to regard the Greek problem as simply one
among many. "Throw out the revisionists," "No more con-
cessions," they chanted in the rhythms of May '68. Then the
night sticks started to connect, and they shut up. But later
that evening a Molotov cocktail, thrown from a car without
license plates, landed on the first floor of the baroque building
that housed the consulate, "in the bowels of which," declared
the accompanying leaflet, "the sergeant and his gang had
sired the crime." "The bomb caused considerable damage
but no casualties," said the next morning's papers.

5

"I rule out the Black Hand."

"What's the Black Hand?"

"A parallel organization abroad, rather like CROC, based
around Frankfurt. Ex-police thugs, hoodlums whose price is
fifty marks, the scum of society, notorious gangsters who
don't mind using knives—but, of course, nationalists to a
man! Before the dictatorship they used to send threatening
letters to the democrats. Then they disappeared until the
murder of K. After that they circulated a list of eighteen
names they said were also going to have to pay."

"But where?"

"Not here. They've never dared show themselves here. In
West Germany, where most of the Greek emigrants are. That's
why I don't think they liquidated him. They've only tried to
exploit it."

"So you think he did commit suicide?"

"Certainly not. I think he was the victim of others, higher up. The night before he was killed, he was in excellent spirits. Two days later he had an appointment with someone important who was going to donate some money for the resistance. Who was that mysterious someone? That's the key to the riddle. I don't know any more about it than that because the whole thing's been lying dormant for four years. And I'm afraid. Yes, afraid. I'll say just one last thing. The autopsy was performed by a major in NATO. A homosexual. And . . ."

"And what?"

"That's all I know."

6

On the day of the funeral they all went to meet the chief at the airport, trying to counterbalance their grief with flowers and songs. The chief waved to them as he stepped off the plane, just as in the days when he was still their parliamentary leader.

Those who were seeing him for the first time since he'd escaped from the dictators' dungeons noticed how much his eight months in hiding and jail had tired, matured, aged him. Or was it that he was overwhelmed by the sudden blow of K.'s death?

In answer to journalists' questions, he said the people behind K.'s death were the same people who were behind the junta. In other words, NATO and the Pentagon. Then he went straight to police headquarters to be officially informed about the progress of the investigations.

The slides of the autopsy sickened him.

"As you see," said the head of the crime squad, "the

coroner's report shows clearly there were no other injuries, although the victim was shot at point-blank range. It makes me think of that picture of the Saigon chief of police, now defunct, aiming at the temple of a frail little Vietcong. Only *he* had his hands and feet bound and couldn't defend himself. But Mr. K.'s hands were free. Why didn't he put up a fight against his murderer? Why should he have let him bring his gun to within a few inches? The only possible explanation is suicide."

The lights went on, and the chief saw the speaker on the other side of the room—a tall Norlander with an astronaut haircut. He put down his cigar and started to explain how K., though left-handed, had been shot in the right temple. And only a fakir or a Kabuki actor could perform such acrobatics. So why all the embroidery?

"This business must not become an issue in Parliament," said the man standing next to him, head of the immigration police, playing with a silver fish with articulated scales that writhed like a snake. "The opposition's just waiting for a chance to attack the government on the subject of the parapolice. And as you know, Norland's a peaceful place. Not like Greece or the Congo. The cows graze quietly, and the people mind their own business—apathetic in politics but active in do-gooding. If you stick to your murder theory there are going to be untold complications. Norland was on the point of leaving NATO when the invasion of Czechoslovakia made it hastily change its mind. The opposition has exploited this. If you're really against NATO, help us for the moment by leaving it to us, and if it really is a question of murderers, rest assured we'll get them in the end. . . ."

"This whole business stinks," said the chief. "Like the Polk affair in another time and place."

"We have a few more slides here," said the head of the

crime squad, switching on the viewer. "Do you think any of
these faces are suspect?"

They were photographs taken at various demonstrations
against the junta. One of them showed K. on the platform,
two microphones completely cutting off his chin.

"No," he said curtly.

"And now I'd like you to tell me what you did together on
the Sunday evening, a week before—"

"I was passing through Koper," said the chief, "to settle
the last details of the Pan-Scandinavian antifascist conference.
He came to meet me at the airport with his friend the interpreter. From there we went straight to the Majestic Hotel,
where they'd reserved a room for me. K. was in exceptionally
good form. He criticized severely but constructively my views
on armed resistance. He was very worried about the factionali-
zation of Greeks abroad, when the colonels were doing their
best to suppress their own differences."

"What didn't he agree with in your views about armed
resistance?"

"He thought the time wasn't ripe yet to say anything about
it. It was to foster the development of such a situation that he
planned to introduce me to someone who would help the
resistance financially."

"When?"

"The next time I passed through here."

"Have you any idea who the person was?"

"None. It might have been some very rich Norlander or
even a Swiss. *I* think that's the key to the whole thing: who
was the go-between linking K. and this, to my mind, non-
existent patron of the resistance?"

"And then?"

"Then we went and had a meal in a restaurant by the canal.
The Albatross, I think it was called. We had seafood. There

was a tourist menu for ten crowns. We drank beer. The interpreter had two more than we did. Then we went back to the hotel and continued discussing the day-to-day problems of the organization."

"Do you think this go-between could have been a member of a resistance organization you don't happen to know?"

"No, impossible."

"You're sure K. wasn't organizing urban guerrillas behind your back?"

"He was loyal and devoted."

"Then why did he attack what you said about armed resistance?"

"Because he thought either that it was being prepared and therefore shouldn't be discussed, or that it wasn't and so was pointless to discuss. The important thing as far as I'm concerned—and I want you to understand this—is that K. felt so deeply committed to the Greek cause that the suicide theory just doesn't hold up for a moment. It's impossible that a man who lives day and night with the dream of seeing his country set free would put an end to himself in that stupid and ignominious way. He'd have preferred to go back to Greece under a false passport, pretend to be a journalist, stuff his pockets with dynamite, and blow himself simultaneously with the dictator and his henchmen to kingdom come at some press conference.

"Anyway, Cretans don't commit suicide. They charge at the enemy and take the bullet straight in the chest. He has all those cousins back in Crete, with black scarves around their heads and knives in their belts—wouldn't he have considered what they were going to think? For true Cretans, suicide is a sign of degeneracy, an insult to the honor of the family. Before, yes, he might have been languishing in his travel agency. But the coup reawakened the Cretan hero in him—

Kazantzakis and all that. That's why the only possible explanation is murder."

"I have written proof here," said the head of the immigration police, "that Mr. K. tried to commit suicide eight years ago with gardenal."

He held out a discharge certificate from an Athens emergency ward. The chief turned white. They've got it all worked out, he thought.

"And here are the papers found on him," went on the Norlander. "Wallet, passport, checkbook, pocket diary—and this note."

He switched off the projector and pulled back the curtains, letting the gray daylight into a room as murky as a top-secret report.

The chief saw with surprise that the note was the same as that published the previous day in Athens by the junta newspapers: "Must go. Can't delay any longer. I love you always. K." The name Karine was written on the envelope.

"That's not his writing," he said. "Any expert can confirm that. K.'s writing was smaller and curlier. But what's most surprising is that this note could have found its way into the hands of the junta when all his belongings were here in your possession. I still don't see what sort of a plot there's been. Frankly, it's beyond me. But this place has become just a crossroads for espionage and counterespionage. I declare Koper an open city. I'm not spending another night here. I'm scared."

And he ran down the stairs. He was just about to get into his car when he saw the door had been forced. At first he thought he couldn't have closed it properly, but when he got in he noticed his briefcase was missing. He looked everywhere for it, but in vain. Nothing else had been touched; the radio aerial and the tires were intact, and so were the old pair of driving gloves, the road maps and the newspapers. Everything was as he'd left it except the briefcase. Fortunately it contained nothing of importance—otherwise he'd have taken it in with him—apart from some xeroxed leaflets on the junta's balance-of-payments deficit. The theft of the case was like one more explosion in a mine field. What next? What invisible hand, doubtless political, had abstracted the case right under the noses of the police? Or was it perhaps the hand of the police themselves? Till now, whenever he'd crossed the frontier he'd been filled with a sense of security and confidence. He'd looked kindly on the representatives of order, from the customs inspector to the lowliest traffic cop. How could he have dreamed that this fraternal country, which had given the junta so many diplomatic thorns in the flesh, could lend itself to these paranoiac machinations? He tried to start the car. The engine turned over, but the car refused to move. They must have sabotaged something, he thought. He pressed the accelerator, but the car only jolted where it stood. Then he realized he hadn't released the hand brake—it was a rented car and he wasn't used to it. Relieved, he drove around the block. Everything worked: gears, brakes, lights, and, most important, steering.

But he preferred to go to the cemetery in the doctor's car. As he sat in the back beside the lawyer, he wondered why K. and not himself. If they wanted to strike at the head, it was he they should have liquidated. And what if K. really had committed suicide, he thought with terror. Such ideas were reproved by a sign: HALT. WORK IN PROGRESS. They had to make a detour to the cemetery.

They were all there. No priest, no incense. Just wreaths and hymns. The priest had claimed the laws of the Eastern Orthodox Church forbade him to officiate at the burial of a "suicide." How did he know the dead man had committed suicide? By the note he'd left for "the woman." And how did he know about the note? Through the consulate. But the note was in the hands of the police. Yes, but they'd asked the consulate for a sworn translation. It was there the goat-priest had seen it and convinced himself that by "go" K. had meant "pass on." Few among this medieval priesthood bore any resemblance to the underground Secret School of their predecessors under the Ottoman Empire. Most tried to eke out their official stipends with gratuities from weddings and baptisms. This one was a former black marketeer disguised as a priest. His great fear was that the Holy Synod might depose him and force him to go back to Greece, where he'd be jailed for debt.

"The junta and the junta alone is responsible for K.'s death," said the chief in his funeral address. "Either they slaughterd him, as we believe, or they 'self-slaughtered' him, as our foreign friends maintain—they're incredibly sentimental about their own affairs, but set themselves up as 'objective observers' of everyone else's. So their inquiry has flagrantly excluded all those who knew K. and might really have helped find his murderers. . . ."

His voice choked, and he stopped. How could he speak so coldly of someone he loved, who'd hardly had time to digest their last supper together? Like Polk, he thought again, trying to repress nightmarish thoughts of K.'s last moments, when he must have realized that there was no escape from the trap he'd fallen into. He tried to master his emotion; the colonels had caused such communal grief that private lamentation was out of place.

A few slogans made themselves heard, like a distant echo of other funerals at which a whole people had bade farewell to its hero. But the words were soon lost; this northern clime stifled expansiveness. The blood soon thickened in the veins here, as the ice formed early over lake and river.

He resolved on the need to carry on the struggle. The octopus had reached out of its hole, and today they were burying its first victim on foreign soil. If they were not to mourn new victims they must deal decisive blows so that Greece, set free from its nightmare, could arise and look to a better future.

The Greeks were comforted. To understand the warming effect of a speech like that you have to know what loneliness is, and distance, and the lack of any saving daily contact with reality. Today everyone was burying a part of himself with K. Tomorrow the struggle in Norland would embark on a new phase. Some thought the change would be for the worse. Then, instead of the national anthem, students and workers began to sing passages of the "Romiosini": "This land, it is theirs, it is ours"; "And though they are slain, life grows on." Meanwhile the sun tried to break through the sullen clouds. Just before setting, it reappeared to warm him who had died in this cold land. Every land is cold when it is not one's own country—when it lacks the special temperature that makes a man's skin one with that of the earth.

The same evening, in the club's assembly room, the chief read them, instead of an obituary, the last part of an article K. had written for a Scandinavian political review. It was called "Greece and the Balance of Power in the Southeast Mediterranean."

". . . Norland's geographical position within NATO should not be forgotten. Behind the NATO technocrats' plan to build a bridge over the sea separating Denmark and Sweden—what they term a 'tehnological advance' to replace the old ferryboats—is the intention of blocking the Soviet fleet's outlet from the Baltic to the Atlantic, leaving it with only the arduous North Pole route.

"But what has all this to do with our problem—the Greek problem? That is the question. As everyone knows, the descent of the Soviet fleet into the Mediterranean constitutes a serious threat to the omnipotence of the American Sixth Fleet. It indicates that the Russians are anxious to stake their claim in the Mediterranean, and ultimately, by tacit agreement with the Americans, to turn it into a neutral zone. That is why it is the duty of small countries like ours to take our destiny into our own hands, independent of the parceling out of the world into spheres of influence.

"After the Six-Day War the question of Yemen came up again. The Soviets has always longed for an outlet into the Persian Gulf and Indian Ocean. Bottled up in the Black Sea, they could do little. So they exploited the Arab-Israeli crisis and appeared in the Mediterranean, at first only timidly with sonar ships, then more and more openly on the pretext of backing up Egypt, to the great dismay of the 'policeman of the Mediterranean.'

"Not many people know that the admiral of the Soviet fleet is no old sea dog but a young cybernetics expert aged thirty-eight. They don't confront the Sixth Fleet with ships of the same displacement—they employ smaller ones with a more powerful striking force. If you replace *Coral Sea*-class aircraft carriers with 'copter carriers you can automatically adjust the balance of power, even if the Americans have sixty ships and the Russians only six. Their six are electronically equipped and can neutralize the Goliaths on the other side.

"So, with the balance perfectly held, who is going to win? Can a million Israelis hold out in the long run against fifty million Arabs? They will break and have to relinquish the occupied territories in return for recognition of their independence. Then the Suez Canal will be reopened, and all the Russian fleet has to do is set its course for the seas beyond and Yemen's oil.

"To compensate for this, the Pentagon's electronic brains want to build a bridge between Denmark and Sweden, barring the Soviet exit from the Baltic. It's the loser's natural comeback. Already, around the negotiation tables, the players are showing their cards. 'What have you got?' 'Ace of diamonds. And you?' 'Straight flush. I win.' So the problem of our little Greece has to be set in a much wider context, and we must start to plan now for the struggle ahead. The Americans, driven away from everywhere else, will hang on more and more grimly to our ports."

7

"This year, the fourth since his death, we wanted to hold a memorial service. The latest priest sent by the junta is trying to stay in with both sides. His one desire is to be made bishop of Magnesia. But we drove him right into a corner over this service. He sat here in this very chair.

"I've never had and never shall have any time for religion. For me it is and always has been enemy number one. We put the priest in a dilemma. If he did what we wanted he'd be thrown right out by his own bunch. If he refused he'd be at our mercy when things changed in Greece. He was caught between the devil and the deep blue sea, so he pretended his father was at his last gasp and split twelve hours before the service. He stayed in Volos about a month. We found out his father was in perfect health. Finally we conducted the service ourselves. All the resistance organizations brought wreaths."

"What happened to the other one, the black marketeer?"

"The goat-priest? He was sent to prison. Some say he handed over the consulate's code book to the East Germans.

Others say it was some monkey business to do with drugs—
ten pounds hidden under his cassock. . . ."

8

"Did K. take hashish or marijuana or LSD?"

"Never touched them in his life."

"So the theory that he committed suicide under the influence of drugs . . ."

"Doesn't hold water. He often found himself in an awkward
position with friends who did use drugs. He had to give up
seeing them. People who use dope regard those who don't
as 'class enemies,' though the converse isn't always true. So
he stopped seeing them even though they were nice people—
intelligent and very progressive. But he hated being put in
any category."

"Who did he get his instructions from?"

"From the chief, of course. But only regarding organization. He did everything else on his own initiative. He
wouldn't submit to the rigid discipline of the left-wing parties. And he was often in conflict with the central bureau of
his own party. What bothered him most was being away,
having only indirect contact with those back home, only
secondhand information. He was tortured at the thought of
time passing for him outside Greece. But he used to say your
country is where you eat and sleep."

"Was he panic-stricken about it?"

"About what?"

"Was he obsessed by how time passes and no one can
stop it? Panic comes when you suddenly realize a year or
five or ten have gone by and there's nothing you can do about
it. You feel you want to run after the years and catch them
by the tail. It's a common case among exiles; we can't make
history or plant milestones to mark the distance. Even our

decisions are translated into action elsewhere. And so time, undivided, becomes a nightmare."

"Yes, that was what he felt. I've got a letter here he wrote from Utrecht on September 7, 1968. I'll read some of it to you.

" 'A year ago, in Holland, one had hope and the energy to discuss and pass judgment. But now everything is known, written and said, and the only thing left is the question: What's to be done? When that stage has been reached, not many people even bother to cut the pages.

" 'Later, reading the literature put out by the Portuguese émigrés, I was staggered at the resemblance with ours. They too demand the liberation of political prisoners—even the names are rather like ours. They too denounce carnivorous foreign investment. What the Americans are to us, the English are to them. They attack Gaettano and his so-called liberalization and say he's Salazar's best pupil. They condemn the foreign press for presenting the dictator as the champion of democracy. The relationship between Greece and Greek-Americans is paralleled by that between languishing Lisbon and the brave new world of Brasília. The only difference is that their colonial wars are nothing like the Cyprus problem. And seeing all this, I was afraid—as when I first went into exile and happened to see a special issue of *Europe* on Catalan literature. At the end there was a huge list of militants and artists and intellectuals who'd died in prison or exile, or were still living in prison or exile. It was like a credit list of all the actors in a film. And I had a vision of a similar issue of *Europe* on Greece thirty years hence. . . . It's at moments like that I see the imperative need for action. . . .' "

"It's at moments like that that the lurking panic of time leaps at you and seizes you in its claws. . . ."

"And the Portuguese are still asking for a tourist boycott."

"Did he drink much?"

"Not at all. It didn't agree with him."

"What did he look like? What did he say?"

"He used to say we'd go back to Greece one day and wouldn't recognize it."

"What did he mean by that?"

"That the dictators had time on their side. That was why he set himself deadlines. He was running a silent race with the junta: Who was going to outstrip the other? Like the rest of us, he was a good runner, but he was off the track. Whereas they, however slowly they went, were on it. And that's why the longer they stay in power, he used to say, and manipulate the people with their idiotic slogans stuck up everywhere, and their newsreels depicting themselves as the saviors of the nation . . ."

"But people hiss them in the dark."

"He knew that. But he was afraid that habit would bring a time when they wouldn't hiss any more. He was afraid of how a daily diet of fascism can warp human consciousness. He made a distinction between dictatorship and dictatorism —untranslatable in Norlandese. He said there's a dictatorship now, martial law, military courts. Tomorrow all these things could be abolished yet still exist in people's minds. The suppression of freedom and civil rights could be institutionalized."

"He was referring to the famous second phase?"

"No, he wasn't so much contrasting present and future as comparing a military regime with its demilitarized twin— Tweedledum and Tweedledee. He was afraid people's apparent indifference—the crowded restaurants, the pursuit of a life that seems superficially the same—might one day cease to be just superficial and apparent. Might become real, fundamental indifference. Do you see?"

"I think so."

205

"It was this deep distress of his he was expressing when he said we'd go back to Greece one day and not recognize it. He was afraid of time, time the catalyst, the vehicle of change. Not just normal growing old or visible scars on the body, but the deeper change caused drop by drop by the poison of fascism, trying to turn a whole nation into waiters and guides and lackeys of international vacationism. That's why all he did gravitated toward a single goal: no more words and meetings and antifascist jamborees—everyone must go into action."

"Did he reject the old parties completely?"

"No, but he believed the resistance would produce its own leaders, that they were already emerging from the dim background of trials and imprisonments. Every time there was a trial—the Patriotic Front, Democratic Defense, the Panhellenic Liberation Movement, the Proletarian Front, the Movement of October 20th—the sentences made him ill. He couldn't eat. He felt excluded, outside it all. And that's why he believed in more active participation. Not just 'I'll find you the money and you do the job.' He made up his mind to go himself."

"He didn't seem to worry about the political prisoners before. His own travel agency used to send tourists to Aegina. Why did he suddenly become concerned? Had the fire spread to his own house?"

"No fire could take hold with him unless he lit it himself."

"Well, then?"

"A difficult question, especially when the person involved isn't here any more. It's hard to give a complete answer just from the few notes he left and what I remember. The essence of the matter is that like many others, like myself, K. woke up with the coup. April 21 was a blow in the face. He took the tanks as a personal insult. Even I, only an interpreter who knew Greece mainly from the tourist point of view, felt something crack inside me that day."

"Did he have any Greek phonograph records?"

"Dozens. That was the only thing he listened to. He used to work day and night and always to the music of Theodorakis. Another thing—he found everything here insipid."

"Insipid? How?"

"Our fish, our meat, ourselves—so clean and blond. The silence. Empty streets. No one selling lottery tickets. Sundays with no soccer and no pools. Fruit wrapped up in paper, like soap. He used to say nothing had any smell here. Sometimes he would sniff the odor of his boots. He said you might be years abroad and never feel like an exile until the moment someone tells you you can't go back. I don't know whether he'll figure in history. I know in your country lots of heroes have disappeared without trace. The ruling class has always paid its historians instead of paying for its mistakes. In any case, he was a man apart, strange, full of contradictions. . . ."

"Could it have been homesickness—incurable longing for home? Could everything else have been only to hide a loneliness that at its worst drove him to the final extreme?"

"No. Unthinkable. Homesickness is a subtraction from reality. *He* made additions, multiplications, divisions—but subtractions, never. Perhaps you'll understand better from some of these notes.

" 'Summer 1967. Today I tried to define who I was. I tried to find my geographical co-ordinates, and all I found were those of my country. My country is here in the form of a flag on a yacht, probably some shipping tycoon's. Today I saw the sea again, I dived into water almost like ours, and all of me became . . . involuntary return. We are not made for northern climates and lowering clouds, for life in the jungle of cities. . . .

" 'Exile is a state without perspective. You walk along

paths made by others; you can never make one for yourself. . . . We're where no glossary can give the text any meaning. We abandon the few paths we know to be ours and come to the sea, the shores heaped with its secrets. Resistance—talk. Things happening in exile—for exiles. The law of the city— prisons in revolt. Automobiles—mobiles in a landscape. The secrets of the sea are heaped on its shores. The seaweed—a precipice and wall of stench.'

"And so on. I've only touched on the question of homesickness. Of course he felt it. Which of you people does not? The fibers, the pores, cry out for the climate that fashioned them. Sometimes the feeling goes so deep it can cleave you in two.

"But it didn't cleave him. On the contrary, it unified him, transformed him into an avenging sword. His homesickness receded before the dreadful reality: the crowded cellars of the Asphalia, the overflowing camps and prisons. He made a list of torturers, to be tortured exactly as they'd tortured others. As for the dictators, 'the most cynical impudent wretches our country has ever spawned,' they would have to deliver the same speeches, but now the audience would be able to react. The punishment would be to have to hold out to the end. He used to talk like that when he was in good spirits. For meanwhile he was secretly preparing the great uprising."

9

"Cows are awkward," said the peasant. "Wait a minute till I've finished."

He was pulling at the cow's udder with his gnarled hands. As far as the eye could see the country was green as baize.

The policeman waited, feigning indifference. He'd come to

search the peasant's barn, where, according to information received, K. had hidden the arms he intended to send back home.

The milk foamed into the big wooden bucket. When the man had drawn the last drop he gave the cow a friendly tap under the belly. She started forward, then stopped and looked back at her deliverer with an expression of melancholy and relief.

"Now what can I do for you?" he said.

The policeman showed his badge. The peasant froze. The cow stared fixedly at the stranger, like a dog. The peasant picked up the bucket, and they walked together towards the house.

Absolute stillness reigned except for an occasional moo. The sun was melting the frost crystals. Leaves and grass smoked as if on fire.

"I've come to search the farm," he said. "Stables, barns and house. We've been told K., the Greek who committed suicide, used to hide arms here for Greece. I'm from the NATO special police. Our duty is to protect the countries of the alliance from anarchists like that."

The peasant put down the bucket and looked at him.

"There must be some mistake," he said. "I don't understand a word you're talking about."

The policeman searched everywhere but found nothing except a carbine dating back to the resistance, in which the peasant had played an active part. He still used it now and again to keep off the wolves, he said.

10

"No, he wasn't a wolf, at least not when he and I were together."

"When did you meet?"

"Just before the coup. I went to his agency, the Rhodes Travel Bureau at the corner of Heinekenstrasse and Alleesagat, to get a plane ticket to Greece. I wanted to spend Easter there. I saw him; he saw me. There was something in his look. I hung around deliberately, pretending to be looking for something in my purse. We went out together that evening. We ate in a Greek restaurant and then went to my place. At that time I was sharing an apartment with two girls studying architecture. And so instead of spending Easter in Greece, on Good Friday I found myself at the Koper central station with him and the Greek workers on their way home for the holidays. That year the Orthodox Easter fell a week later than ours. The workers were stuck at the station because the frontiers had been closed and no trains were leaving. I remember how completely disoriented they were. They didn't know what was happening. They stood in the hall listening with rustic skepticism as he explained about the coup. Some expartisans, he told me later, had muttered that their people had already taken to the maquis. He was deeply impressed by their sense of tradition and responsibility as they camped there in that huge station. "I can't bear not to be there"—the words became engraved on his heart.

"Naturally the junta exploited his movements that day, and their papers accused him of 'preparing an armed invasion and supplying arms to Greek and foreign workers.' That's why they'd set up a prohibited zone along the frontiers. According to the papers, the same thing had happened at other stations in Western Europe: 'Gangs of anarchists handed out guns to poor emigrants who only wanted to spend Easter quietly back home with their families.' *Hestia* even demanded K.'s head on a platter."

"Do *you* think he was murdered?"

"I don't think anything. Anything's possible. He could have killed himself; he could have been murdered."

"But if he was so ardent in the cause, why should he have committed suicide?"

"He was a strange man, emotionally unstable. Once he told me there were two people fighting inside him, one good, one bad. He didn't know which would finally win. He confessed that soon after we met, in a moment of weakness. I remember another time—he put his hands over his eyes so as not to see the 'shadow.' "

"What shadow?"

"A sort of cloud he said came up in front of him. He told me he often saw it—it came on like a migraine. It was divided in two like a typewriter ribbon, black on top and red underneath. To deal with it he'd have had to move a little rod here on the right temple."

"The spot where the bullet's supposed to have hit him?"

"Yes."

"Is it true you withdrew your statement?"

"I didn't make any statement. I just said what I had to say the first and last time I had anything to do with the police."

"What about the interpreter?"

"I haven't seen him since that morning."

"The note was addressed to someone called Karine. . . ."

"Let's not talk about that. The truth about K. and me is very simple. We got along very well together until the coup. From that day everything changed. Something happened to him—what, I don't know. Anyway, he wasn't the same any more. That day, before he went to the station, he put up a notice at the agency: CLOSED FOR MOURNING. The Norlanders were surprised, wanted to know who'd died. When he told them they stared at him. Even the television people came. He'd suddenly become a legend. Some people whose reserva-

211

tions had fallen through were furious and tried to sue him. I stood by him as best I could. I loved him, but my position soon became unbearable. I hardly ever saw him, and when I did it was always with other people. They all spoke Greek—I didn't and still don't understand a word. I tried, but your language is very difficult. Often he didn't come home in the evening because he said he had to see people at the club or meet the committee or the union or the members of the majority. He was all nerves. Until then he hadn't ruled out the possibility of our getting married, but after April the mere mention of the subject drove him wild. He wouldn't even bother to listen. He hit me in the stomach two or three times —the last man I'd ever have expected to raise his hand to me.

"I tried to be patient. I told myself it was just a storm that would blow over. In the summer of 1967, I went to Majorca to give our relationship a breather, see if he'd miss me and so on. When I came back I found the house invaded by Greeks. They were wanted men, from the underground, with forged papers. I went to stay with an aunt of mine. That went on all autumn. It wasn't a house any more; it was a hostel for émigrés.

"And I was bored to death! I couldn't bear it, sitting there for hours not understanding a word! Of course, every so often someone would explain something to me in English. But the endless conversations and debates and altercations and shouting—they were enough in themselves to show me the dictatorship was likely to last a good long while.

"He wasn't angry at first when I told him I was leaving him. We tried to remain friends, but it didn't work. And then he took up with another girl, the Karine you were talking about. You know, the great revolutionary who managed to establish herself in the Greek resistance in only a matter of months."

"Did you cook for him?"

"Sometimes. Why?"

"What sort of things did he like?"

"Nothing *I* cooked. He liked oil, but here it's only used for salad. Why do you ask? Are you going to write something about him?"

"Perhaps."

"I'll tell you a typical detail. He had a passion for sesame. Whenever he found it on a biscuit or on bread he'd scrape it off with his teeth—like this. It was difficult to get sesame in Koper. One day on the outskirts of the town where it's full of Turkish immigrants, I found a grocer's where they sold it loose. I bought two bags—one the ordinary yellow, the other black. He didn't like the black. He was superstitious and it reminded him of the 'shadow,' the cloud. He threw it away. . . . But you must go. My husband will be back soon. He's a Turk, and he's jealous of Greeks. . . ."

11

The murderer couldn't possibly have been a Turk, whatever the old crippled woman said who lived on the mezzanine in the same apartment building as K. All day she stared out at what was going on in the street, and in the evening she gaped at television, that other window on the world. And it was there, on the small screen, that two days after the funeral she saw the static crystallize into K.'s photograph and heard the announcer say the inquest had returned a verdict of suicide.

The old lady was uneasy. She was sure it was murder. She'd seen with her own eyes.

"What did you see?" asked her son. He was sure she just sat at the window making things up to pass the time.

"The murderer," she said. "A Turk." Then she went on: "I know all about K.'s comings and goings and all the colored people that went in and out." By "colored people" she meant the dark-skinned Greeks who worked upstairs building the offices of the New Resistance. "That day, Tuesday afternoon, I saw him stop his car outside the door without parking it. He got out first, toying with his keys as he always did. Then another dark man got out—I'd never seen him before. I said to myself, 'Who's this?' Didn't like the look of him at all. He was short and thickset, shaved bald as an egg, with boots and a waxed mustache. He looked like an Asiatic. A Turk from the depths of Anatolia. K. went upstairs, and Genghis Khan waited for him below. He walked nervously up and down and around the car, casting suspicious looks in all directions. Of course, he couldn't see me—I was behind the curtain. When he saw K. come down again his expression suddenly changed. He put on an idiotic grin and got back in the car. Then they drove off."

"Would you recognize him if you saw him again?"

"Certainly."

"What made you suspect him?"

"His looks."

"You didn't ever think the other dark-skinned people might be murderers?"

"No, never. Perhaps because I was used to them. I'm always bothered by a new face, and then when I've seen it two or three times it doesn't worry me any more."

"How can you tell, then, that you weren't suspicious of this one just because you happened to see him for the first time the Tuesday of K.'s suicide?"

"If you prefer to think your poor old mother's crazy, suit yourself. But I'm going to tell everything to the police."

The policeman at the other end, thinking this was some opposition maneuver now that the result of the inquiry had been announced, was very polite on the phone. After he'd interviewed the old lady he took her son aside.

"Long experience in the crime squad," he said, "has taught me to be very careful when third parties try to muscle in on a case just out of boredom. What does the old lady do all day? Sits in her wheelchair, poor thing, and watches what goes on in the street without being able to take any part in it. Then one day she sees on television a neighbor's committed suicide. And since the inquiry leaves certain question marks, she clutches at them like a drowning man at a straw and tries to find the answers. It gives her a chance to participate, to stop being alone and cut off from life for a while. . . ."

Her son tried to dissuade her. In vain. She wouldn't be put off. A big popular daily published an "identikit" portrait of the "murderer" based on her description, with a request for anyone who knew anything about such a person to telephone or write in. But the whole thing threatened to degenerate into a witch hunt against all the dark-skinned workers in Norland, and the government had to intervene. For the first time, the smear campaign against foreigners was touching on hysteria. According to an opinion poll published by the paper in question, the Greeks were second on the list of those considered undesirable. The Norlanders placed them after the Turks but before the Portuguese, Spaniards and Italians.

12

"The Czech pistol—where did he buy it?"

"From someone passing through."

"Did he have contacts with Prague?"

"He intended to get arms from the socialist countries and forward them to Greece through Bulgaria."

"Describe his last day for me."

"He was proud and happy that morning because of the news from home. Not only had Panagoulis not flinched, but he was on his way to becoming a hero. And that's what did happen later when he defended himself before the court-martial. He said, 'A fighter's only swan song is the rattle of the firing squad.'

"Mitsos, Panayis, Menios and Pavlakis were there. We were drinking coffee we'd made in an improvised *briki* before going back to work on the new offices. We were discussing the meaning of the junta's attack on Yorgatzis and what sort of danger this implied for Cyprus. K. was particularly concerned and yet at the same time optimistic.

"His optimism was because he'd just received a cassette of Papandreou's funeral from Athens. He said it was the best possible answer to anyone who talked to him about the torpor and passivity of the Greek people. We'd already seen pictures of the huge crowd, but it was another thing to actually hear the slogans that sprang up from it, like strophes in ancient drama welling up from the eternal heart of the people. 'Rise up and see us now.' 'This is the way we vote.' 'Down with the junta.' 'No!' 'At last you are free.'" This last had a double meaning: Papandreou was free not only from the junta's claws but also from what had paralyzed him throughout his political career—his dependence on the imperialists. It was a psalm on tape, a swell breaking into roars that climbed skyward, a human sea echoing and re-echoing through endless caves. Strangely enough it was through his death that Papandreou, the 'Old Man,' was most useful to the movement. That may sound cynical, but it isn't. That concourse of people was the best possible answer to the junta's lies about the referendum. Ah, they were poignant moments, fighting moments. Even now, four years later, I still tremble whenever I think of it. The last writhings of the fish before it expires."

"Was K. liable to depression?"

"He got depressed quite often. As a nontraditional leftist, he had his share of melancholy. But he wasn't depressed then.

When we'd had coffee he left us and went out. He must have just walked around the streets, lighthearted. No possible witnesses but himself. Not even his shadow. There was no sun. It was one of those dull gray days you get at the beginning of winter. . . . He probably went and picked up his mail from the poste restante, where he had letters and contributions for the movement sent. Then he must have gone to the New Resistance offices. They were temporarily in the same building as the club then, with its wheezy elevator, while the new offices were being prepared.

"Oh, I forgot to mention that before he went to the club he stopped in at his barber's. His hair had been falling out, which made his forehead look very high. He connected even losing his hair with the dictatorship, and we used to kid him and say he'd be all right if he used 'Mao,' the hair restorer advertised all over Greece. Of course, when he was asked to come forward, the barber denied having washed and anointed him on the eve of his death. The poor guy was an immigrant from Sparta and afraid of getting into trouble.

"The two fellows who worked the Xerox machine at the club found K. there at around eleven, bent over his desk, writing. Tuesday was the day they brought out the Greek newssheet distributed throughout Scandinavia. He'd already drunk three Turkish coffees and was smoking his pipe. The phone rang. He signaled to them to stop the machine and picked up the receiver. Perhaps it was so the person at the other end wouldn't know where he was. They spoke in English. As soon as he'd put down the phone he got up, checked his pockets, tidied himself and went out.

"From that point on we lose track of him. We pick him up again at three o'clock with a Greek acquaintance by whom his mother once sent him olives, wine, raisins and honey from Crete. They talked mostly about personal matters. The junta, which had deprived K. of his nationality, now threatened to seize all his property. His father wanted to disinherit him so that his trees and land wouldn't go to relatives of Cretan collaborators. We saw this acquaintance after the funeral. He's a Scandinavian furniture dealer in Heraklion. He looked inconsolable. He wouldn't hear of suicide—he considered the very word an insult. He said a man who bore all Greece within him wouldn't stoop to such a way out. He told us what K. was like as a schoolboy in Heraklion, always carrying his satchel on the left, always withdrawn, apart, already whetting his sword.

"All the rest is just a negative no one can develop. Since K.'s death even the interpreter has kept, or we've kept him, so much apart we hardly ever speak to each other."

"And what became of the Czech revolver, finally?"

"It went through various hands, but everyone was afraid of trouble with the police. I don't remember who kept it in the end."

13

"Did K. feel he was a man apart?"

"What do you mean?"

"There are three stages of alienation, apartness, which in the case of the Greeks would correspond to the use of 'we,' 'them,' and 'those.' "

"I don't follow."

" 'We' is the geographical and social expression of a people that acts and moves in a specific context. Everyone who uses it feels part of a society. He may be for or against the dictatorship, but he always relates to a common term of reference, he's an organic member of society. In other words, not an outsider.

" 'They' belongs to the first degree of apartness, disorientation, alienation—call it what you like. The type that says, for instance, 'They're a nation of footballers,' has found a kind of golden section within which he and his country *can*, but not necessarily do, coexist. He's a word of the same root but with a different meaning; at this stage the wound, the burn, though not negligible, is not incurable. You can always bring up the logical argument against it. 'Wait a minute! Who are *they*? Who are *you*—a Latvian?' If the person you're talking to is decent he comes to his senses and gets back on the rails.

"But with people who use 'those,' the gangrene's reached the bone, the tooth's beyond saving. The speaker's completely alienated from his origins. You see this most often in those who've lived a certain length of time abroad and claim they have nothing to do with the underdeveloped Balkan country known as Greece. The wounded ego, wanting to feel secure in its adopted country, is not content with just throwing away its own nationality. By using 'those,' the speaker wants to show the distance he sets between himself and all the factors that formed him or forced him to retreat in disorder. 'Those Greeks don't know what they're doing'—that's the sort of thing he'll say."

"In this analysis, where would K. stand?"

"I don't think he belonged to any of the three categories. He was closest to the first, to those who say 'we,' but only when he was talking to foreigners. For the rest, he was no wild anarchist, no merciless dissector of Greek society cut off from reality. Nor had he anything in common with the gray-haired disciples of Trotskyism who've remained true to it because for them it's a reflection of their own adolescence. Or with the internationalists who use internationalism as a loophole, an excuse for not doing anything concrete for their own country. He tried to cast a cold eye, but only because he was aflame within. He didn't like amateurism. . . ."

"Was there anything he dreaded?"

"Becoming like the Spanish exiles in *La Guerre est finie*."

"What do all these fears and imaginings have to do with Greece?"

"When our politicians were squabbling over the electoral system and whether there should be direct or proportional representation, a set of gangsters was plotting to usurp power. . . ."

"What did he look like? What did he say?"

"He said time stopped for him on April 21, 1967. And he looked like the Scandinavian cattle that still, even when they're dead, even when they're in the oven, bear the stamp of the government inspector."

14

The lawyer found nothing absurd in the old crippled woman's claim to have seen K. with an unknown "colored man" on that Tuesday afternoon. His own conclusion from the file was that K.'s last girl friend, the lovely, proud, charming, revolutionary, romantic Karine, was the agent of a foreign power, perhaps of the First Oil International. And if K. had told her about his plan for blowing up a wing of the Pappas refinery at Salonika, there was no doubt about who stood to gain by his death. But he couldn't prove anything. He had no evidence at all.

He himself didn't agree with K. about "active resistance"; he didn't see how you could solve the problem just by wiping out a few of the regime's hard-liners. It would have been a different matter if it had been just a one-man tyranny. But he saw how foreign companies vied with each other to invest in Greece, not because they necessarily agreed with the regime or because they felt protected by the new constitution, but because the regime stifled the development of any democratic movement in the country. In other times the same companies had halted their investments, not because they feared the bourgeois government of the center, but because they were afraid of the possibilities it offered for the development of a popular movement. So for the moment, in his view, any terrorist action could have only disastrous consequences; it would simply give the dictators the excuse they needed to prolong their usurpation indefinitely.

"But do they need excuses?" K. would answer. "And if they do, what's to stop them from fabricating them? It's they who ask the questions *and* give the answers. Your argument would make *sure* their usurpation would be extended indefinitely."

And now the lawyer could find nothing to hang on to. Greece had vanished from the news like a coin withdrawn from circulation. The media's attitude seemed to be if you don't resist, if you don't kill, if you don't contribute to the international blood bath, you're not worth mentioning. Even Czechoslovakia was almost forgotten. As for Biafra . . . The only thing that still rated was the continued bloodletting in Vietnam. And one trial followed another in Athens, all exactly the same, as identical as the supermarkets all over the world. At each, the same jail sentences were handed down, snowflakes from the inexhaustible clouds of fascism. "Built-in fascism," as K. would have said. And the lawyer remembered the eyes, Cretan, anxious, sad, avoiding his own. The lawyer, listening to a record, lit one cigarette after another, leaving them to burn themselves out in the deep ash tray of petrified wood. Until one day someone knocked at the door.

The plain-clothes man with the astronaut haircut told him this time they'd gone too far—the last leaflet openly accused the Norland police of hushing up the case. Because the leaflet was unsigned, they could complain only to the antifascist committee that had sponsored it. The policeman knew, of course, having looked up the file, that the lawyer himself wasn't liable to expulsion, since he'd acquired Norland citizenship by marriage. But if the committee didn't change its tune, they'd be obliged to take severe measures.

The lawyer had his civil rights at his fingertips, even if they were only those of a second-class citizen. He answered, playing with his wedding ring, that he wouldn't pass this indirect threat on to the press for the simple reason that he considered the police another victim of the same plot, hatched and directed from above. What they hadn't understood about the leaflet, he said, was that the suspicions it expressed were of the "parallel" and not the "legal" police— of the secret police of NATO, the CIA, and the oil companies and refineries. Unfortunately he didn't yet have any proof. He knew the average Norlander thought of the Greek as frivolous, sentimental, Mediterranean, passionate and picturesque and that in serious matters like this the Norlanders were cautious and required evidence for everything. Only the chief, with his economic expertise and political flair, could convince Scandinavians. He himself had only circumstantial evidence. As soon as he had something conclusive . . .

The policeman, duly impressed by the Greek's eloquence, bowed politely, apologized and withdrew.

A few days later the lawyer sent for Theodoris, the bartender at the club, to initiate him into the "plan."

15

"Talking about the K. case, one must begin by eliminating the legendary element altogether. There *is* no legend. If we let it go as political murder at the time, that was first and foremost for reasons of local expediency."

"So you think he committed suicide."

"Hold on a minute! K. was a Nietzschean. A mystic. His

spiritual sources are to be found in the superman theory. He had a boundless admiration for the Slavs and for everything blond. But at a metaphysical level. Just as he had a metaphysical hatred for the Turks and everything dark. Ideologically he was rather hazy.

"That was why he liked hazy people. I found out that one of them was here on the eve of his death. A great bull-necked fellow shaved bald as an egg. I had to translate his request for political asylum into Norlandese—that's how I got to know him. He was of 'unknown origin'—adopted by an English couple in Greece and then by some Greeks in England, and he lived in Germany for a time before the war. He was a Buddhist and believed in nirvana. He was very intelligent, with shrewd eyes. I said, 'You might go easy on the Buddhism! You just use it as a pretext.' Under the occupation he acted as agent for the Intelligence Service but was dismissed for left-wing sympathies. He went to the socialist countries but had to leave. He was accused of being an agent of Western imperialism. So having seen both sides of the coin he became an advocate of the middle way. This went down very well with the student movement in Norland, though he was parachuted into it in a rather mysterious manner. But the young all came to him for directives. A word from 'Buddha,' as they called him—the 'defector,' *I* called him—was tantamount to an oracle. He offered both the guarantee of the experienced and the imagination of the seer. It was through the student movement that K. met him. They clicked; birds of a feather. . . . After the accident he disappeared. Some said he was *persona non grata* in the NATO countries and had gone to Sweden; others said he'd gone off to Pakistan. I didn't know he was with K. during the last days. When I found out, frankly, I was scared!"

"Where did K. stand politically?"

"He said himself, 'I started out apolitical, or, in other

words, right-wing. Then I wanted to move up, so I joined the Center Union Party. Then I saw the absurdity of trying to make a career in capitalist society, and I joined the left. Now I want to overturn capitalist society, so I'm a revolutionary.' He'd taken a crash course, you see, in the whole range of left-wing alienation. And even after that he couldn't be regarded as a leftist, as much as he might have liked it, because there'd always be someone to the left of him."

"How?"

"The left could be defined as a wall, the mass of humanity, the people. The people, organized, form a party. Someone suspended in the void, accusing others of dogmatism or revisionism, can be accused by others again of the same things, so he can't really be regarded as a leftist. Unfortunately it's true: 'However far left you are, there's always someone lefter.' It's proved every time there's a political upheaval— take May '68 in Paris. Even the situationists were called revisionists by some. No, as a manifestation of revolution, the left is amorphous. It takes on form only when it's incorporated in the masses."

"You mean K. changed from a political innocent to a great revolutionary overnight?"

"Not exactly. Unlike some unblushing imitators, he distinguished between Che the guerrillero and Che the product of the consumer society. He saw the writings of Giap and Ho in their historical and social context. In that, he was 100 per cent Greek. His symbol was Aris and his gospel was Glinos."

"Yes?"

"But you soon find yourself on the slippery slope when you mix with characters who say you have to liquidate first the bourgoisie of the left and then the bourgeoisie of the right. In a free Greece, splinter groups like that might play a useful part by puncturing the complacency of the left. But here, abroad, in no social context but internationalism, with no co-

operation between them and no equipment but a lot of books
only students can afford, such groups are grotesque. It's as if
the storm of the dictatorship had blown the pollen to the four
winds instead of to the pistils it might have fertilized. And it's
certain that almost every one of these 'groupuscules' contains
an informer."

"Where was he supposed to turn, then? Whom was he to
join with? He wanted modern, electronic resistance against
the computer dictatorship of the Pentagon, and all you in the
party had to offer was leaflets and slogans on walls."

"What you say doesn't apply to the left at the time when K.
belatedly became a revolutionary. Then, in February 1968,
well before the split in the socialist camp over Czechoslovakia, our party was already divided in two. Its members were
offered a choice between Vice and Virtue: either they stayed
loyal to the monolithic party—the party bogy, the party idea,
the party sword, the party crown, the dogma that exists independently of its members—or else they joined the section of
the left which accepts the principle of the minority—which
is antidogmatic, born and bred of a local reality."

"Which side was he on, then?"

"Neither. He deplored the fact that the split gave the junta
media an opening. He thought it hampered the struggle. But
since he didn't belong to the party he declined to comment.
He believed, with Sartre, that you only have the right to criti-
cize from within. If you're outside it's your duty to keep
quiet."

"Was he in a depressive phase when he committed suicide?"

"Not at all. He was on top of the world. He *had* been badly
broken up—by nature he was liable to depression—when
they arrested a friend of his, a Scandinavian journalist, in
Athens. He was carrying some addresses K. had given him.

He was followed from the moment he stepped off the plane at Hellenikon airport. He didn't realize it until the very end. They just let him go about his buiness until one day he was called in to the police station at Maroussi. There he found all the people he'd contacted. They looked at him in silence, feet swollen, arms broken—like one of those pictures of the inmates of concentration camps standing in their striped uniforms looking out across the barbed wire. When K. heard about it he fell into despair. The journalist must have been squealed on from here. But by whom?

"Another time K. was depressed was when the Warsaw Pact armies invaded Prague. Not because he regretted socialism's inner complications, its pangs in bringing its latest child to birth. He felt it because NATO used it as an excuse to close its ranks and redouble its insolence. Norland had been almost on the point of withdrawing from the alliance. The Norlanders were infuriated when a thermonuclear bomber crashed on their territory scattering radioactive fallout all over their pastures. *I* think if K. had had a friend to confide in we wouldn't have lost him prematurely like that. I think it was loneliness that got him."

"What about the interpreter? Weren't they inseparable?"

"I meant someone Greek. The interpreter was a very nice fellow, but like every good Norlander he was more interested in his own country and its king. I've known Norlanders of the left so steeped in propaganda they think the sun shines out of their king's behind."

"And Karine, the girl they say his farewell note was addressed to?"

"He didn't leave any note. All that was invented by the police to make the suicide story stick. I suppose you know it was published the same day in the junta papers."

"I know."

"But it's true he was living with her. I didn't know her myself, but I know she was one of those pseudoanarchist girls who reduce everything to their ass, if you'll pardon the expression. Even the resistance attracted her sexually. No one knows exactly what their relations were, but after the accident she let it be known he committed suicide because she'd refused him her favors that night. She considered the suicide a sort of decoration, a supreme honor. And before six weeks had passed she'd taken up with another Greek, Theo—he was on the same side as K. politically. Sort of a rough diamond, but a good buy. He was killed in a car accident later, and the girl . . ."

16

Karine had dreams. All the time. Strange dreams. Because she couldn't sleep without tranquilizers, her dreams were tinged with barbiturates. Psychedelic dreams: the forest, K., the lake—they sank, she woke.

A girl friend told her she should go to the Psychic Research Institute and talk to K.'s ectoplasm. After death, said the friend, people's souls floated about disembodied in the air, so she could get in contact with him. At first Karine laughed. But after a few days she asked for a medium's address.

So then came the Ouija board and long-distance calls to the beyond. The islands of real life got more and more lost in the archipelago of metempsychosis.

K. had left some papers and a lot of records at her place. She couldn't understand the papers, but the records had been like alcohol to him. When he was seized with hopeless homesickness he would use them as a spring to drown his longing. He listened to them so often they became part of her life too, the accompaniment to which she ate, cooked, woke, went to the toilet.

Now she was listening to them one by one before giving them back to the club. Alone in her apartment, with the stereophonic loudspeakers amplifying them, she was helpless, vulnerable before the invasion of sound, before her own longing for K. with *his* longing for his own lost country. She bent down, rolled herself a cigarette. Hashish soothed her loneliness.

One record followed another, often different versions of the same tune. Afterwards she wiped each one with the velvet pad and put it carefully back in its cover, then in its jacket. She wanted to hand them back in good condition.

Gradually the pile of unheard ones grew less. In the room, time had stopped. She'd unhooked the telephone. The trace of hash in her cigarette had helped her take off. She was in another, resurrected, world. K. was there before her with his Cretan boots and his Cretan look—direct, harsh, uncompromising.

The music filled the room, the country, the world. Forbidden in its own home, it spread and came alive here like a horla. Nothing ever dies, she'd learned from her sessions with the medium. Now she was like a cosmonaut out of his capsule. A cable linked her to the cabin, but she was walking in space, weightless, freed from gravity, without the least sound. The music was a planetary vacuum hermetically sealed.

Suddenly the cable was cut, and she fell. Then she put on another record and continued her voyage. The Earth showed one cheek only, a white curve on a black background. The other planets were outside her reach.

The doorbell rang. It was someone from the club to collect the dead man's records.

17

Theodoris Karatheodoris, or Theo Karatheo, bartender at the club, was a stonemason from Alonissos. He was good looking, full of charm and warmth, with dark eyes and a delicate, tormented face in which Byzantine asceticism tempered the languor of Roman decadence. His skill on the bouzouki and in dancing the hassapiko made him popular with the Norland women, who swooned over him and called him "Zorba the Second."

Theodoris had belonged to the left since he was a small boy. After the civil war there'd been a camp of political prisoners on Alonissos, his native island. The inmates were all educated men—doctors, lawyers, engineers—and he'd learned a lot from them. He sold them fish, or, rather, exchanged it for the chickens they raised in their experimental poultry yard. He relayed to them all the news he had picked up in the village café. At full moon they had to survive without news because the fishing boats didn't go out. When the elections came, the whole village voted "red," and the camp had to be transferred to some barren, uninhabited rocks so that the "innocent" fisherfolk would no longer be exposed to infection. The next year Theo went to Volos to work as a mason, but unfortunately when the wave of earthquakes stopped, building stopped too, so he took the road of exile to Germany. The dictatorship made him assume a more active part in the struggle.

He had sent to Greece for his mother to come and live with him, feeling sorry for the poor old woman with neither husband nor child within reach—his brother worked in Belgium, and his sister had gone to Canada and gotten married. The doctor and the lawyer had sent for him to let him in on their plan. They knew his story and liked him. He was a touchy little big man with an oriental mustache—quick on the draw with a knife, but with the sleepy expression women find irresistible. But the bourgeois lawyer and doctor had difficulty bringing themselves to explain what they wanted him to do. They were afraid they might offend his sensibilities, as delicately receptive as a TV aerial. . . .

"Right!" said Theo, who got the idea at once. "I'll lay the bitch."

"The thing is not to lay her but to find out enough for us to trace things up as high as possible," said the lawyer. "We don't have any proof, only suspicions. She used to work for the Pappas Standard Oil Company. You'll have to play your part well if she isn't going to suspect."

"All the world's a stage," said Theo.

"Has she ever met you?"

"No. And don't worry. I won't slip on any banana peel. I'll turn her inside out and uncover everything."

"Will your English be up to it?"

"I can make out with half English and half Norlandese. And she must know a bit of Greek. We'll manage. . . ."

"She'll be expecting you tomorrow," said the lawyer. "To collect K.'s records. Here's the address."

"Right!" said Theo again. "Oh, I meant to tell you, Doctor —my mother has pains in her right side. The damp here doesn't agree with her."

"Bring her to see me whenever she likes," said the doctor.

"And try to cheer her up," begged Theo. "Living abroad's turning her into a hypochondriac."

18

When the NATO captain found out Karine had taken Theo to live with her, he lost no time informing her that Theo

was an active member of the Norland movement against
the dictatorship and a close friend of the dead man. She
must be very careful with him. Karine didn't pay much attention to her boss's warning; he was a homosexual, and she
assumed he was eaten up with jealousy.

She herself was seriously smitten, and like all women in
love wouldn't tolerate anyone speaking ill of her man or
allow anyone else into her life or house. Even the interpreter
got on her nerves. She had only one interest now, and lived
only for when she could leave the office and go home to her
Theo.

Theodoris had installed himself in the high-ceilinged, ample
apartment with sheepskin from Delphi on the floor and walls
covered with portraits of Ho, Lin Piao and Mao, and cari-
catures of Lyndon Johnson and Papa Doc. He'd even sent his
mother to stay with his brother in Charleroi so that he could
concentrate on the job.

He was fond of comfort. For years he'd shared draughty rat
holes with other workers. Here he enjoyed the pleasant uniform warmth from the network of pipes under the parquet—
the cold weather had by now closed in. He would go to sleep
on the floor and purr voluptuously from its subcutaneous
heat.

And then there was the lavish bathroom, with shining blue
tiles and filtered light, like those he'd seen in Hollywood
movies. It was all his now, to swim in whenever he liked.
Karine had a mania for cleanliness, and there were rows of
bottles of foam and expensive essences for his bath. She
washed his hair every three days.

And she fed him well—steak or fish every day. She always
came home from the office to give him lunch. She tried to get
him to do the dishes or at least make the coffee, but he wasn't
having that and told her to go to hell. Then she called him

an uncivilized boor but said that was what she liked about him.

The only snag was having to hit her. She didn't have an orgasm unless he beat her, and if he didn't feel like beating her she'd make a scene until he got mad and lashed out anyway. She was slight, active, sure of herself, with huge green eyes. She was vulnerable only in bed. There she became transformed into a decadent creature, shouting and howling hysterically.

Theodoris put on four and a half pounds in one week. His face rounded out. He dropped in at the club sometimes for a game of backgammon, and his friends would tease him, saying, "Fallen head over heels, eh?" Theo was always throwing doubles. The others didn't know any details, but they could see he'd drawn a lucky number.

One evening—Christmas and New Year's were approaching and the preparations were making him tense—he got into the mood and started to play the bouzouki. The neighbors had already complained twice in the last few days. This time they sent for the police. Half an hour after midnight two toughs in plastic raincoats came and rang the bell. They said the other tenants had complained that the scratching and grinding of what sounded like some oriental instrument was keeping them awake. The cops wanted to come in and search the apartment for drugs. Then Karine took a tiny card out of her purse, and Theodoris saw the two cops bow, apologize and leave, as if the card had magic properties.

"What was that you showed them?" he said as soon as the door had closed behind them. He seized her by the throat. Karine pressed herself against him and tried to kiss him on the lips. But he didn't let go. His fingers ringed her neck. He meant to find out what it was she'd shown them. Karine was gasping for breath and tried to drag her lover over to the bed to interrupt his interrogation. But he got hold of her purse and emptied it out on the sheepskin rug. At first he found nothing. Then he discovered the card in an inside compartment but couldn't understand it. Karine, like a courtesan who holds the secret that her master has been given poisoned wine, then told him it was an identity card issued by the secret service. She had left Estonia as a girl with her family when the Soviet army moved in. Ever since then she'd lived in exile. Her parents were dead, and like Theo she was engaged in a struggle—to free her country from "red imperialism."

Theodoris knew one word from her could get him thrown out of Norland. The same thing had happened to his friend Panayis. Elka had accused him of living off her and threatening to kill her. He'd been given twenty-four hours to leave. And he hadn't even been allowed to defend himself. The authorities relied so implicitly on the word of a Norland girl—even though Elka had acted only out of spite because she thought Panayis was cheating her with her best friend—that they'd thrown him out there and then.

Suddenly the blood flew to Theo's head. He remembered all those who'd mixed with the occupiers on the pretext of finding out their secrets and who'd had an easy life because of it. What was he doing here? Who'd sent him into this wolf's lair? True, he'd rested his bones, taken the edge off his hunger, but he'd had enough. And for the first time he struck her with hatred. He called her "informer," "police spy," and in her blissful ignorance of his language she kept asking, "What do you mean? What are you saying?" The ultimate vibrations of pleasure oozed out through her fingertips. Numbed and languid, she fixed her eyes at the level of his navel, her mouth full. He pressed her head downwards. His hands had slid back around her neck, squeezing it like a loose bouzouki string. Her eyes closed in on themselves. She was dying of asphyxiation and desire. Unable to speak, she signaled to him to let her go. Her fingers stuck up like the antennae of a panic-stricken insect. Then, exhausted, she disgorged, told everything. The NATO captain who'd performed the autopsy was her boss. He could find his name on the telephone pad. The password Theo must use was that he'd been sent by Dimitri from Greece.

Theodoris and his bouzouki left the next morning for good. When Karine came home at lunchtime and found him gone she fell into a depression with fits of hysteria and soon after had to be put away. Madness was nothing unusual in Scandinavia. It was rather like malaria in Greece just after the war. It was called "Norlanditis" and usually occurred during winter, when there wasn't any light. In accordance with modern architectural principles, the mental hospital was in the center of the town, so the inmates wouldn't feel rejected by society. They drew, organized concerts and plays, and worked in the garden. One day Theodoris, walking past the fence, saw her watering frost-black flowers. She didn't recognize him. And for the first time he felt sorry for her. But when she came out in the spring, cured, it was too late. Theo had already joined K.

19

"I can't say any more. I'm afraid to speak. I knew K. well. *I* think he committed suicide. But he couldn't have done it on November 9. He had an important appointment on the eleventh, and something else on the fifteenth. He would have waited at least till then."

"So you *don't* think he committed suicide?"

"Call it what you like. Even after all this time I'm still scared. I had an appointment with him the day before. He didn't come. I called him up. There was no answer. Then I called up Karine, and she said he'd gone to the club. I went there and was told he'd been in that morning but not after. I didn't suspect anything, though our appointment was a very important one. It was only the next morning, before I left for the factory at six-thirty and he still didn't answer his phone, that I began to get really worried."

"Did you know 'Buddha'?"

"I certainly did! They called him 'Puss-in-Boots' too, because he always wore big hunting boots. He was a brilliant devil; I've had many a talk with him. A walking encyclopedia. He was in the Middle East during the war. Immediately after, he went to China. He'd been to India and studied Buddhism. It was there he shaved his hair off. He'd been all around the world. A marvelous conversationalist."

"An agent?"

"Maybe, but for whom? A double agent, perhaps. He'd settled in East Europe but left after a spell in jail just outside Moscow. Do you think he was sent by those in the East to spy on those in the West? Anybody might be a spy. He was in the Foreign Legion briefly, in Algiers. He sent arms to the FLN through Brussels. Maybe he was an agent here for the junta or NATO or even, on a higher level, for both at once. At a certain altitude distinctions melt."

"Did he really believe in metempsychosis?"

"Of course. How could he have been 'Buddha' otherwise? I was impressed one day, talking to him, by how much he knew about it. He even knew the case of a boy of six in Uzbekistan who could tell about events that happened a hundred years ago. He made fun of *Pravda* for providing a materialist explanation for it. They said he must have heard people talking about it when he was an infant. Buddha regarded it as a classic case of metempsychosis."

"And did K. agree with him?"

"Up to a point, yes."

"And after that he disappeared?"

"Let's get out of here. I don't like the look of the guy who's just sat down over there."

He stood up slowly, holding his back. He'd had an accident at work, slipped a disc snatching a couple of sacks of cement out of the way of a crane. He'd spent four months in bed, and then the doctor told him he could go back to work. But the first time he tried to lift anything—it was a load of tiles—the pain started again. The second time he couldn't move and was taken away in an ambulance. The third time, the doctor told him, he'd be an invalid for the rest of his life. And he wasn't a mason by trade—he was a professional diver. K. used to say it was the very thing for the resistance. You need divers and frogmen for sabotage. He said the atomic base at Souda could only be reached from the sea.

"And now I'll tell you something you don't know—that very few people know. He went to Crete in secret in the summer of '68. The man who'd brought him oil and honey from his mother was his contact. He was an importer of Scandinavian furniture in Heraklion, an ex-partisan, completely reliable. He was left alone this time because he'd kept out of politics. Of course, they arrested him the first day after the coup, but after a few inquiries they let him go; he had signed a paper saying he wouldn't give them any trouble. It was he who told me all about it. He was inconsolable about K. He was here when it happened and couldn't face having to go back and try to tell his people. Up until then, I thought K. was at a commando training camp in Jordan in the summer of '68. In fact, he went to Crete, where he was born. . . .

"He went by train as a tourist with a German passport. He was all on edge. From Belgrade he traveled with a couple of workers going back home to their village at Nea Santa, near Salonika—they'd been working for years in factories in Germany. They'd bought an apartment with their savings and kept talking about their new life. K. nearly died of heat and of frustration because he couldn't talk to them.

"He didn't stop in Athens. He took the night boat and was in Heraklion by the next morning. He took a room at the Madame Hortense Hotel. In the morning he went to the museum; he used to know the doorman, but he'd been replaced too. He went for a swim in front of the old cadet school; then he rented a donkey, like a tourist, and went to see his friend in the village where he was vacationing. There the policeman took to him at once; in this drought of tourists one swallow made a summer. K. pretended to mumble a few words of Greek. He was very careful not to give himself away by the slightest detail. But when he saw the slogans on the wall of the café—soldiers, phoenixes, labyrinths—he had difficulty, he told me later, in biting back an Orthodox Christian oath. All the time he sat there drinking his raki and looking at the poster he was shaking from head to foot. Later, when he'd traveled around on the island, he realized their propaganda had all the characteristics of American marketing. 'It's so methodical and psychological there must be a Greek-American staff working on it night and day. The brainwashing in the villages has reached criminal proportions.' That was why it was so necessary to act at once—he was always saying time was on *their* side. The mass action recommended by the left—factory committees, strikes—could only be applied in big towns. Other tactics had to be used in the country.

"There was one village nearby, at the extreme southeast of the island, where no invader had ever set foot. It was a godforsaken place, and the few old men who were left there had erected a huge aerial like a flagpole in the middle of the square. All day they used to sit there in the shade, without stirring, listening to the radios of ships passing by on the Libyan Sea. In the evening they listened to all the Greek broadcasts from Cologne and Moscow and London. The village policeman didn't say anything.

"K. must have sat for hours in the mountains under the stars, near the sheepfolds, breathing the bitter smell of hot stone, watching the rough mountain villagers, like heroes out of Kazantzakis. He even managed to pass himself off as a reporter from *Spiegel* and talk to the twelve, or, rather, eleven, 'maquisards' of Sfakia, who hadn't come down from the mountains since 1945, because they wouldn't believe the war was over. They were armed to the teeth. The police didn't bother them—they knew they wouldn't do any harm. They asked K. what was the use of wiping out two or three informers if you couldn't reach the people at the top? So they were biding their time and waiting for a 'starry night.'

"The last afternoon before he left, he visited his parents. Later his mother went to the friend's furniture shop—she knew he was the only one who'd seen him—and cried. She'd found him so changed. It was as if she had had a presentiment that she'd never see him again.

" 'Bitterness inside, bitterness outside,' the friend said to me; but it becomes intolerable when those bastards have the audacity to strike abroad. Where is anyone to feel safe? I wish I could tell you more about the people he saw there, the things he did and said. But the organization was made up of cells of two, without any links between them. I'm sure what he did in Greece has nothing to do with his being murdered here. If you ask me, it was people here that got him.

"At the funeral his friend, a marvelous patriot, brought a wreath with the words 'To a worthy son of Crete, mother of heroes.' He mourned him deeply; he knew how much K. loved the scorched and barren stone of the country that was taken away from him."

"But by whom?"

"The junta."

"So you think they killed him, too?"

"I didn't say that."

"But I'd like to know what you think."

"I've told you; I support the suicide theory."

"Why?"

"They might have blackmailed him."

"Who?"

"He was in Intelligence in the army—couldn't stand the military ever since. They put him in Intelligence because he'd graduated in law."

"Go on."

"I've known similar cases. They might have threatened to rake up old scandals."

"And to escape, he committed suicide?"

"Something like that."

"Did he talk to you about arms?"

"I knew he had lots of contacts. Even a general in NATO. They found a letter of introduction on him addressed to the general in Brussels. I made a note of the name and address at the time. But I burned everything. I was afraid."

"Did he often talk about armed struggle?"

"No, at first he just gave lectures. That was when he still thought it was possible to influence public opinion abroad. He used to visit towns and universities and always give the same lecture about the second American escalation in Europe."

"Which was the first?"

"The Truman Doctrine of intervention. And the foreigners listened, stupefied, meek as lambs. At the end they'd ask what they could do. They were stirred by his passion and wanted to work off their guilt feelings. He used to say, 'The best way for you to help us at the moment is to realize the dangers you yourselves run by staying in NATO. The American escalation will spread in your countries too.'

"He hated the way the organizations against the dictatorship passed the hat around. 'Support the families of political prisoners'—it was as disgusting as collecting for the church. He loathed charity. He thought the game was lost unless other countries saw the Greek problem not merely as a moral but also as a political question.

"The game *was* lost in so far as, with the passage of time, the temperature cooled off. People are really interested in another's problem only inasmuch as it affects themselves. And who felt that Greece concerned them? You couldn't claim it was a bloodless Djakarta or make people understand that a slap from a gloved hand can be worse than a naked blow. Every society has its own problems, and after all Greece was indispensable whatever its regime, whatever its fate. It was the oxygen tank of industrial Europe—low cost of living, hospitable people, nice warm climate and first-rate studs. What were these émigrés going on about, with their American escalation and all the rest of it?

"So he gradually realized the futility of what he was trying to do and withdrew. Besides, the worse things got back home the less point there was in wasting one's life in vain agitation and talk."

"And then—after his death?"

"The movement here just nose-dived."

"And the others—what became of them?"

"The workers elected a new council, the students split up into even smaller groups, the doctor and the lawyer continued the struggle within the legal framework of emigration. Every so often the chief would come to see them, but he never spent the night in Koper.

"In Greece, the situation got worse. More and more trials.

People forgot their surge of unanimity at the funeral of the 'Old Man.' After his moment as a shooting star, Panagoulis was swallowed up in the darkness of prison. The interpreter went to Chile in search of new excitement. In Norland the cows calved peacefully and no one bothered any more about whether they grazed on NATO property or not. The winter days were arctic again. The heart was soon enveloped in darkness and cold.

"And one night the old crippled woman's apartment was burglarized. The thieves broke in, gagged her with a nylon stocking, and stole all her valuables. It was a terrible shock for the poor old girl. She maintained the thieves were 'dark.' At first the police tried to connect the burglary with her state-ment about having seen K.'s murderer through the window on the famous Tuesday afternoon. But they finally got the thieves, who turned out to be Norland 'provos,' fair as flax, with leather jackets and motorcycles. They'd had their eye on the old woman's place ever since she was interviewed in the paper. And since the son wasn't there they had no difficulty getting into the mezzanine. . . . I could tell you a lot more, but I'm afraid."

"You don't look like the scared type. You want to make me think you know more than you really do."

"Me? I've burned all my files. When I say I'm afraid I mean I don't want what happened to Theodoris to happen to me. Do you get it?"

20

Theodoris finally decided to go straight for the target, using the password "Dimitri." He went to the offices of NATEF and asked to see the captain, despite the advice of the lawyer, who thought it would be safer to meet on neutral ground. But

Theodoris had had enough of exploring Koper's gay night clubs. The captain was bound to use another name there anyway.

To get to the captain's office, Theodoris had to pass three girls, laughing up their minis about their boss's tastes. Then he opened the door and saw him—cold, stiff, with his uniform and his eighteen-carat virility. For a moment he thought he'd come to the wrong room. Then he saw a glitter in the washed-out eyes. And Theo, though he may not have been educated, had an eagle eye himself. He knew people, and now he was sure he hadn't come to the wrong room. To give himself time to check with "Dimitri of Athens," the captain asked him to come around to his place that evening for a drink.

He was waiting for him in a sky-blue robe.

"Whisky?"

"And soda."

The captain went over to the bar and opened it. It was full of bottles and lit up like a bowling alley. He pressed a button and a bucket of ice emerged from the wall.

"What do you want to see me for?" he asked, his back turned as he mixed the drinks. "Dimitri doesn't know you. You were sent for K."

He suddenly turned around. He was smiling now. With damp, plastic, disgusting lips.

"You're nice," he said, coming over and stroking Theo's cheek.

Theodoris' stomach turned. The captain sat down in the leather armchair, deliberately letting his robe fall open.

"It's funny," he went on calmly. "All things come to him who waits. I've been wanting to meet you. I knew you were living with Karine. I even called one night especially to see you. But she wouldn't let me in. She was jealous. She knew how successful I am with the boys. . . ."

He laughed coyly. "She was a nice girl," he said.

"Was?"

"She committed suicide the other day in the asylum," he said, trying to look solemn. "It was a good thing you gave her those two weeks of happiness. They were the last she had."

Theodoris drained his glass.

"An intelligent girl, a conscientious worker too, but of course not strong enough to bear the weight that was put on her. She broke. I mean, in telling you to come and see me. A great mistake. But what can you expect? It was love, passion, that broke her. Ecstasy. How well I understand it.

"I had a very simliar case a few years ago. A girl gave the signal for a coup d'état in some little central African country. Three thousand people were killed in one night. When she found out she'd pressed the wrong key on the computer, got the wrong country, she killed herself. In my autopsy report . . . But let's talk about something more cheerful."

He went over and switched on the record player. The room was filled with bouzouki music.

"I'm homesick for Greece," he said. He began to cry.

When Theodoris returned from the toilet—on the door of which was a NATEF table, dated April 30, 1968, of "methods for dealing with various poisons"—he found the captain in a hysterical state. He wiped away his tears and started to tell the story of the great love of his life—Dimitri. He'd met him in the flower of youth. Dimitri was doing his military service as a cadet assigned to the MAMA, which then had its offices over the Zonar in the middle of Athens. Dimitri was a Macedonian from Pravi. He'd learned English in Salonika and become an interpreter through a general he knew. The captain took him out of the hovel he was living in—his pay as a cadet was only enough for him to exist on in Athens—and installed him in his superluxury apartment on the corner of Skoufa and Homer streets, with a view of both the Acropolis and Lycabettus. "And he still lives there, the wretch," said the captain. "While I . . ." Then, when Dimitri left the army, the captain, to keep him close at hand, had got him a civilian job in the same outfit, with a higher salary. And the bastard had shot straight up the ladder. Not that the captain minded his success. But Dimitri cheated on him with other officers, his superiors in impudence as well as rank. That's what killed him, that's what tortured him, that he'd done it with his own hands—transformed a nameless Greek cadet into the confidant of the allied services, and all so that the ungrateful son of a bitch could play around with gay generals and great queens of colonels. And to think this Rasputin used to sell himself for a hundred drachmas to the first dirty old man in Omonia.

The captain beat his breast and danced wtih rage. He took another drink.

Then Dimitri had actually got rid of him, his patron, by having him transferred here. After the revolution of April 21, that viper he'd nourished in his bosom knew so many secrets he'd been taken on by private firms. He'd wormed his way up to become special adviser to Esso Pappas, charged with protecting their refinery on the outskirts of Salonika. He cunningly fed rumors of sabotage to exaggerate his own importance. So in five years he'd gone from penniless in Pravi to the top of the ladder. He was one of those unscrupulous elements who avenge themselves on society for having been born poor and having been wounded in their childhood. Everything they do is motivated by resentment for their early humiliation. He, the captain, asked nothing of life but love and understanding, and all he got was barefaced exploitation. It was all very well—he liked to suffer—but that didn't "fulfill" him completely. He often used to fly to Athens for the weekend on the duty plane. And then what did he find? An exorbitant Dimitri always asking "What did you bring me?"

He wanted to fill his apartment with Norland furniture, now the rage in Athens. Everything had to be from Koper, from armchairs to nutcrackers.

"If I'd brought him something he'd go and stand in front of the mirror and exercise his muscles. . . . And then undress. Cynically. Without a trace of feeling. But if I didn't bring him anything, not even that."

In Athens, went on the captain, having overcome his distress, at least he'd been able to work off his inhibitions. A trip to Syntagma or Piraeus and he could pick up some very nice stuff, quite cheap. For ten dollars they kissed your hand as well. He must say the Turks had more pride than that. Once in a cinema in Taxim they'd stripped him naked and stolen every penny he had—and without so much as touching him. It gave him the biggest kick he ever had in his life. Well, as he was saying, he could at least find some distraction in Greece. Whereas here, in Koper, they were all blond cockroaches, cold as ice. And the professionals cost a fortune. What did Theo think of the idea of being his butler? A butler wasn't a servant. And now, anyway, they were bound together by more than one secret. It wouldn't be easy for him to go.

Theo's head was spinning. The various objects in the room whirled by as if he was on a merry-go-round. The record player was playing some choruses from *Axiom Esti*.

> They waited for me out at sea
>   And attacked me with three-masted mortars.
> Is it a sin for me, too, to have a love,
>   Distant lover, immortal rose?

"You see," said the captain, "I even have songs of the resistance. . . ."

Then the captain was felled with two blows, each with a whole year of anger and bitterness behind it. Bleeding, he tried to get to the phone, but Theo rushed and wrenched it out of the wall. Then he spat in the captain's face; the spittle spread over his chest like a medal. The captain thrashed around, howling like a lovelorn seal, rolling over the floor in his sky-blue robe. Theo's head went on spinning; it seemed to him that he too was now lying on the floor. He thought of the scene in a documentary on the occupation; in the YMCA in 1943, a blond Aryan wrestler was being flattened by Vassiliadis, a carpenter from Salonika. The huge German was carried out of the ring, writhing, by the Gestapo—a northern man-eater fallen among Mediterranean fishes, smaller but more agile. . . . When he tried to get up he saw the boots. The boots of the other Gestapo. He raised his head. The boots reached to the ceiling. He just had time to see a waxed Genghis Khan mustache and to hear echoing around the quarry of his skull the last words:

> The tears of love have lapped me in red . . . .
> Distant mother, immortal rose.

On December 22, Theodoris Karatheodoris, aged 27, unmarried, Greek Orthodox, met a tragic death on the road when struck by a refrigerator truck coming in the opposite direction. The impact was so great that it was two days before the identity of the victim could be established.

—Press Release

October 1971